FROM
ROME
WITH
LOVE

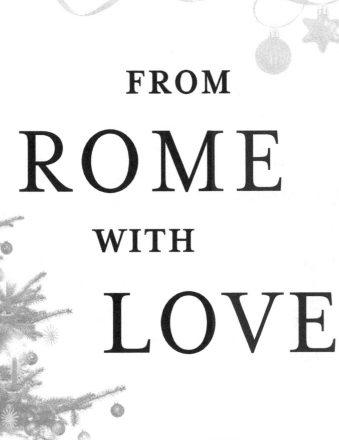

FROM

ROME

WITH

LOVE

Kate
Lloyd

UNION BAY
PUBLISHING

Union Bay Publishing

From Rome With Love

© 2020 by Kate Lloyd

https://katelloyd.com/

ISBN 978-1-7352411-2-8

Cover Design: Monica Haynes, The Thatchery
Interior design: Colleen Sheehan, Ampersand Book Interiors

Printed in the United States of America

To Lisa-Ann Oliver

CHAPTER 1

"**I**S YOUR PASSPORT up to date?" I'd thought it was an odd question for my new employer, Gretchen Williams, to ask me a couple months ago when she hired me to look after her quirky fifteen-year-old daughter, Tabatha.

"A valid passport is a requirement of the job," Gretchen had said, her gaze piercing into mine.

"Yes, I believe it's current." After the interview, I'd hurried home to check my passport and was pleased to see it was valid for another six years. I hadn't checked its expiration date for years, to give you an idea how often I traveled. And then only up to Canada from Seattle.

Until days ago, Gretchen never mentioned their trip to Rome over Tabatha's Christmas vacation. My chance to escape my humdrum existence and explore a city rich with history and intrigue I'd studied about in college, even if it meant leaving Mama by herself over the holidays. Which I hated to do, but I was so excited and filled with anticipation I could think of little else.

Inching forward to check in at the bustling Sea-Tac Airport, Gretchen said, "Lucy, did you remember your passport?" She glared at me as if I were a pesky gnat.

"Yes. Right here." My hand dove into my purse, then held up the blue booklet for her to inspect. I checked the expiration date again just to make sure.

In her midthirties, Gretchen wasn't much older than I was, but I almost added *ma'am*. She stood five feet ten, towering over me, and her black mane hung straight like the pop singer Cher's in her younger years—unlike my short stature and brown wavy hair.

I'd spent the night in the Williamses' guest room so I wouldn't be late. No time to spruce myself up before leaving their house. Plus, I'd decided to wear comfy clothes—flats; stretchy, black slacks with an elastic waist; a teal-colored, long-sleeved T-shirt to match my eyes; and a black puffy jacket. Mama had assured me that on a long flight, comfort is king. But according to my newly purchased tour book, I might need warm clothing in Rome in December.

Seven hours later, the giant aircraft took a dip. I felt my stomach lurch to my throat. It was a bumpy ride; we'd been restricted to our seats most of the time since switching aircrafts in Chicago. Riding on airplanes had rattled me since my early teens—make that scared me to death after my father's demise in his single-engine Cessna 172. I shouldn't be surprised I'd remained awake while the rest of the passengers around me snoozed.

I finally gave in and took a Benadryl, hoping it would help me sleep, but thoughts still ricocheted through my head. I wished I could leave my past behind in Seattle, but I couldn't. If the Williamses knew the truth about my battle with opioids, they never would have hired me. Thank goodness I'd never been arrested. No police record to hound me. But I craved a shot of Scotch or a sleeping pill right now. Not that I dared.

I clamped my eyelids shut and saw a shadowy outline of Brad Helstrom, at one time my sweet darling. I struggled to put his image aside but couldn't help wondering if he'd found my replacement. Since Boeing transferred him to Japan six months ago, he rarely contacted me. At first, texts or an email arrived every day, but it had been weeks. Get real, Lucy, I told myself. I might as well give up on a future with him.

Flight attendants clinked glasses as they prepared breakfast. The aroma of fresh coffee floated my way. All I wanted to do was stretch out and sleep for eight hours, but too late now.

Never had I dreamed I'd be traveling with the Williamses as their daughter Tabatha's au pair to Rome. Not that I was really an au pair, but Tabatha hated the word *babysitter*. Which was pretty much what I was.

The Williamses and their daughter had most likely enjoyed a relaxing night up in first class. Even the man sitting next to me was sleeping, his seat back tilted. No doubt a seasoned traveler, what with his earplugs and his eye mask. Before nodding off, he'd spoken to me in English that betrayed an Italian accent and mentioned that he knew most European languages, one reason Amazon hired him. I, on the other hand, knew no Italian. My mother's side of the family was from France. Why couldn't the Williamses have chosen Paris instead of Rome so I could use the French I'd studied at the University of Washington?

Nothing new. The Williamses carried an air of mystery about them, always getting off a call or closing their laptops when I entered the room. Sure, I knew they owned and operated a posh art gallery down in Pioneer Square, but when I brought their daughter in, I rarely saw customers. Maybe art collectors arrived for private viewings or on opening nights to make their purchases. Apparently, no big deal for some to spend $500,000 on a painting or piece of sculpture. Or possibly their interior decorators did the choosing.

The Williamses' home in Windermere was splendid, with its black marble entry, chandelier, and curved staircase. I didn't know houses like theirs existed in Seattle until I'd come to work the first day a couple months ago. And security was tip-top—cameras and burglar alarms armed twenty-four seven. I assumed the Williamses lived there to protect their fabulous art collection, better than most Seattle museums. Since I'd minored in art history in college, I recognized some of the artists and tried to keep my jaw from dropping when I saw signatures such as Cézanne, Matisse, and several Picassos. Not to mention the room in the basement I wasn't privy to but figured contained more works of art too valuable to be stored in their gallery or around the walls of their dining room, living room, and master bedroom.

They kept their house locked up tight and the security armed.

I wondered if they didn't fear for their daughter's safety. Tabatha was fifteen, but her parents claimed her IQ was sky-high. She had apparently taught herself to read at age three. A bright girl, but no friends from what I could tell. I'd encouraged her to invite someone over after school, but she always declined, saying she was too tired.

Back in Seattle, my job was to deliver her to her prep school, pick her up, and then keep a close watch on her. During the day, I shopped and prepared the family's meals and did light housecleaning, steering clear of their art collection.

The man in the seat next to me yawned, then covered his mouth. "*Mi dispiace*—I mean, I'm sorry." So he was indeed Italian. "Did you sleep well, *Signorina*?" he asked me as he raked his fingers through his thick nutmeg-brown hair.

"I've had better nights." No need to tell him what an inexperienced traveler I was. Inexperienced at everything would be more like it. At age twenty-nine, I still lived at home with my mother. How pathetic was that? Not that I hadn't lived in the dorms during college. But when I hunted for an apartment and discovered the budget-busting rents, Mama encouraged me to stay at home until I could afford something better.

"What brings you to Rome at Christmastime?" the man asked.

I stifled a yawn. "I'm traveling with a family . . ." I wondered what the Italian word for nanny would be.

Not that I owed him an explanation. Mama had often warned me not to trust men.

The flight attendant served us coffee, and he took a sip. "Again, I must apologize," he said, his choco-late-brown eyes capturing me. "Where are my manners? I haven't introduced myself. My name is Mario Russo." He tipped his head toward me. "And yours?"

I'd heard Italian men loved to think of themselves as Casanovas but decided it couldn't hurt to tell him. "Lucy Goff."

"Ah, Lucia." He pronounced my name Lucheea. "From Donizetti's opera *Lucia di Lammermoor.*" He stroked his chin. "One of my favorite operas by Donizetti. Do you know it?"

"No." I'd never attended an opera but smiled as if I understood what he was talking about.

"It's fantastic but tragic," he said.

"You mean everyone dies in the end?"

"I'm afraid so." He gazed into my eyes with intensity. "Are you staying in Rome over Christmas?"

"Yes." Again, I felt bad leaving my mother alone. Not that Christmas was a big deal at our house anymore. A pint-size tree—ever since my father died—and an unlit menorah Mama had owned since a girl perched on the fireplace mantle. We'd decorated a tree reaching the ceiling and exchanged presents. Mama said Papa had put the nix on attending synagogue over Hanuk-kah. "Go if you like, but don't expect me to," he'd said. Church was out of the question, too, even though we all loved Christmas music. I remembered him singing "We Three Kings" and "Joy to the World" in the shower.

He had a glorious baritone voice I'd do anything to hear again. My father was vigorous and fun—the zest of our family.

Mario checked my left hand, I assumed for a wedding band. "You and I should attend an opera some evening while you're here. Until you've heard an opera performed in Italy, you haven't lived." This guy was beyond handsome. I reminded myself I was in love with another man. What on earth was I thinking?

CHAPTER 2

"WHERE ARE YOU staying?" he asked.

"I think it's called the Hassler." I'd looked up the contact information to give my mother in case she needed me. "Or something like that."

"Ah, very nice." A smile bloomed on his handsome face. "And not far from my apartment."

I could hear Mama's voice in my ear telling me to not trust strangers and to keep my lips zipped.

"I could be wrong," I said.

"No matter." He brought out a pen and then handed me his card. "I wrote my number on the back should you want anything. Maybe we can get together. I'll show you the sights. Museums. Or meet for a drink."

I slipped the card in my purse, then let my head sink back as the Benadryl kicked in. I floated into slumber, as if cushioned on a pillow of clouds. Even in my half-sleep, I mused about my great-grandfather on my mother's side—a man I'd never met because he died in a concentration camp. Mama told me he'd been an accomplished artist and an art collector, but she owned only one of his paintings, hanging in a bedroom away from prying eyes. She said the rest were stolen by Nazis, amassed for gluttonous Hitler's collection, and never seen again.

She'd encouraged me to study art history at the university and to get my teaching certificate so I could make a living. "Art history is interesting, but with teaching you will always have a good job," she'd told me. Not that I did. I wish I'd found my elementary students adorable and teaching fulfilling, but I hadn't.

Before I knew it, I was waking up, hearing the flight attendant instructing us to put our seat backs up and remain seated. We'd landed.

Mario tugged his leather bag from under the seat in front of him, then stood and pulled his carry-on out of the overhead bin. "May I help you with yours?" he asked.

"Thanks, but I checked my suitcase." Standing five feet three, I would have been happy for his assistance. How could Mario look so good after such a long flight? I imagined myself in his eyes and thought of the word *rumpled*, my mousy-brown hair flattened on one side and a crease across my cheek.

I followed him out the jammed aisle and soon found the Williamses waiting to find their bags and go through customs. Neither Gretchen nor Stan asked me if I'd slept, but I reminded myself they were my employers. I was not here on a holiday.

"Lucy!" Flaxen-haired Tabatha wrapped her arms around my waist, then dropped them and scanned the crowd, probably to see if anyone was watching. I smiled as I recalled being her age, when I thought everyone was looking at me.

Minutes later, a throng of travelers milled in the crowded area, inspecting the baggage carousel. Gretchen pointed to several suitcases, and a porter lifted them onto a cart and followed her. I tagged along behind them, lugging my wheeled suitcase as we cleared customs, then exited the bustling airport. I wanted to say goodbye to Mario, but he'd vanished.

A man in a dark suit and a cap stood with a placard with the name Williams on it.

"*Buongiorno.*" He greeted the Williamses as if they were old friends. "Good to see you again." He introduced himself to me. "My name is Lorenzo. Welcome to the city of seven hills." He opened the doors, then crammed the suitcases into the trunk of his black Mercedes-Benz.

As we clambered into his sedan, I wondered if I'd see Mario again. I didn't expect to spend every moment with the Williamses and might have a free evening. No, I had a boyfriend—sort of. I slid onto the front passenger seat, which seemed to please Lorenzo to no end.

He spoke in English as he maneuvered us through zany traffic, all the while pointing out marvelous historical sites I'd seen only in school textbooks and my Rome guidebook.

My gaze swept from right to left, trying to capture each monument and ancient ruin. The city was decked out for the holidays—glistening lights and Christmas trees.

Finally, we pulled up front of a splendid building. Lorenzo turned to me. "Here we are. The Hotel Hassler Roma is located at the top of the Piazza di Spagna—the Spanish Steps—in the heart of Rome."

Christmas splendor adorned the hotel's entrance. Greenery entwined with sparkling white lights framed the front door, and two Christmas trees stood on either side like sentinels. Several staff members, meticulously dressed and coiffed, hurried out to meet us and took our luggage. Minutes later Tabatha and I entered our luxurious room on the third floor. Tabatha flopped down on the bed she wanted, plugged in her earbuds, and read from her Kindle—a historical fantasy she'd told me—off into another world.

I scanned the room and decided it was the most beautiful place I'd ever seen. The flowered bed comforters matched the wall paper. I brushed my hand over the pillows and bedspread. The fabric felt of the highest quality. If I'd had more energy, I would have examined each piece of furniture and admired the magnificent view of the city, but I was zonked and ready to drop to the bed and sleep. It was morning here, but my internal clock told me to sleep.

After the Williamses settled into their suite several doors down the hall, they poked their heads into our room. Gretchen had changed into a slinky floor-length dress. Her long hair was swept into a stylish bun. "We have a meeting." She glanced at her diamond-studded wristwatch. "I hope you've reset your watch, Lucy. Nine hours difference."

My head spun, but I tried to maintain an air of sophistication. "Thanks, I'll do it right now."

"As I said, we have an appointment, and we expect you to look after Tabatha. This hotel has very good security but keep an eye on her. I don't want her wandering outside unescorted. Lorenzo will stop by later to take you two on a short tour of the city." She jabbed my upper arm with her acrylic fingernail. "Lucy, are you listening?"

Oh dear, had I closed my eyes? I blinked them open.

"It's best to stay awake if you want to avoid jet lag." She handed me a tour book, though I already had one I'd been pouring over yesterday and last night. But I'd better use hers.

"Thank you," I said.

Her gaze turned severe. "As I said, I don't want Tabatha wandering around unescorted."

"No, of course you don't. I'll keep a good eye on her."

"Maybe she could do some Christmas shopping."

"Sure." I needed to shop myself. I planned to buy Mama a Christmas present or two. And maybe something for Brad. Or was he a lost cause?

Tabatha stretched out on the bed. "I'm hungry," she whined as she turned off her Kindle. "I could die of hunger if I don't eat right away."

"Lucy can order room service for you, honey." Gretchen's glance moved to me. "The hotel has several restaurants if you'd rather eat there."

"No, Mommy, please don't make me."

"I'm fine eating here too." I scanned the opulent space and couldn't imagine any restaurant more beautiful than this room, with its floor-length burgundy velvet curtains and what looked to be antique furniture.

"Stan and I have a busy day tomorrow, Lucy," Gretchen said to me, jerking me into the present. "As I said, we've hired Lorenzo to take you and Tabatha around to see some sights." She turned to her daughter. "Anything in particular you can think of?"

"Nah, I don't want to spend the day walking through museums." Tabatha folded her arms across her flat chest. "Can't I just stay here and read?" She adjusted her Kindle. "This is my Christmas vacation."

I wouldn't have minded a day of rest myself but fabricated a perky expression on my face. Here I was in Rome, a city I'd studied, but I was too fatigued to go out exploring today.

After the Williamses took off for their meeting, our room's telephone rang. I was surprised to hear a man's voice on the other end.

"Lucia?" He paused for a moment as if formulating his next sentence. "*Ciao*. It's Mario Russo, from the plane."

"But how did you get this number?"

"You mentioned the name of your hotel, fortunately, because you left your cell phone on the plane."

Nothing made sense. I reached into my purse and dug through it, hoping to find my phone. I felt my sunglasses, thank goodness, but my phone was gone.

"Thanks so much." I really did need my phone—a birthday gift from my mother. "But how will I get it from you?"

"How about if I swing by the hotel?"

"Did I mention I'm here working for a couple looking after their teenage daughter?" I said. Tabatha flipped her long bangs and glowered at me.

"Yes," he said. "And I saw you all in the luggage carousel area and at customs."

"Why didn't you give me my phone then?" I asked.

"This may sound strange, but I located it at the bottom of my carry-on bag. It must have slipped in . . . Honestly, Lucia, I have no idea how it happened."

Was this guy for real?

I recalled popping that Benadryl in hopes of inducing fatigue. Ten minutes later, right before Mario woke up beside me, I'd stuffed my paperback in my purse and thought I'd done the same with my phone. Did I shove them in his bag instead? Maybe the Benadryl really did make me wonky.

"I could come by right now and give it to you," he said.

"Or leave it at the front desk at the hotel?" I said.

"Whatever you like, Lucia." My name rolled off his tongue like a melody. "*Ciao*."

"Goodbye." I returned the phone to its cradle. Maybe I should go see an opera with him after all. Surely the Williamses would give me one night off.

"I'm hungry," Tabatha whimpered. "If I don't eat, I'll faint."

I knew better than to ignore her for fear she'd fly into a tantrum. Yet half the time she was compliant. No, make that, she moped around and verged on depression.

When I lifted the handset from its cradle again, a woman said, "*Pronto.*"

"Uh— I want to order dinner to our room." I hoped the woman could understand English.

"Of course, what may we bring you?" Her English was flawless.

"I want a hamburger," Tabatha said. "And fries. Lots of them. And ketchup and extra mayonnaise."

"How about some vegetables?" I asked Tabatha.

"I hate vegetables, and you know it. Why are you always so mean?"

"Did you hear that?" I asked the operator. "About the hamburger and the fries."

"*Sì*, I did. And what may we bring you?"

Should I just order the same as Tabatha? No, not in Rome, once known as the eternal city.

"What would you suggest?" I asked the operator.

"We have several specialties. Do you prefer fish, chicken, or beef?"

I was too drowsy to think. A long pause ensued. Finally, I said, "Chicken. No—make that beef." I yawned. "You decide. Okay?"

"Yes, *signora*. We'll select something we hope you like. May I suggest a small salad too?"

"Sure, that would be great."

"Get off the phone so they can bring me my burger," Tabatha said. "And a Coke with a maraschino cherry."

"*Sì, signora*, and would you like a glass of wine?"

"No, thanks." I dared not. I couldn't handle alcoholic beverages; they'd lead me to something stronger. Not that I'd brought oxycodone with me. I'd disposed of every opioid I owned.

I wondered if they had AA meetings in Rome. NA—Narcotics Anonymous—would be a better choice. I should call my sponsor, but she'd be sleeping.

"*Grazie*," said the operator.

After I'd hung up the phone, I realized I hadn't thanked her. Well, too late now.

CHAPTER 3

TABATHA AND I ate our meals in silence. Airpods plugged Tabatha's ears as she listened to an audiobook and gobbled her hamburger and fries. Room service had brought me an elaborate meal of what the server called *frutti di mare*—a cold seafood-type concoction—veal scallopini, and the best pasta I'd ever eaten. For dessert, delicious creamy tiramisu. It seemed like enough food for supper, not an early lunch, but I'd read in my tour book that the Italians ate their largest meal midday and then often closed their shops and napped.

While in the powder room, Tabatha sang some pop song I'd never heard before. Her voice rang clear and beautiful, a lovely soprano I'd rarely heard in Seattle. She was full of surprises.

I envisioned our clock in the kitchen and realized it would take me all week to become accustomed to this time zone. And I'd gain ten pounds.

The room's phone jingled. I stretch to my feet and answered it to find Gretchen on the other end.

"Bad news," she said. "Lorenzo can't drive you today. A sudden death in the family, and he says he must attend to his mother's needs."

"That's all right. I was thinking of taking a catnap after I call my mother to let her know we made it okay."

"No, I want Tabatha to get the most out of this trip. She's supposed to write a report by the time she goes back to school. It's a mandatory assignment."

I yawned. "Maybe she can start gathering information tomorrow." Not that I didn't want to explore this fabulous city, but I was half-asleep. A walking zombie.

"I'm serious when I said it's best to jump into this time zone as quickly as possible while the sun's shining and the sky is blue." She sounded like Mama when grouchy. My poor mother had plenty to be cranky about, but for the most part, she kept her disappointments hidden.

After I hung up, I let my body flop like a rag doll onto the bed. All that food needed to be digested, and Tabatha was reading again. My lids slid shut across my dry eyes.

A gentle rapping woke me with a start. I canvassed the room and noticed Tabatha, now lying on her back and deep in slumber. I figured room service was here to pick up our dirty dishes. A few biscotti remained on a plate; I set the dish aside before opening the door to find Mario.

"*Ciao*, Lucia. Hello."

My jaw dropped as Mario handed me my iPhone. I'm glad he couldn't read my mind, which was assessing my appearance. I wished I'd checked myself in the mirror before opening the door. I assumed mascara ringed my eyes and I looked like an owl. But too late now.

"Thank you," I said. I hadn't forgotten how handsome he was. I didn't want to stare like a country bumpkin. To keep myself from gawking, I glanced over to Tabatha, who was sucking her thumb as she often did when sleeping. I'd heard some adults sucked their thumbs in secret for fear of ridicule.

"So this is *la ragazza* you're looking after?"

I assumed he was referring to Tabatha. "Yes. I need to wake her up and get her ready to go on a tour of the city."

"I would be delighted to drive you."

"I doubt her parents would approve, but thanks for the offer."

"Maybe later this evening?"

I could feel the weight of exhaustion slump my shoulders. "As I told you, her parents have hired me."

"But certainly, they don't need you twenty-four hours a day."

I hadn't agreed to any amount of time, but no need to tell him that.

He smoothed his strong jawline. "Perhaps I could take both you and *la ragazza* to see the sights. I know the city well. And then an opera tomorrow night. We could take *la ragazza* with us."

WouldGretchen and Stan allow me to take Tabatha with Mario anywhere for any reason? I couldn't vouch for his character.

When the phone rang again, Tabatha tugged her pillow over her head and curled into a fetal position. I hurried to answer.

"Everything's going down the tube," Gretchen said. "First Lorenzo can't drive you, and now his friend has an obligation. You might have to use Uber or take a cab." She sighed into the phone. "Did Tabatha eat her meal?"

"Yes, but I'm having a hard time keeping her awake. Are you sure she can't take a nap?"

"She slept on the plane for eight hours on the way over. She needs to reset her inner clock, no matter how sleepy she is."

There went my snooze. "I'll try to get her up and out. We can maybe take a walk."

Gretchen chuckled into the phone. "She hates walking, but who knows, maybe you can get her to at least leave the hotel and spend time out in the sun. Sunlight is a key to overcoming jet lag."

"I could use a boost of energy myself." I glanced over to Mario who smiled and kept quiet.

"I've got a great idea," Gretchen said. "Take a cab to St. Peter's Basilica. That should keep you busy for a while. I'll ask at the front desk for tickets and a guide to the Vatican if they're available."

"That sounds wonderful." I felt myself waking up. I'd always wanted to go there.

"Keep a good eye on her." Gretchen's voice turned somber. "Promise?"

"Is there something I should know?" I asked.

"No—not a thing."

I wished Gretchen would tell me why she was so worried about her daughter. To me, Tabatha had a case of being a spoiled teenager who enjoyed stretching the truth.

After I hung up, Mario suggested, "Why not let me drive you there? In fact, I would enjoy walking through that marvelous church and protect you two from beggars and pickpockets."

"Don't you have someplace to be?" I asked him.

"Not really. A meeting in three days, but nothing until then." He tossed me a little lost puppy look. "I was wondering how I would entertain myself all alone," he said.

I didn't buy his explanation. "You don't have friends in Rome?"

"A few, but my family is from Tarquinia, north of here. Any friends living in Rome would be at work."

I checked the clock on the bureau and saw that it was almost two in the afternoon. I started to calculate what time it was back in Seattle but stopped myself. I needed to dive into Roman time.

"I'm afraid I'm going to have to pass up your generous invitation," I said.

"*Che peccato*. I mean, what a pity. I have a car. A red Alfa Romeo Giulia. A sedan. Plenty of room."

"With a back seat?" Tabatha asked, proving she was listening in on our conversation.

I turned to her. "We must do what your parents wish, and that is take a taxi."

She let out a groan. "No one ever asks me what I want."

"I'm sorry, sweetie." I felt a pang of pity for her. I recalled when I was her age; the last thing I wanted to do was what my mother demanded. Yet I should have. After breaking my leg skiing in my late teens, a cocktail of prescription painkillers had taken over my life. I was lucky to be alive.

Not that I would ever be really free.

CHAPTER 4

WHEN I CAUGHT a glimpse of St. Peter's Basilica, I was filled with unexpected joy. Adrenaline invigorated me. I paid the cab driver, who had taken us to the nearest entrance and a long line, after assuring us in broken English that twice the number of people would be here in spring or summer. I tried to recall what I knew about this marvelous church that I'd learned about in college. Given extra time, I would have researched more, but too late. I was here.

Tabatha exited the cab in slow-motion. "Are you sure we have to go in there? Look at all those ice cream shops down the way."

"Tell you what," I said, "after we stroll through the basilica, we'll go get you some ice cream. How's that?"

"Okay. I guess."

The interior of the church was beyond spectacular and heavily populated. I heard a myriad of languages.

Nothing I had studied had prepared me for the grandeur and elegance.

I stood admiring and explaining Michelangelo's statue the Pietà to Tabatha, who showed no interest. I wished my mother were here to see this masterpiece. I should have called Mama when we were back at the hotel. I took a moment to text her to say I made it and would get back to her later. She was a woman who carried many uncertainties, which unfortunately lapped onto me. Her husband—my father—had died leaving her debts and nothing in the bank. No wonder Mama told me not to trust men.

"Lucia." I recognized Mario's voice.

I whipped around. "You followed us here?"

"I didn't exactly follow you . . . Well, the truth is I had nothing else to do today and was hoping to run into you. With all these people, it's amazing I found you."

Tabatha beamed up at him and said, "Hi, I'm Tabatha."

"*Ciao*, Tabatha." He shook her hand. "Since I've run into you, may I give you a tour?" he asked. "I've been here many times."

"That would be fabulous," Tabatha gushed. Suddenly, she was fascinated with the basilica. Or was it the man? Well, in any case, she was beyond elated, so I went along with it.

After thirty minutes of strolling through the magnificent church, Mario asked, "Would you two be interested in walking up to the top of the dome? There's a splendid view of the city."

"That would be cool," Tabatha said.

"There's no charge," Mario assured me. "It's wonderful exercise, not that you need to worry." He glanced down to assess my figure, then looked away.

"Please, Lucy. Please." Tabatha tugged on my arm. "Let's do it."

I was afraid of heights at a gut level ever since my father's death, but agreed to go. After all that sitting and eating, I could use the exercise.

Mario showed us the entrance, and we began our ascent, following a throng of tourists. The circular stairway was cut of stone, and the steps, worn down by thousands of feet, became shallower the further we went. Tabatha sped ahead of us in spite of my calling her. In a moment, she was out of sight. I tried to hurry as my heart beat double-time with anxiety. The steps became even smaller, and the walls curved in until I felt as if I were suffocating.

"Don't worry," Mario said. "We'll catch up with her at the top."

There was no way to squeeze past the slow-moving people in front of us. Mario traveled on my heels. As the steps became smaller, I grew more and more nervous and was panting by the time I reached the apex. Up ahead, a group of uniformed men hovered around someone I couldn't see.

Shrill voices entered my ears. I recognized Tabatha's.

Mario strode over to the men. "*Che cosa sta succedendo qui?*"

I forced my way between two of the men. "What's going on?"

"This girl threatened to jump off," one said.

Tabatha turned away as if she couldn't hear them. She took hold of the bars and gazed through the barrier to the city below. "Look, down there. Is that where the Pope lives? I know him. If I had a parachute, I could jump from here."

"Shush." Was she teasing us? Gretchen had warned me Tabatha had mood swings, but nothing like this. I'd assumed the teenager had the usual hormonal roller-coaster ride that was typical of this age.

Mario spoke in my ear. "We had best get her out of here. I heard one of the guards say something about taking her to the police station."

Images of Amanda Knox's trial ricocheted through my brain. The young woman spent four years in prison after her conviction of murdering her roommate right here in Italy. All of us in Seattle had watched the roller-coaster trial unravel until she was finally proven innocent and set free.

I needed to get Tabatha down to the first floor and to safety, but that meant descending the staircase. I turned to Mario. "Would you help me?"

"But of course. I'll lead the way."

The thought of descending those narrow stairs made me woozy, but I said, "Thanks, that would be great. Please don't let her get past you."

"I won't. Let's sneak out of here while we can."

As the guards argued, I latched onto Tabatha's elbow. Keeping my voice low and hiding my fear and vexation, I said, "It's time to leave. Right now."

"No, I don't want to go yet." Her voice turned snarly. "You can't make me."

"But I promised ice cream, remember?"

"Oh, yeah. That sounds delish. And I'm thirsty too."

"Then we'll buy you a soft drink."

One of the guards noticed our attempt to escape. "*Aspettate tutti voi!*—wait."

Mario handed him a fistful of paper money and assured him everything was okay. I held onto Tabatha until Mario had entered the stairwell.

"Don't even think about running away again," I told Tabatha. She tried to wrench out of my grasp, but I held her tightly.

"I wasn't running away; I was waiting for you at the top, you slowpoke." She struggled to break free, but I clamped onto her elbow with all my might.

"Ouch, you're hurting me, Lucy. I hate you." She squirmed and twisted. "I wasn't really going to jump. I was just kidding."

Her words pierced into me, but I knew I was doing the right thing. Mario glanced over his shoulder and chuckled. What would I do without him here? Those guards could have hauled Tabatha off to jail.

Minutes later, we found a café serving ice cream— what they called *gelato*. Tabatha said she had no appetite. I asked her what her favorite ice cream flavor was and ordered her a dish, but she only picked at it.

"Are you feeling okay?" I asked her from across the table.

"I'm so tired I could fall asleep right here." She let her head drop forward until her forehead rested on her hands.

"Maybe jet lag," Mario offered.

"I'll bet you're right," I said. "I feel ready for an extended nap myself."

"Tell you what." His elbow touched mine. "I'll give you two a ride back to your hotel."

"No, we can't accept."

"What, you don't like red Alfa Romeos?"

"I do." I wanted to see his car. "But Tabatha's parents wouldn't approve."

Tabatha's head snapped up. "What are you talking about?"

I HATE TO admit how little persuasion from Mario and Tabatha it took for me to agree to accept Mario's offer to drive us. Through traffic, we crisscrossed the city and entered a large square.

"This is Piazza Venezia." Mario brought his car to a halt. "That huge marble structure is il Monumento a Vittorio Emanuele II." A colossal and gorgeous Christmas tree stood at its feet.

"Wow" came out of my mouth before I could formulate an intelligent reply. "It's incredible." The white monument dwarfed the tree.

Mario shifted his gaze to the right and pointed his finger. "See that balcony up there?"

I tipped my head and spotted a small balcony jutting out from a larger building.

"That's where Mussolini gave his famous speeches," Mario said. "Il Duce is what they called him. Thousands would come to hear him speak."

Had I heard Mario correctly? The fiercely hateful anti-Semite's balcony?

I opened the guidebook and read aloud. "From this balcony, the fascist dictator delivered many of his most famous speeches that would determine the course of history, such as the declaration of the Italian Empire in 1936 and a declaration of war on France and Britain in 1940."

"I know all that." Tabatha chortled. "Mom and Dad talk about Mussolini when they don't think I can hear them."

I didn't buy her story—not after what we'd just been through. Tabatha had a tendency to stretch the truth, to put it mildly.

"They talk about how Mussolini's girlfriend hid his art collection away," Tabatha said. "Paintings worth millions. That's why we're here, so they can buy some of them." She brought out her cell phone and snapped a few photos of the balcony. "I'll write my school report on Mussolini."

I recalled what I knew about the fascist dictator and shivered. "Are you sure you want to write about him?" I asked Tabatha. "He was a brutal man."

"So? It's not as if we don't have dictators all over the world today." She lowered her window and craned her neck to get a better look.

I imagined the square crammed with cheering admirers and felt a wave of nausea sweep through me.

"Alas, he's part of our history that can't be ignored," Mario said to me. "That balcony was restored several years ago."

I wasn't surprised the Williamses had come to Italy to purchase works of art for their gallery, but I hadn't considered the possibility of stolen art. It had been so many years since World War II. Maybe art taken by the Nazis was up for grabs, which meant some of my great-grandfather's paintings might be located. My mother would be over the moon if she could find even one.

Oh dear, my imagination was growing as squirrelly as Tabatha's.

Tabatha took one last shot as we cruised out of the square. "Please don't mention anything to my folks," she said. "They'd kill me if they knew I was eavesdropping. They don't think I can hear them when I'm wearing earbuds."

CHAPTER 5

AS WE PULLED up in front of the hotel and got out, Gretchen and Stan were exiting an Uber. They moved toward the front door until Gretchen caught sight of us. She swooped over to Tabatha.

"What's going on, darling? Are you okay?"

"I'm fine, Mom." Tabatha's animated voice turned flat.

Gretchen pivoted to me. "How dare you?" Her face contorted. "I told you to take a cab. Who is this guy?"

Mario jumped out of his car and came around to our side to open the doors. "I assure you, I'm a very careful driver," he said.

"We met on the flight over." I immediately regretted my statement.

"Look," Gretchen said to me, "if we weren't in Rome, I'd fire you on the spot. How dare you pick up some guy on the plane and take my daughter with you?"

"The fault is all mine," Mario said. "May I introduce myself?" He brought out his passport. "My name is Mario Russo."

"I don't care who you are." Gretchen grabbed the passport and reviewed it. "We should do a background check on this fellow," Gretchen told Stan. "Whose car is this?"

"It's mine." Mario leaned against the Alfa's polished fender. "I keep it in Rome when I'm out of the country doing business. I work for Amazon."

"Hey, I like Mario," Tabatha said. "He gave us a tour of St. Peter's."

Thankfully, she didn't mention the climb up to the top of the basilica. Her erratic behavior there still boggled me. The Williamses owed me an explanation.

Gretchen turned to me. "Did anything unusual happen?"

"Yes." Tabatha broke into the conversation. "We had gelato—Italian ice cream." She rubbed her tummy. "It was so-o-o good. Why don't you buy it for me at home?"

"We will, dearest," Stan said.

"I might write my report on gelato."

"That's a terrific idea." Stan seemed to be putty in her hands.

"No, never mind, I won't," Tabatha said. "I'd rather write about Mussolini."

Stan looked stunned, his face pale. "Why on earth? How do you even know who he is?"

"From history class. We just drove past his balcony. I took photos with my phone. I'll google him later." She turned to Mario. "Will you drive me there again?"

"No, he will not." Gretchen gave Mario the evil eye, then glanced to Tabatha. "In this beautiful city, I can think of a hundred better topics."

"That's what's so neat about it. I'll be the only person in the whole school who's ever written about him."

"I forbid it," Gretchen said.

Tabatha shrugged her petite shoulders. "We've studied about him in school. Are you going to tell my history teacher she's not allowed to speak his name? You and Dad talk about him more than she does."

Stan and Gretchen exchanged sideways glances.

"I've heard you," Tabatha said. "And about his girl-friend, Clara. I mean Claretta." She turned to Mario. "Will you take us back to that square? Oh, no, I can't recall its name. Piazza Venezia?"

Mario nodded. "I still have a couple days off. But we need permission from your parents."

"You've got that right." Gretchen menaced in Mario's face. "We're not running a dating service here."

"Of course not." Mario aimed his words at Stan. "I assure you I have impeccable credentials—you can do a background check on me if you like. I was only trying to help your daughter, who seemed to be having some trouble."

"He was a wonderful help," I said.

"I best bid you all farewell." Mario's gaze lingered on mine for a moment.

"Thanks for the ride and everything," Tabatha said.

"I was glad to be of assistance." Mario gave a slight bow, then slipped into his car without saying goodbye to me. I doubted I'd see him again.

GRETCHEN ASKED STAN to take Tabatha to the hotel's gift shop so she could speak to me in private.

"Come on, baby doll." Stan guided her through the hotel's front door. "With Christmas right around the corner, we need to buy presents."

If they fired me, what would I do by myself in Rome? How would I get home? I imagined myself in the vast Fiumicino Airport days before Christmas hoping to catch a flight. Not that I could afford to without dipping further into my savings account.

Once we were back in her room, Gretchen spit her words at me. "I'm serious about firing you. I thought I could trust you."

I assumed she'd checked my resume when they'd hired me. I'd seen the Williamses' job listed on a neighborhood app, Next Door, and the private school I'd worked for had assured me they'd given me a stellar recommendation. Why had I gone to all the trouble of getting a teaching certificate if I wasn't going to use it? After we got home, I might try again at a different school.

"Listen," I said, "I don't think you've been up front with me. What is Tabatha's problem?" I scanned the opulent suite—twice the size of our room—and saw a cylindrical container, the kind you might hold a map in, only smaller.

Her lips flattened. "I know she can be mouthy—"

"That wasn't her problem today, unless mouthy is what you call claiming she knows the Pope and contemplating parachuting down to his dwelling place."

"Good Lord. She actually tried to jump?" Gretchen wrapped one hand around her throat.

"Not really." I didn't want to cause unneeded worry. "But she talked about knowing the Pope."

"What happened?"

"Don't worry. She couldn't get through the metal barrier." I shuddered as I recalled the whole incident. "But she sure got the attention of the guards."

Gretchen shrank back. "I was afraid something might happen."

"She could have gotten hurt. If Mario hadn't been there, she could've ended up in jail."

"I should have thanked him, but I had no idea." She tossed the cylindrical tube into a closet and closed the door with her foot. "In fact, I should've accepted his offer to drive you. Lorenzo is still unavailable tomorrow."

I wondered if my job continued to be in jeopardy.

As if reading my mind, she said, "I'm sorry I snapped at you, Lucy."

"Thanks," I said. "Gretchen, you still haven't answered my question about Tabatha. Is there something I need to know about her?"

"We're not sure." She sucked her lips in for a moment. "She's always been a moody girl. But over the last six months, she's changed. One minute she's on top of the world, but the next she seems depressed. We've wondered if there's a girl at school who's teasing her or what."

"Have you taken her to see a counselor or psychologist? Spoken to her teachers?"

"Not yet, because no one at school has complained." She glanced at the closet door. "Our daughter's behavior today wasn't your fault. In fact, if you'd like the evening off, you can have it. We'll take Tabatha out to dinner with us. Maybe we need to spend more time with her. Stan and I have been so busy, and we will be again tomorrow."

"Really?" But what would I do? I recalled Mario's business card, still in my purse. But he'd no doubt think I was chasing after him.

Once back in my room, I found Tabatha dressing for dinner. She seemed downhearted as she looked at herself in the mirror. "I'm ugly," she said, the corners of her mouth angling down.

"No, you're not. Quite the contrary."

"And fat."

I glanced at her slim frame. "You're not fat in the slightest." If anything, she was skinny. "Where did all this come from?"

"I saw a beautiful girl downstairs in the lobby . . ."

"So what?" I knew where her mind was headed. I'd looped through that slippery slope too many times myself. And soothed myself with a pill.

"Don't try talking me out of this. I know what I know." She hurled herself onto the bed and sobbed into her pillow. Now what should I do? I had no idea how to comfort her.

I longed to hear Mama's voice, but what time was it in Seattle? Too early. I'd wake her up.

A rapping at our door broke into my thoughts. I opened it to find Stan and Gretchen.

"What's the problem, Princess?" Stan asked Tabatha.

"Come on, let's go," Gretchen said. "We're heading out for dinner." She looked like a movie star strutting off to the Emmys.

Tabatha turned her head toward her mother. "I'm not hungry, and my feet hurt. Please don't make me go with you."

"But I just told Lucy she could have the evening off."

"That's okay," I heard myself say as I felt my heart sink. "I'd be happy to stay here with Tabatha." Not really, but what could I do?

I was surprised Gretchen and Stan didn't offer to stay in for the evening, since their daughter was in obvious distress. But they left in a flurry, Gretchen's stilettos clacking down the hallway and her long hair swaying.

Minutes later, the room's phone chimed. I was pleased to hear Mario's voice on the other end asking me if he could drive Tabatha and me anywhere tomorrow.

"Okay, sounds good," I said, glad I hadn't called him. He'd made the first move.

After our conversation ended, I lay the receiver in its cradle. "Maybe we should spend time on your school project," I suggested to Tabatha.

"You really want to ruin my day, don't you?"

"I just thought you might want to get a start on it." I admit, I wanted her to know that spending time in this hotel room with me wasn't going to be all fun.

She chuckled. "Once my parents figure out what I'm going to write about, they'll have a hissy fit."

"What do you mean? I thought you told them."

"I didn't tell them that I know about the art stolen and hidden by Mussolini's mistress. Clara amassed quite a pricey collection and gave it to her brother to hide. Someone—my parents say it's Clara's nephew—is selling the pieces. Mostly paintings."

"Is there a problem with that?"

"Duh. Like, they're stolen works of art worth millions."

If true, I wondered how the Williamses were planning to get stolen art out of the country. I sure didn't want to be involved with any of it. Maybe I already was, just by knowing the facts. Or maybe Tabatha's story was fabricated. She had, after all, claimed she knew the Pope.

Tabatha's mouth twisted. "Promise me you won't say anything to my folks. They'll punish me something awful."

"I highly doubt that." Gretchen and Stan had been nothing but patient with her. And yet where were they right now? Relaxing on their Christmas vacation. Enjoying the sights of Rome, what I wished I could be doing.

"Please promise me, Lucy," she said, "or I won't be able to sleep all night."

"Okay, okay." What else could I do? If the Williamses were tangled up in something illegal, I wanted no part of it.

CHAPTER 6

M Y CELL PHONE rang, but I switched it to silent when I recognized Brad's number. He hadn't contacted me for weeks or replied to my texts. Well, it was his turn to wait for my call. I was officially done being his doormat.

I wondered what it was I liked so much about Brad to begin with. Good looks and smooth talking weren't everything.

I drifted off to sleep for what seemed like moments before the phone by the bed rang. When I answered, Gretchen's voice sounded like pebbles in my ear.

"Good morning," she said. "Is Tabatha up yet?"

I glanced to the window and saw a sliver of sunlight slanting through the velvet curtains.

"No, not yet." I rested my head in my hand. "Tabatha, it's your mother."

"Please don't make me wake up yet." Tabatha ignored the phone as I tried to hand it to her. "Can't you tell

I'm still asleep?" She clamped her eyelids shut. "And keep your phone turned off."

"You got a call?" Gretchen asked me.

"Yes, on my cell phone. But I didn't answer."

"That Italian fellow, Mario?"

"No, it was someone calling from the other side of the world, many time zones away." When she didn't voice an opinion, I said, "Do you have a problem with Mario? I was hoping you'd give us permission to go with him today."

Tabatha sprang to life and snatched the receiver from my hand. "Please, Mommy, let Mario drive us." A long pause ensued. "Thank you, you're the best mother in the world." Tabatha's voice practically sang. "Yes, yes, and he promised to help me with my report."

I figured she was lying to her mother but decided to let it slide. What harm could it do?

"I don't want to go to a dumb museum." Tabatha sighed, followed by a pause. "Oh—okay. Anything you say, Mommy."

Tabatha hung up, turned to me, and stretched her arms over her head. "Would Mario take us to the Vatican, do you think? That would count as a museum, wouldn't it?"

"I assume so." I wanted to go there, along with a hundred other places. The Colosseum, the Pantheon, just to name a few.

"Cool." She came to life. "I want to pay a call on the Pope."

Was she serious or playing some teenage mind game? In any case, we needed to eat breakfast, even when she said she wasn't hungry. I called Mario and arranged for him to come by the hotel in an hour to pick us up. I wondered why he had so much free time on his hands, but he assured me he did and that it would be a pleasure to drive us.

"First, I need to call my mother," I said. I scooped up my phone and dialed her number.

She answered with a yawn. "Everything okay, dear?" she said when she heard my voice. "I figured you'd be too busy to call your mama."

"I have been. Oh, I don't know . . ."

"Would you try to enjoy yourself and quit worrying?"

"Okay. I just—"

A man's voice chuckled in the background and said her name, "Gladys."

"Mama?"

"I've got to run, Lucy. Bye-bye, dear." She giggled as she hung up.

AN HOUR LATER, Mario pulled his vehicle away from the hotel with me in the passenger seat and Tabatha in the back.

"As you will find, this entire city is a museum," he said when I asked him about taking us to one. He glanced into his rearview mirror to speak to Tabatha. "Where are your parents today?"

"Scoping out some galleries. For them, this is a business trip."

"I hope they find what they're looking for." He rubbed the back of his neck with one hand.

He took a right, then maneuvered us into frantic traffic I wouldn't dare drive in. "It's such a lovely day, maybe we should go to the Borghese Gardens," he said. "Or perhaps wander through the Colosseum."

I pulled my sunglasses out of my purse and was grateful I'd remembered to bring them. The day was coolish—in the fifties—but bright, and the sky a hard-cobalt blue.

"If only I could see the Pope," Tabatha said.

"I heard he's giving an audience today." Mario checked his watch. "If we're not too late. We probably won't be able to get very close to him, but you could see him from afar."

"That would be way cool." Tabatha draped an arm around him from the back seat. "I've spoken to him before. Several times." She wore skinny jeans and a white hoodie.

Mario's eyebrows lifted. "How wonderful. Few people get that opportunity." He glanced to me, and I shrugged.

Minutes later, he parked the car. "Come on, we'll have to walk a couple blocks."

The closer we got to St. Peter's the thicker the crowds grew until they formed a human wall. Finally, we could see over their heads the source of their excitement. Like a magnet, they swarmed around what must be the Pope in the distance, standing in a motorized vehicle. Both Mario and I stopped, but Tabatha dropped to all fours and crawled forward, out of my grasp and soon out of sight. Mario and I tried to keep up with her and were met with glares of disapproval. "We've been standing here for two hours," one woman said in a crisp British accent.

Tabatha had done it again. There was nothing I could do but wait. After an agonizing hour, the crowd dispersed as the Pope's vehicle returned to the Vatican. I finally caught sight of Tabatha who beamed with delight.

"He remembered my name! I told you I knew him."

I was filled with both relief and anger. Tabatha had proven again I had little control over her. Make that, no control. Maybe it would be better if her parents fired me before some catastrophe occurred.

As the three of us sat eating at a nearby café, Mario asked Tabatha, "What's your parents' gallery like?"

She licked her fork clean. "Just the normal kind."

"No special interests?"

I had to wonder why he cared. Did he believe Tabatha's anecdotes about Mussolini's girlfriend's hoard of paintings? Apparently she had a tendency to fabricate stories I didn't know about. Let's face it, she did not know the Pope. So why believe any of her other tales?

"If they find something they like, how do they know it's genuine?" he persisted.

"So many questions." She tilted her head. "You'll have to ask them yourself."

Mario received a text. After scanning it, his features took on a look of disappointment, the corners of his mouth drooping. "I'm afraid I'll have to cut our outing short. That was my new boss. Something's come up."

"You mean we have to go back to the hotel?" Tabatha asked.

"Unless you two would like me to drop you off some-where else."

Was this goodbye? I was surprised to feel a sense of loss. Followed by dread. How would I keep control of Tabatha by myself?

"Is there somewhere I could take you?" he asked me.

"Anywhere but the hotel." Tabatha sounded dis-traught. I could feel her toes kicking the back of my seat.

"I know a wonderful area," Mario said. "You could wander around, have lunch, and then take a cab or Uber back to the hotel."

"Okay." I sounded pathetic even to me. Because I'd grown fond of him in a short time. Which made me feel immature. I was hoping he'd lean forward and kiss me goodbye, but of course, he couldn't and wouldn't with Tabatha here.

Maybe he had no desire . . .

CHAPTER 7

HE DROVE US forward over cobblestones. "There is a very interesting area. Good food available and small shops. The Jewish Ghetto."

"How did you know?" I kept my heritage under wraps for a number of reasons. My mother had often repeated, "Beware, anti-Semitism is alive and well." And I knew this fact to be true from watching the news.

"Everyone should add the Jewish Ghetto to their list of must-sees in Rome," he said.

I recoiled at the suggestion. "A ghetto?" The word made me shudder.

He must have noticed distaste in my voice. "It's not what you think. The area is most enjoyable and not located far away from other sights. It's nothing like a ghetto anymore. A charming part of the city I think you'll enjoy. It's filled with small restaurants, shops, and ancient ruins. And it's located only a stone's throw from Piazza Venezia and Capitoline Hill."

"Then why is it call a ghetto?" I asked.

"In the sixteenth century, the area was walled off as the residential area for Rome's Jews, a common occurrence across Europe. In fact, the word *ghetto* is an Italian word." He slowed to take a turn. "It's the rectangular-shaped area just west and south of here,"

"I want to see it," Tabatha said. "We can take a taxi back to the hotel."

"Or even walk," Mario said.

Tabatha moaned. "Nah, I hate walking."

"Let's see how we do," I said.

"Maybe wandering is a better word." Mario seemed at ease maneuvering his Alfa in the hectic traffic. I glanced over to evaluate his classic profile. He was gorgeous, if I was honest with myself. But I didn't trust my instincts when it came to men. Brad had strung me along for years.

Ten minutes later, Mario dropped us off in what I found to be an extraordinary area, alive with shops, restaurants, and tourists—not at all what I expected.

He jogged around the car and opened my door. "I really am sorry to leave you stranded, Lucia." I felt a buzz of attraction—a zing between us as he brought my fingertips to his lips for a brief kiss.

He grasped my hand and helped me exit the car. "Call me if you need me."

"But you'll be busy."

"A call from you would be a great excuse to get out of the meeting," he said with a wink. "You have my number, no?"

After Tabatha climbed out of the back seat, he shut her door. "I bid you lovely ladies farewell," he said.

Tabatha giggled. Mario was a flirt. I scolded myself for thinking I was anything special in his eyes.

Tabatha and I strolled into a fascinating area lined with small outdoor restaurants, churches, and syna-gogues. The square was teeming with tourists. My nos-trils were hit with a myriad of luscious aromas, but I turned my attention to Tabatha. I needed to focus on her.

I used my stern teacher voice. "If you don't stay close to me, we're going straight back to the hotel. Do you understand?"

She let out a dramatic sigh that scaled an octave. "Yeah, I get it. Like why are you being so mean?"

"I'm not. Do you want your parents to fire me? I'm looking after you the best I can, but it hasn't been good enough."

She snorted. "That's what happened to the last two women."

I felt foolish for not asking Gretchen about Tabatha's previous caretakers when I took the job.

We ambled across the square, stopping into small shops to buy Christmas presents. An hour later we found ourselves back in the Piazza Venezia. My eyes zeroed in on that balcony where Mussolini spoke to his adoring crowds.

Tabatha followed my gaze. "Do you think we can go up there?" she asked. "Maybe it's open to tourists. Wouldn't that be cooler than cool?"

"My hunch is your parents wouldn't think so." I sure
didn't want to. I thought about my great-grandfather—
executed in northeastern France by the Gestapo, Mama
told me. He was an art collector and a painter. What
Hitler had hoped to be but had little talent; instead,
he'd stolen great works of art from others.

Tabatha tugged on my elbow, pulling me into the
present. "Oh, come on and don't be such a fraidy-cat."

"Mussolini was a terrible man," I said. "I'd rather
head up to the Victor Emmanuel." I stared at the fabulous white structure. Surely, walking up all those steps
would wear Tabatha out. "I'll bet there's a beautiful
view from the top. You can take pictures to show your
parents. Or maybe do a report on that."

"I guess so. It looks like a huge wedding cake, doesn't
it?"

"Yes, that's an excellent description."

She grinned. "I'm smarter than people think I am."
She leaned closer, spoke in my ear. "For instance, that
man who's been following us doesn't think I've noticed
him."

My goodness, this girl had an imagination. But no
use trying to argue her out of it.

We crossed the square, avoiding zooming cars and
scooters, and began our ascent to the top of the enormous white marble monument. Halfway up, I brought
out my tour book—partly to catch my breath.

I read aloud. "It says here this place was built to com-
memorate the first king of Italy, Victor Emmanuel II
(1820-1878). He worked to free Italy from foreign
control and became a central figure of the movement

for Italian unification. When he died in 1878, he was buried in the Pantheon. We'll have to go there too."

I doubted Tabatha was listening. A breeze had come up, and she stood swiping her blonde bangs out of her face as she scanned the view. I closed the guidebook and did the same. I breathed in thousands of years of ancient history. I would make the best of this trip, my chance to broaden my horizons. I felt exhilaration careening through my veins. Until I looked down the many stairs and saw a man staring up at us. He turned away and commenced reading a folded newspaper.

No doubt just some guy. A plainclothes guard? Tabatha's overactive imagination was rubbing off on me.

"Come on, Lucy." Tabatha pivoted. "Are you coming or not?" She took off like the fifteen-year-old she was. I pulled myself together and followed her.

"Just a second, I want to take some pictures." I dipped into my purse, exhumed my phone, and took a half a dozen photos. I admonished myself for not taking more earlier to show Mama when I got home. And to remind myself of Rome's many attractions. Including Mario.

"This place is cool." Tabatha was content to admire the view for a couple of minutes but quickly grew weary. "Come on," she said and ascended several steps.

I had hoped to catch my breath and enjoy the magnificent view for a few minutes more but knew better than to let her get too far ahead of me. I noticed the man with the newspaper was chatting with a woman who was laughing. He was probably just a cabdriver or tour guide looking for customers. We might need him ourselves.

Tabatha increased her pace. As I sped up, I caught my toe on a step. In what seemed like slow motion, I flew forward, my hand flying out to cushion my fall. I landed with an undignified thud.

For a moment, I couldn't breathe. I'd heard the term *knocked the wind out*. Had I broken a bone or injured myself in any way? I recognized the metallic taste of blood. I ran my tongue around the inside of my mouth to make sure I hadn't broken a tooth, but they all seemed intact. I must have chomped down on my tongue.

I noticed Tabatha turning on her heel and coming back to help me. She slowed as she retrieved the contents of my purse. Several women arrived and asked me questions I couldn't understand. I assumed they were Scandinavian.

"Should we call you an ambulance?" one of the women asked in broken English.

I wiggled my toes and fingers. "No, thank you, I think I'm okay." I assumed my hip and ankle would be bruised, not to mention my aching wrist. Pain screamed up to my elbow. I needed a white pill to lessen the pain but didn't wish to revisit my old friend. Make that enemy.

"Can you find my phone?" I asked Tabatha, and she handed it to me.

"Thanks." I rang Mario's cell number. I couldn't think of what else to do. I didn't wish to call the Williamses for fear they'd decide I was incompetent.

"*Pronto.*" Mario answered immediately. "Is there *un problema?*"

"I feel foolish bothering you during a meeting."

"Not at all. We were just wrapping things up. I saw your number—"

Where to start? "Would you be able to drive us back to the hotel?"

"*Certo*. Certainly. Where are you?"

"At the Victor Emmanuel. I fell . . ."

"Do you need to see a doctor? Can you walk?"

"I think so." I feigned a laugh. "The only thing I wounded is my pride." I hoped. "I'm on the steps."

"Don't try to come down on your own. I'll be right there."

By the time Mario reached the Victor Emmanuel, I had scooted most of the way down the hard marble steps on my rump. Tabatha carried my purse. She seemed pleased to help me. And who was I to refuse her?

Mario sprinted over to us. "Are you sure you didn't break anything?" he asked.

"It happened so quickly . . . I feel foolish."

"Let me carry you."

Before I could give him an argument, he lifted me up as though I were weightless. Mario didn't seem that strong, but he obviously was. His cheek grazed mine as he settled me into his arms.

My hands naturally moved around his neck. My head fell against his chest. I was glad to see Tabatha at his elbow.

"Where shall we take you?" he asked me. "To the hospital?"

"No, I hate emergency rooms."

"I could take you to the walk-in clinic near my place. I know a doctor who works there. Friends since childhood."

"I'd rather just elevate my wrist and try an ice pack."

He glanced to Tabatha for a moment, then spoke in my ear. "If we were alone, I'd take you to my apartment and try icing your wrist."

I gave my head a shake as my mind spun with possibilities. I didn't want to go back and sit in the hotel room. "Her parents would have a fit."

"They won't mind," Tabatha said, her voice giddy. "I want to see where you live, Mario. Let me try to get them on the phone." Tabatha handed me hers. "I already dialed Mommy's number."

"Thanks." I reached for her cell phone, put it to my ear. But it went straight to voice mail.

Now what? I didn't want to spend hours in an emergency room full of sick people when all I'd done is twist my wrist. I could wiggle my toes and fingers. And I had Tabatha to think of.

"We'd better take you to my place," Mario said. "Well, really, it's corporate housing, owned by Amazon for use by employees while staying in the city."

I had trouble entering his car but finally got situated. In ten minutes, Mario cruised up front of an eight-story apartment building. He glanced over as I craned my aching neck to count the stories.

"What floor are you on? Maybe this wasn't such a good idea."

He chuckled. "Don't worry, Lucia, we have an elevator."

"Oh, but—" I still wasn't sure I shouldn't insist we go back to the hotel.

"Come in, since we're here," he said. "You look pale."

A spasm of pain made me wince. "My wrist."

With their arms around my waist, he and Tabatha helped me hobble to the elevator and then to his apartment on the sixth floor. I made it to the couch and collapsed.

"Put your feet up on the table and relax." Mario pointed to an ultramodern glass coffee table. In fact, every piece of furniture looked new, as if a decorator had placed them around the room. Not a speck of dust anywhere.

Magazines fanned across the table. Mario swooped them up and placed a pillow on my lap. "I'm going into the kitchen. I'll be right back." Minutes later he returned with an ice bag.

"How's the pain?" he asked.

"Better." But I felt weak, as though I'd been in a car wreck.

He placed the ice pack on my wrist. "We can get you to a doctor if this doesn't work," he said.

"That would be great." I craved a pain reliever.

I tried reaching Gretchen and Stan again, without result. Finally, I called the hotel to see if the Williamses had left me or Tabatha a message.

"*Mi dispiace, signora,* I'm sorry, we haven't heard from them all day," the concierge said.

"Where could they be?" Tabatha glanced up to me. "Nothing new, I'm always the last to know."

"But surely, they'd tell me. Wouldn't they?" I hung up and canvassed the room: tall bookshelves filled with leather-bound books that all seemed to match too well. I reminded myself a decorator had assembled this apartment.

He lay the ice pack across my wrist. "*Ecco*—I mean, here. I'll get you an ACE bandage when we're done icing."

"You have one on hand?"

"Yes, several. I run . . ." He let out a sigh. "I took a fall last year. Nothing serious."

"This apartment is so neat it doesn't look as though a man lives here," I couldn't contain a smile.

He chuckled. "*Grazie*. This is the first time I've been told I'm too neat. Truth is, a cleaning service came this morning. Amazon pays for it."

I admired the swirling blue and green glass vase in a window.

Mario followed my gaze. "You like?" he asked.

"Very much."

"Then you must visit Murano, in Venice."

"I'd love that. Maybe on another trip."

"I wish I could take you there."

"How about me?" Tabatha piped in.

"Yes, of course, you must go too and ride in a gondola. Perhaps with your parents."

"You trying to get rid of me?" Tabatha asked.

"Not at all. But your parents would enjoy the trip immensely."

My phone chimed.

"That must be them. Finally."

I recognized the number. Brad. I was tempted to ignore the call again but started to worry something might be wrong. Why would he call me after so long?

"Hello?" I said.

"Hey, Lucy, what's going on with you?"

Hoping Mario couldn't hear, I pressed the phone to my ear. "I—this isn't a good time."

"I've got a big surprise, sugar. I'm flying into Rome tomorrow."

"You are?" I should be overjoyed.

"Yeah, I called you at home, and your mother told me you were there."

"I am, but I'm tied up."

"You have your boss standing right there? Tell them you need some time off."

"I'll call you back later, okay?" I said.

"That won't work. I'm sitting on a plane on the tarmac, so you won't be able to reach me. Aren't you excited about seeing me?"

"Uh, yes, but I'm working."

"Never mind that. If they don't give you the time off, you can quit. I'll take care of you."

I'd waited three years to hear those words, but they rang hollow.

I glanced to Mario and weighed the two men. I hardly knew Mario. But I was attracted to him. What woman wouldn't be?

CHAPTER 8

"HOW IS MY favorite patient feeling?" Mario lifted the ice pack off of my wrist. "It's been twenty minutes. I'll put this back in the freezer. Has your pain improved?"

"Not perfect but much better." I wasn't used to being fussed over and appreciated the attention. The fact was, my wrist pain had practically disappeared. I should be thrilled, but I wasn't ready to get back to work looking after Tabatha, who was more trouble than expected. But she'd been my conduit to Rome.

I bent my legs and placed my feet on the plush carpet.

"Excellent," Mario said. "I'll fix you a snack if you're up to eating."

"Always," I said. "I was born hungry."

Minutes later, he presented us with a sumptuous antipasto platter—salami, sliced cheeses, crackers, and olives. He placed it on the table at my knees, then turned and disappeared into the kitchen again, this time for plates, flatware, and napkins.

He proceeded to arrange items on a plate atop a tray and handed it to me.

"Thank you."

"*Il piacere è tutto mio*—the pleasure is all mine."

"Hey, how about me?" Tabatha said.

"Help yourself," Mario said, but she curled her lip. "Nothing you see to your liking? I've got fruit and cookies in the kitchen. Go in and sample whatever you like."

"Okay." She popped to her feet and skipped into the kitchen.

"How about a glass of wine?" he asked me.

"No, thanks, I'd better not. But you go ahead." Wine sounded heavenly, but I didn't dare take a chance.

"I can wait," he said, sinking down next to me.

Finally, my chance to be alone with Mario. I turned toward him and found his eyes gazing into mine.

"Tell me about your family," he said.

"Not much to tell. My father died when I was a young teen." Why had I blurted that out?

"I'm so sorry."

"That's okay." No, it wasn't. Papa left Mama and me under a mountain of debt. "I shouldn't have said anything."

"But I want to know everything about you."

His stare shifted to my lips in a way that told me he longed to kiss me. The world seemed to stop revolving.

"These cookies are fabulous," Tabatha said, bursting into the room.

Mario leaned back, lifted his brows, and sighed.

She plopped down next to me. "They're stupendous," she told me. "You should try them." She gnawed into one, then passed me the container.

"Those are biscotti," he said. "I'm glad you like them."

I took one, nibbled into it, and savored the almond flavor and texture. Everything in Rome tasted better than back home. "Yummy," I said. "I should get the recipe and make them when we get back to Seattle."

"Please do," Tabatha said. "I want to take this whole city home."

Mario chuckled.

I decided to buy some biscotti for Mama for Christmas. Mama said she'd be okay, but I worried about her being all alone and wondered how she'd spend her time. Probably watching classic movies such as *Holiday Inn* and *White Christmas* on TV. Too bad it rarely snowed in Seattle at all, let alone at Christmas.

"Does it ever snow in Rome?" I asked Mario.

"Rarely. But we do get snow further north."

"Let's go there," Tabatha said. "I want to play in the snow on Christmas morning."

I imagined what we would do here on Christmas Eve and on Christmas Day. Stay in the hotel? Maybe I could find a way to be with Mario. Unlikely.

FROM MY PERCH on the couch, I tried calling Gretchen several more times. Finally, I called the hotel again to see if she'd left a message for me. Apparently,

Gretchen had called and told the staff to put all our charges on their credit card. She wasn't sure when she and Stan would return.

"What?" I was flabbergasted. "Did she tell you where they are?"

"Sorry, no."

"What's wrong?" Mario asked when Tabatha was in the powder room.

"It looks as though my employers have disappeared. What kind of parents would simply not answer their phones? Where are they?"

Mario shrugged one shoulder. "I've never been married nor had children."

"I'd better get Tabatha back to the hotel."

He checked his clock on the mantelpiece. "Let's ice your wrist for another twenty minutes first. Then I'll wrap it in an ACE bandage. Unless you want to have it x-rayed. Have you changed your mind about that?"

I wiggled my fingers, initiating a spasm of pain. "No, I think I just twisted it. Nothing's broken."

Tabatha collapsed onto a love seat and closed her eyes.

"I think we should stop and get it x-rayed on the way to the hotel," Mario said. "It won't take long. In fact, I insist."

Mario whisked me and Tabatha to a small clinic, where the radiologist pronounced my wrist okay. No fracture anyway. But pain throbbed up to my elbow. Thanks to Mario, a physician recommended in broken English that I take pain medication, which I dared not do. I feared even ibuprofen or aspirin after years of breaking free from my drug addiction. I never considered myself free because I wasn't. I still attended a meeting once a week, which I was missing this week. I'd convinced myself I'd be fine. I could call my sponsor any time I needed her, but I couldn't. Not now. I glanced at the wall clock and calculated the time. Sharon was probably still in bed. Not that Sharon wouldn't drop everything to help me. She'd been my NA sponsor for five years.

The doctor scribbled out a prescription and handed it to me. Against my better judgment, I slid it in my purse.

Then Mario and the doctor fell into Italian—I surmised chatting about a soccer game by the way they were snickering and kicking the air—while Tabatha rolled around the room on a rolling stool.

"Dr. Fiorino recommends you take it easy and elevate your wrist when possible," Mario said. "I'll stop by a pharmacy on the way back to the hotel."

I got an itchy feeling and was tempted to tell him to go ahead. But I stopped myself. "That's okay," I said. "I'd rather not."

"The doctor said you'll sleep better tonight if you're not in pain." He glanced over to me "Why suffer needlessly?"

As Mario drove, he turned to me. "How are you feeling?"

My arm throbbed but I said, "Fine."

"You should listen to the doctor's advice and get the prescription filled. Look, there's a pharmacy there on the corner. I'll stop."

I recalled breaking my leg skiing years ago. The physician had prescribed painkillers that quickly became an addiction. "Really, I'd rather not."

"Be practical. Just one pill couldn't hurt." He reached out his hand. "Where is that prescription?"

I retrieved the prescription from my purse and gave the paper to him.

CHAPTER 9

BACK AT THE hotel with Tabatha, I first went to the busy reception area to reconfirm that the Williamses had not returned. And no additional messages. I took a moment to admire the festive Christmas decor.

"It shows they have great confidence in you," Mario said, also scanning the lobby.

Tabatha leaned against me. "Yeah, we're fine without them. I don't care if they don't come back. Ever."

"I wonder what they'll think when they return and find you here," I said to Mario. "You worry too much," Tabatha said as we wended our way through the lavish hotel to our room. "They're the ones who are acting irresponsibly, not us." Her voice turned whiny. "I'm hungry." Her shoulders slouched.

"Okay. I'll order food up to the room," I said. "A burger? Or do you want to try something Italian?"

"Nah, I want a burger and fries."

"Do you have a key to the Williamses' room?" Mario asked me.

"No. What are you thinking?"

"Nothing, never mind." Mario spoke in my ear. "I'll see if I can help track them down."

"Call the hospitals?" I whispered.

"That's one thought. I have many friends . . ." He opened the door and stepped out into the hallway. I could hear the rumble of his baritone voice as he spoke on his phone.

Twenty minutes later, knuckles rapped on the door. I opened it to find room service pushing a cart. Mario rang off his phone and followed the server into the room. Tabatha sat on the bed against several pillows, buds plugged her ears, and she hummed. She was off in another world but sniffed the air when the tray came to her bedside.

I sat on an overstuffed chair, a pillow elevating my wrist.

"You poor thing," Mario said to me. "Are you in pain? I have your medication right here."

"Half of my problem is jet lag." Although my wrist and arm throbbed. I was used to living through pain. "It's not unusual for the Williamses to stay out late, but usually, they tell me ahead of time."

"My parents would have a cow if I acted that way," Tabatha said.

The corners of Mario's mouth tipped up. "I'm sure they want only what's best for you."

She shrugged off his remark. "Whatever."

"They may be out on a business meeting. You said they collect art?"

"Yes, and I bet you're right," I said. "They mentioned something about driving up to Florence, but it seems they would've told me ahead of time."

He rubbed his chin. "You know them far better than I do."

"I thought I did."

Tabatha swished another french fry through her ketchup and chomped into it. I wondered if she was listening to our conversation. If so, she was putting on quite an act. I myself would be beyond upset. Well, they'd hired me to look after her, not scare her needlessly.

"Do your parents ever take off like this?" I asked her.

"Not exactly like this, but they don't keep me updated on their comings and goings."

"I should leave you two to rest," Mario said and set the pill vial on a table near my elbow. I wanted him to stay. I didn't trust myself.

He opened the door and stepped into the hallway. "Please come back soon," I said to his departing form.

I turned to Tabatha. "Hey, cutie. You okay?"

"I feel so tired." Her head sunk into the pillows.

An hour must have passed. I realized I'd been sleeping too. Tabatha stirred and stretched. "I want to go out somewhere. To go shopping for Christmas presents. Mommy gave you a credit card, didn't she?"

"Yes." And Gretchen hadn't given me any limitations. "What would you want to buy?"

"I don't know. I can't go home with nothing."

"Understandable. You need souvenirs at least. We'll ask the hotel where to buy something nice."

I hid the pill vial in a drawer in the top bureau with my lingerie. I imagined the employees of this fine hotel being tempted to take it, which, actually, would be a favor to me.

My phone chimed. I scooped it up and glanced down at it, expecting to see Gretchen's number but recognizing Brad's. His timing couldn't be worse. Perhaps an overstatement, but it felt as if I were sinking into quicksand. Too many uncertainties at once.

"Aren't you going to answer?" Tabatha asked, proving she was listening in on every word.

"Hi, Brad," I said.

"Hi there, sugar," Brad said. My chest was not fluttering with butterflies. But my brain was flapping with worries about the Williamses. I assured myself they'd show up. Hadn't I gone out on all night binges in the past? The alcohol I could handle, for the most part, but the narcotics had taken over. I'd woken up in strange places, to say the least. I'd disappeared for days, leaving my mother frantic.

"Lucy?" Brad said.

"Yes."

"Where are you? I just landed."

"Oh?"

"You don't seem excited to hear from me." His brittle voice told me he was losing patience.

"I am, but I'm just leaving the hotel." I didn't know what to think. My emotions were engaged in a tug-o-war. Brad adored staying out late, carousing—having a good time, which always included alcohol consumption. And maybe a snort or two of cocaine. In other words, double trouble for me. He'd argued that he didn't drink for a whole week every month, evidence he didn't have a drinking problem, and he'd all but given up cocaine and never flew with a stash on hand.

"Once I'm in town, I'll call back," he said. "Can't wait to see you, Lucy."

"This isn't a good time."

"How about dinner tomorrow? Where are you staying?"

"The Hotel Hassler."

"Whoa. Uptown. I've heard about that place."

"It's very nice."

"To put it mildly. I've seen pictures."

"Brad, I'm working."

Tabatha got to her feet and stood at my side. As I wrapped an arm around her shoulder, I thought about the term poor little rich girl. I couldn't desert her. She tipped her chin and looked up at me. "Well, can we go out shopping now?"

"Look, Brad, I can't talk."

His voice grew surly. "Can't or won't?"

"Got to go." I hung up.

Tabatha had already lost interest, though. I watched her topple onto her bed and insert her earbuds.

"Hey, girlie, are you falling asleep?"

"What do you care? If my parents weren't paying you, you wouldn't even be here." Her words were laced with bitterness. Had I done something to hurt her feelings?

"Sweetie, they are paying me, but I'm delighted to spend time with you."

"No, you're not. No one likes me."

"I don't believe that."

"If it wasn't the truth, why didn't they bring a friend along?"

"Well, maybe they thought I could handle only one young woman."

"Nah, I don't have any friends at school. No one to invite."

"I bet that's not true."

"I changed my mind. I don't want to go anywhere."

I snatched up a french fry and savored the taste. "Have you noticed that even the fries taste better here? We should call them Italian fries."

She didn't answer. This time she really was asleep. I ate her untouched salad, then pulled out my guidebook and sat on my bed. My eyelids were so heavy I couldn't keep them open. And my neck couldn't keep my head from falling back.

Before I knew it, I was sound asleep, deep in a cavern of crazy dreams about when I was a girl and my father was alive. I struggled for consciousness and glanced over at Tabatha's bed. She was gone.

CHAPTER 10

MY FIRST THOUGHT was that she was in her parents' room. They had returned even if I hadn't heard them. How could I be so lame? How long had I been sleeping? I glanced at the clock and saw six o'clock. Time for dinner?

I opened the drapes, saw blue sky, and realized it was the next morning. I couldn't believe I'd slept that long.

I examined my phone. No missed calls or text messages. I texted the Williamses but got no answer. They were probably sleeping. I tried Tabatha's phone, but it switched over to "Like, leave a message, already," which I did.

"Where are you?" I asked. "Please call me immediately."

My first priority was to find Tabatha. As I took a quick shower and got dressed, I admonished myself for not hearing her leave. No time for makeup or to fix my hair. I gathered it into a ponytail. I scooped up my purse and key and hurried to the Williamses' door. I knocked. No answer.

A hotel employee strode down the hall—I assume after delivering room service. Fortunately, the stout woman recognized me and said, "*Buongiorno.*"

"Good morning. I got locked out. Can you help me?"

She must have known this wasn't my room, but she knocked, then opened the door. One pillow lay atop the king-size bed, and the velvet spread was slightly mussed. Someone had slept here, it seemed, but the room was empty.

"Thank you," I said to the woman as I left and closed the door behind me.

I hastened down to the first floor and inquired at the front desk to see if anyone had seen them come in last night or knew where the Williamses were, but the shifts had just changed. I did my best to describe Tabatha, but the staff stared at me with bleary eyes. One pointed down a hallway. "Maybe in the restaurant?" he said.

But no sign of her there.

I scoured the first floor, jogged up and down several flights of stairs, and asked every staff member who spoke English if they'd seen a blonde fifteen-year-old girl. Finally, back at the front desk, I inquired again.

"A young woman did leave about an hour ago who might fit that description," the man said. "I don't know. I'm sorry. I am just coming on shift after a few days off and didn't recognize her." In Italian, he asked the other hotel employees, but no one knew.

Another one of Tabatha's shenanigans? Where were the Williamses? Should I call the police? I felt fear laced with anger taking over. The stores weren't open yet. Maybe Tabatha was exploring the Spanish Steps. I hurried to my room for a jacket then left the hotel. As annoyance threatened to overcome me, I tried to look on the bright side. This might be my one chance to take a walk in solitude. According to my guidebook, I had missed a multitude of monuments and fountains.

I left a written message in my room and at the front desk. Outside, the air was fresh and invigorating. The madcap morning traffic hadn't started up yet. I could cross streets without feeling as if I was going to be mowed over. I wandered down narrow side streets. I heard a man crooning with a superb tenor voice and followed it until I found a fellow sweeping the cobbled street. It occurred to me that people in the United States don't sing, except at birthday parties and in church. And yet here was this man who sounded like he could sing in an opera. He was handsome too.

"Excuse me," I said. "Do you speak English?"

"A little. Do you need help?"

"I'm looking for the Trevi Fountain."

A smile took shape on his handsome face, revealing crooked teeth. He pointed and explained in Italian until he realized I couldn't understand him. Finally, he said, "Down that way and around the corner."

"Thank you. *Grazie.*" I decided to try out my meager Italian.

He fell into his native tongue, what must have meant, "You're welcome—*Prego.* Anything else I can help you with?" He waited with what seemed to be an expectant expression.

Mama always warned me not to speak to strangers, but I was grateful for the directions. It seemed the fountain was close by. And what could it hurt? He must talk to tourists all day.

"*Mille grazie.*" My pronunciation was improving.

"Come back this way again tomorrow morning. I'll be here." A flirtation if ever I'd heard one.

I took off in the direction he'd pointed and soon came to the magnificent Trevi Fountain. I stood admiring its grandeur and listened to water splashing down. More music.

Just for fun, I reached into my pocket for a coin and tossed it in among the many other coins. The words to "Three Coins in the Fountain" circled through my head. I felt like singing the first few bars. I saved singing for the shower and when listening to the oldies channel on the radio in the kitchen or car. I'd been told many times that I had a good singing voice and was in the choir in high school until it wasn't cool anymore. Why had I always cared so much what other people thought of me?

I realized I should make a wish but wasn't sure what to ask for. I would have to watch the movie again. Maybe tonight on my iPad. But why wish for someone else's dream? Didn't I have one of my own? What would I wish for if I could have anything? A husband, children, a passion? If nothing else, Tabatha was passionate. When she wasn't down in the dumps. I could use some of her enthusiasm. At least I hadn't succumbed to the little white pills beckoning me.

Thinking about Tabatha jerked me into the present. I needed to get back to the hotel. I felt all turned around and finally asked a woman on her way to work for instructions. She pointed and spoke in Italian. I'd have to do my best. I zigzagged my way back to the bottom of the Spanish Steps, climbed to the top, and was relieved when I saw the hotel's elegant facade, Christmas lights illuminating the doorway.

Which reminded me I needed to purchase a gift for my mother. Hanukkah had turned into Christmas thanks to my father's demands. Times like this made me miss him down to my bones. I cursed his stupid little plane, which must have run low on oil or fuel before it crashed near Mount Baker. Mama said she'd tried to get him to sell the Cessna, but he wouldn't.

I should buy a small gift for Tabatha, too. Perhaps an audiobook. I'd loved reading at her age. Maybe choose one of my favorites? A classic like *Wuthering Heights* or a Jane Austen. Most likely she'd hate them. Getting into her head was beyond me.

I felt a wave of guilt for leaving her. I texted her again, and to my surprise, she responded right away and said she was doing research for her paper on Mussolini.

Are you in the hotel? I texted.

No!

Where are you? I cringed when I thought of her out on the streets by herself.

At Mussolini's balcony waiting for it to open.

Stay there, I wrote. *I'll meet you.*

I hailed a cab, which whisked me off to the Piazza Venezia, toward the notorious balcony used by Benito Mussolini to address his adoring crowds. I contemplated what evil meant. What if someone kidnapped Tabatha? It could happen in a gigantic city like this.

The closer the driver zeroed in on the square the more anxious I got.

"Stop, I see her—over there at a table." I pointed to a café, and the driver jerked to a halt.

Tabatha sat sipping on frothy cappuccino. When I spotted her, my heart filled with love and gratitude. Yes, I loved this rambunctious teenager. My mother had seemed overbearing when I was a teen, but Gretchen gave Tabatha little attention. I thought having a father solved all your problems, but Stan often ignored Tabatha. Maybe this was his second marriage and she was not really his daughter. Come to think of it, she didn't look like him. I, on the other hand, resembled my father. I kept a framed photo of him standing by his Cessna in my bedroom. Strange that Mama had no others in the house.

The moment I paid the driver I leaped from the vehicle and jogged over to Tabatha. I was glad to see she wore her lined denim jacket and an orange knit scarf.

"Lucia." She finger-waved. "You have got to try this cappuccino."

"Do your parents know where you are?" I asked.

She tipped her head. "A better question would be, do I know where they are?"

"You didn't see them last night?"

"No. I slept in their room waiting for them." She wrinkled her nose. "But they never showed up."

"How did you get in?"

"A cleaning woman opened the door."

"Have your parents ever done this before?" I was flummoxed.

"No, they always come home by morning," she said.

The city brimmed to life as the sky brightened. People congregated at the café's bar, sipping coffee and eating pastries. A waiter with a white apron tied around his waist strutted out and asked me what I wanted. I'd learned: no sitting without ordering.

"*Un cappuccino doppio*," I said, hoping he could understand me. I guess I'd been practicing in Starbucks without knowing it. Minutes later he brought me a frothy cappuccino with a heart on top made of white foam. Was he flirting with me too?

"*Grazie*." I gazed up into his good-looking face. My, these Italians were a handsome race.

"*Colazione*?" the waiter asked. "Would you like breakfast?"

"Yes," Tabatha said. "I'm starving. I'll die if I don't eat. An orange juice, *per favore*. And some of those fancy rolls."

"*Certo, signorina*." Minutes later, he presented us with freshly squeezed orange juice for Tabatha and a platter of pastries: fruit-filled croissants and other tasty morsels that would no doubt expand my waistline.

The pale blue sky showed promise, but a chill permeated the air. I was glad for my warm jacket. I glanced up at the balcony I recalled from the black-and-white

photographs in history books. Crowds of chanting sup-
porters followed by photos of the grisly deaths of Mussolini and his mistress spun through my mind.

I imagined my great-grandparents being carted
off to a concentration camp during the same era. I
wondered if they'd died together, clutching onto each
other, or if the men and women had been separated
in a further act of cruelty. More than ever, I wondered
about my great-grandfather's paintings. The framed
pastel drawing my mother had was beyond beautiful
and also tragic: a pregnant woman leaning against a
wall, wearing a pensive expression on her face. Mama
had specified in her will that I was to inherit it. Maybe
so I'd hurry up and get married and have a child.

"When does Mussolini's balcony open?" Tabatha
asked the waiter, yanking me out of my ponderings.

He shot her a doubtful look. "Why would you want
to go up there?"

"I'm doing a school report," she said.

"With so many beautiful antiquities in Rome, why
go there?"

"Why work almost across the street from it?" she
shot back. "I know." She tipped her head. "Because it's
good for business."

She had a point. Like it or not, Mussolini's balcony
was a landmark.

"*Mi dispiace*—I'm sorry. It's not open today. *È chiuso*."
The waiter glanced at a portly couple seating themselves at a nearby table who jabbered in what sounded
like German, then he returned to us. "May I bring you
anything else?"

"Do you have something with chocolate in it?" Tabatha asked.

He sent her a smile. "Hot chocolate or a pastry?"

"Both." She grinned as he hurried back to the kitchen.

I wondered why the waiter had ignored the German couple. Did bad blood still flow from World War II? Why would German tourists want to see Mussolini's balcony in the first place? I reminded myself they might not even know what and where it was.

Minutes later, the waiter brought Tabatha a cup of hot chocolate and a plate mounded with chocolate-filled pastries.

"Thank you, thank you," she said.

He continued to ignore the German couple until they flagged him down. Then he slowly approached their table and took their order.

I tried calling the Williamses again, but both of their phones were turned off. As I was slipping my phone back in my purse, it chimed.

"Finally," Tabatha said.

I glanced down and saw Brad's number. I paused. Should I just let it ring? Yes.

"Not my parents?"

"Sorry." I shook my head.

Tabatha rested her elbows on the table, then her chin in her hands.

"I'm sorry, sweetie." I rubbed her rounded shoulder.

"I think they'd be happier without me."

"I'm sure that's not true." What was she trying to tell me?

"I've never said this to anyone, but I've thought about ending it all to make things easier for them. For me. Living's too hard."

I gulped. "You mean commit suicide?"

"Yeah." She let out a sob.

"Please promise me you won't." What should I do or say? Not that I hadn't contemplated suicide when I was in the clutches of addiction. I'd considered snuffing myself out like a spent candle.

"I've learned not to make or believe promises." She sniffed. "My parents never keep theirs."

"It may seem that way . . ." Much as I wanted to defend them, as was my tendency, I couldn't, because where were they now? Had they mentioned something I missed? Was this mix-up all somehow my fault?

"Come here, puppy," Tabatha suddenly gushed. I noticed a small mutt wandering through the tables. It was underweight, its ribs showing.

"*Va via!*" The waiter yelled at it, sending the canine skulking away.

"Hey," Tabatha said, her hands on her hips. "That's my puppy." She turned to me. "We can keep it, can't we?"

"I doubt the hotel will allow it." Fact was, I knew they wouldn't. The animal looked as though it hadn't been bathed for its entire life.

Tabatha tore off a piece of pastry and hopped to her feet. "Come here, puppy. That's her name. Puppy. Or is it a boy?"

"Tabatha—" I said.

"You'd let it starve to death?"

I loved dogs and missed my mother's and my cairn terrier, Sassy. But this scenario would never work out. I went through all the logistics in my mind and couldn't come up with a happy ending.

CHAPTER 11

"I'M NOT LEAVING this place unless we bring Puppy with us," Tabatha said.

I assessed its size and clumsiness. "I bet it's only eight or nine weeks old."

"Then it'll die if it's out here all by itself."

"Maybe she needs to go back to her mother," I said. "She might still be nursing."

"What do you mean?"

I was going to have to teach Tabatha the facts of life? I thought of the mythological twins Romulus and Remus left on the Tiber River nursing from a wolf. A statue of the trio stood in the hotel's foyer and elsewhere in the city.

No, that wouldn't be a good example of motherly love. Maybe Gretchen had raised Tabatha with a nanny on a bottle. Although that wolf seemed to show more attention to the boys than Stan and Gretchen showed Tabatha.

The pup scurried away and around the corner, saving me from having to explain.

Tabatha leaped to her feet to follow it. I grabbed her arm before she could get away.

"Come back to the table," I said. "If the dog needs to see you, she knows where you are."

"You're right; I'll sit here all day. Who knows, Mussolini's ghost might come out on the balcony."

"Sweetie, you know he was a dictator, don't you? Do you know what that means?"

"Yeah, I know."

"He was a cruel and evil man." I wondered if she knew how he died. His life was barbaric and so was his death.

"Maybe all that was said about him is lies. Why would all those people follow him? They loved him."

"A good question, and I don't have the answer." I wished I did.

We sat at the table and waited. Accordion and violin music from the sound system filled the air. A tenor singing an Italian opera aria joined in. It must have been recorded live at a concert because at the end, voices cheered and yelled, "*Bravo!*" The foot traffic increased, as well as vehicles of all sizes and shapes. Several honked their horns, apparently in a hurry to get to work.

The waiter refilled our cups.

I received a text from Gretchen. *Please take care of Tabatha.*

I will. I texted back. *I am.* I awaited more messages but received none.

Yet I needed to tell Tabatha something. "Hey, Tabatha, I just got a text from your mom. "She wanted to make sure I was taking good care of you."

I texted Gretchen. *Tabatha's right here. Do you want to talk to her?*

Gretchen didn't respond.

Where are you? I wrote but received no answer. Wouldn't Gretchen want an update on her only daughter?

"I hope they never come back." Tabatha brought out her tablet. "Like, I've already started writing my report on Mussolini. Doing lots of research. Wait until my teacher sees this. I'm going to turn it into a fictional piece."

"Will your teacher accept that?"

"Yup, in fact, he suggested it as a possibility—as long as we did our research."

"That's cool."

I wished Mario would contact me. I tried him myself. He answered right away, saying he was tied up in meetings. He'd get back to me later.

Tabatha was writing on her iPad. I texted Brad as a last resort. I should be ecstatic to see him, but he seemed like more trouble than I could handle at this moment. I was still irked he hadn't contacted me for weeks. I didn't buy his story about being too busy at work. How long does it take to send a text or call?

He got right back to me. *Where are you, sugar? I'll be right there.*

Maybe I'd been wrong about him. I gave him our location.

As I texted, I glanced away from Tabatha. When I looked back, she was gone. I asked the waiter, who shrugged and said he didn't know. I asked the German couple, who smiled and pointed down to where the mangy puppy had retreated.

I loped off in that direction, down a narrow, cobbled lane. I called out "Tabatha" and asked people if they'd seen her. No one had. I wasn't sure they understood me.

After ten minutes, I circled back. I scolded myself. A girl who hated walking and a puppy couldn't have traveled very far.

Only yards from the lane's entrance to the piazza, I noticed a steep staircase leading to a closed door. I climbed the steps to the apartment that must be atop the café and knocked on the door. "Tabatha, are you in there?"

No answer.

I rapped on the door with my knuckles until a small dark woman my age opened it and greeted me with deference. Behind her, a half dozen pups nursed from a German shepherd mix with her hackles raised.

"The girl told me she was lost," the woman said, her dark hair pulled back into a bun.

I scanned the shabby room. A Madonna on the wall. A candle in the window.

"Please come in." She opened the door farther.

"Tabatha?" I said. "Where are you?"

"Here." She giggled, then finally popped up behind a couch. I was struck by her immaturity.

"All the puppies are so cute. I want them all. Please can't I take one?"

"*Mi dispiace*—I'm sorry, but they are too young to leave their mother," the woman said in a kind voice. "Maybe in a couple of weeks I will sell you one."

"We can't wait that long," Tabatha said.

The apartment was the opposite of Mario's. Even the Christmas tree was wilted. The aroma of coffee from the café below drifted up into the room.

"That's my brother's shop below," the woman explained. "I rent this *appartamento* from him. My name is Maria." She must have been five feet tall, even shorter than I.

"Nice to meet you," I said, extending my hand to shake hers. The mama dog bared its teeth at me.

"No, no, Bella," Maria said. Tabatha strolled over to the dog and plopped down next to it.

"Be careful," I said, but Tabatha paid me no heed. She stroked the mother dog under the chin, then pet the puppies. "I want one of these pups."

"We can't take one through customs," I said. "We don't even know where your parents are."

"All the better. I don't care if they ever show up," Tabatha said. "They don't love me. I want to move in with Maria,"

"I would take her for a while," Maria said. "I have one little baby who's asleep in the other room. If I could find someone to look after him, I could get a job."

I saw no ring on her left hand. "No husband?" I asked, then regretted my question.

Her cheeks turned scarlet. "No, the man I thought I'd marry, he left me six months ago." She glanced to the floor. "I don't know where he is."

"I'm so sorry," I said. "But Tabatha can't move in here. No parents to help you?" I asked Maria, realizing I was being nosy.

"They disowned me when I moved in with this man." Maria's eyes watered up. "You see, I got pregnant . . . I disgraced them."

"You have no one to take care of you?" I asked.

"Only my brother, Leonardo. Downstairs."

"I think we met," I said. "Seems to be a nice fellow."

"Maybe you two will get together," she said. "I keep telling him he needs a wife."

"Uh, I don't think so." Although I had newfound respect for him.

"He owns his business," she said. "Very handsome, no? And a hard worker."

"Oh, please, let's move in with her." Tabatha cradled one of the pups. "Then I can watch these puppies grow up."

I loved dogs but didn't dare reach my hand over to them. The mother dog kept her gaze locked onto me.

"I'm afraid life isn't that easy," I said.

"I could rent you a room if you need a place to stay," Maria said. "I have a spare bedroom."

I was touched by her generosity, even if she planned to charge me rent. I figured I might be her gateway to moving to America if I married her brother.

"We need to head back downstairs," I said to Tabatha. "I told Brad he should meet us there." I pulled money from my pocket and left it on the kitchen counter as I noted its disrepair.

"No, no, I can't take money," Maria said.

"It's for your baby. We'll come back another day and meet him when he's awake."

"You can't make me leave," Tabatha said and stomped her foot.

"That's no way for a young lady to act." Maria came to my rescue. "You come back and visit me another time."

Tabatha turned to me. "Promise I can come back?"

"My door is always open to you," Maria said.

I was reluctant, but I finally gave in. "Yes, okay."

Maria gave each of us a brief hug and a peck on the cheek as we left. I noticed the money had disappeared. She must have slipped it in her pocket. Well, that was okay. She needed help.

Tabatha and I picked our way down the dark staircase and found our spot still vacant.

"I saved this table for you," Leonardo said.

Tabatha's demeanor brightened. "Thank you."

He brought her more hot chocolate and me a cappuccino and more pastries I couldn't resist. I would need to go on a diet when we got home. If I went home, that is. I noticed the lavish Christmas decorations. Could I stay and live in Rome? There wasn't a thing about the city I didn't like. Except Mama wasn't here. A slice of sadness cut through me when I thought of her spending Christmas all alone. Sure, she had a few girlfriends, but they were married and had extended families.

Tabatha jabbered on about the puppies and how nice Maria was. "I can't wait to go back."

I also wanted to return but knew better than to encourage Tabatha. I sipped the cappuccino and savored the taste of the pastries. Italians did know how to cook better than Americans, no doubt about it.

Fifteen minutes later, Brad arrived driving a white Vespa. He slowed the scooter and canvassed the square.

"There's Brad," I told Tabatha.

"Ignore him," Tabatha said. "Maybe he won't see us." She ducked under the table.

For a crazy minute, I was tempted to hide under the table with her. But I reminded myself I was in love with Brad. This is the moment I'd waited for.

"Over here," I called with a wave.

He grinned as he parked, dismounted the scooter, and removed his helmet. I watched him—tall and manly. Blond hair, blue eyes, confident.

To deny I had feelings for him would be a lie. He was like a magnet, and I a helpless scrap of steel. I noticed people at surrounding tables looking at him too. He was that handsome. Still, I kept a poker face. I wasn't going to get up and act like a teenager meeting a movie star.

"Like it?" he asked me. "It's a rental." He lowered himself on the chair next to me, his arm encircling my shoulder. "Are you happy to see me, sugar?"

"Yes, of course." At this moment, I felt like snuggling into the warmth and safety of his arms. But I introduced him to Tabatha, who acted nonplussed. She brought out her iPad and commenced writing as if he hadn't arrived.

"Want to go for a ride?" Brad asked me.

"I can't." I tilted my head toward Tabatha. "I'm working."

His lips turned pale. "She's old enough to stay here by herself."

"No, she's not."

Tabatha lifted her chin. "Call Mario," she said to me. "He'll come and keep me company."

"Who's Mario?" Brad asked.

"Her new boyfriend." Tabatha gave him a sideways glance as if noticing him for the first time.

"No, he's not." Containing a grin, I frowned at Tabatha. "He's someone I met on the plane. But he's been a great help to us."

"You're hanging out with a guy you met on the way over?" Brad asked, disdain souring his voice. "A complete stranger?"

"Yup, and he took us to his apartment," Tabatha said, the corners of her mouth lifting. "And he's got a red Alfa Romeo and knows everything there is to know about Rome."

Brad scowled—not his best look, but I'd witnessed it before many times. Saying he had a nasty temper would be an understatement. Tumultuous scenes flooded my mind. Always, after a verbal beating, he'd bring flowers, and we'd make up. I walked on egg shells. How could I forget about his tirades?

"We should get back to the hotel," I said.

"No, not without a puppy," Tabatha said. "I'm not leaving here. Plus, I want to work on my report. It's not as if my parents are waiting for us."

"True."

"Maybe there's somewhere we can be alone," Brad said in my ear. "I've heard of the Hassler Hotel—classy, five-star." He put his hand on my knee. "You and I can get reacquainted."

I removed his hand. "Please, I'm working."

"All day and night? That must be against the law even in Italy."

"I'm sure I'll get some time off once Tabatha's parents get back. But I can't get ahold of them." I felt foolish for not negotiating my work schedule with the Williamses before the trip. I had no one to blame but myself.

"We could rent you a Vespa, too, and have a blast scoping out this city," he said.

"That would be fun. Maybe tomorrow." I'd never driven one before but could figure it out.

Leonardo asked Brad for his order.

"Coffee—and don't make it too strong," Brad said. "Gee, this Italian coffee is bitter."

"*Certo*—certainly." Leonardo paused. "Anything else?"

"Nah, now that I've found the love of my life, I've got everything I need."

I couldn't help it. I was flattered. But I kept my cool, sipped my cappuccino.

Brad said, "Maybe we can take Tabatha—is that her name?—to a park to play so you and I can speak in private."

"Like, I'm fifteen years old," she said, anger inflating her voice. "In some parts of the world, old enough to get married. Almost."

Brad sneered. "I don't see a line of men waiting to marry you." With exaggerated gestures, he looked around and behind him, then chuckled. I watched Tabatha's face droop, her neck bend.

I massaged her shoulder. "Hey, Brad," I said, "lighten up."

"Is this how it's going to be?" he asked me. "Always someone more important than me?"

Before I could formulate an answer, a coachman driving a horse and an aged buggy stopped in front of our table. Tabatha sprang to her feet and jumped up and down, clapping her hands.

"It looks as though *la ragazza* would like a ride," the driver in his twenties said.

"Yes, I do. I do." She hopped into the open buggy. "Can we?" she asked me.

I had to admit I was tired of sitting at this table with Brad.

"Will it hold three people?" Brad asked.

"Yes, sir, if you snuggle together." The driver tipped his hat. "I'm sure you and your wife will enjoy the drive. And of course, your daughter has already made her desires known."

Brad turned to me. "Doesn't riding on the back of a Vespa sound like more fun?"

"It does sound fun, but this is a perfect solution."

"Then I'll join you, if you don't mind." His voice was flat.

"But what about your rental?"

"It should be safe for an hour out here." Brad rolled the Vespa toward the entrance of the café and spoke to Leonardo, then handed him some money. Brad returned wearing a grin. "All taken care of." He put out his hand and assisted me when climbing into the carriage, which creaked under our weight.

The driver addressed us. "Where would you like to go?"

"Everywhere," Tabatha said. "I want to see everything in Rome."

He adjusted his hat. "As you like."

"Hold on," Brad said. "For an hour."

"*Sì, signore. Un' ora.*"

"That's not long enough." Tabatha yanked on my arm. "Please say we can go out longer than that."

"I need to be back in an hour," Brad said. "If that Vespa gets stolen, I'm toast."

As the carriage rolled through the streets, Brad attempted to drape his arm around me, but Tabatha sat squarely between us.

"Maybe you'd like to sit up with the driver," Brad suggested to Tabatha, but she crossed her arms and stayed planted firmly on the worn leather seat.

We wended our way up and down smaller streets. Several sporty cars honked, but the driver paid no attention. "This carriage is called una *botticella*, meaning a small barrel," the driver said with pride. "At the beginning of the century, they were used as public transport, the same as our modern taxis."

While he pointed out churches and antiquities, Tabatha begged to go in, but Brad suggested she come back another day—no doubt trying to get me alone. "We don't have time today."

The driver came to a stop in front of the opera house. "Magnificent, no?"

Tabatha said, "That's where Mario is going to take us, Lucia."

"Lucia?" Brad said, his voice laced with sarcasm. "Is that your new name?"

"That's what Mario calls her," Tabatha said, and I felt myself shrink back. "He's taking us to an opera," she said.

"Is that a fact?" Brad swiveled his neck to stare at me. He raised an eyebrow. "Suddenly you like opera?"

His attitude irked me. Then, as if flipping a coin, he grinned and said, "Well, that's fantastic. You'll have one more reason to stay here and live with me when I'm transferred to Rome. Isn't that fabulous?"

"Yes," I said, not sure how I felt about it.

"You mean live together before you're married?" Tabatha said, sounding like my mother. "End up like Maria?"

Tabatha was right. I wanted a commitment. At least a ring and a date.

CHAPTER 12

A S THE TRAFFIC increased, automobiles muscled past us. A car's horn blared, and tires screeched. The coupe narrowly missed the horse, then sped away, its tires spinning. The spooked horse reared up on its hind legs.

The driver grappled with the reins and spewed out rapid-fire words in Italian, what must have been swearing at the car's driver.

The carriage teetered, then crashed against a stone wall. Our driver tumbled out as a wheel spun off and the horse struggled to stay upright. The seats slanted at a forty-five-degree angle. Tabatha and I slid toward Brad.

The driver unhitched the frantic horse. "I'll call my friend to come and get you. No charge from me."

"I should say not," Brad said. "I'm not paying you one cent."

The driver located a cell phone in his pocket. "I'm calling my friend. His horse is very fine. White. Very, very nice."

"Nah," Brad said, "we've had enough. I'll call an Uber or a cab to take us back."

"No-no-no." Tabatha clasped onto me. "I want to see the white horse. My parents are paying for this." Which was true. And I was supposed to keep her safe, not spend time with my boyfriend. If he was one. I didn't know what to think.

"I'm out of here," Brad said, landing on the street. "I've got to pick up that Vespa."

The driver broke into the conversation. "My friend is coming. You don't owe me anything." Cars whizzed past us.

"He could have gotten us killed," Brad said. "These Italians drive like maniacs."

"We're used to it," the driver said. "No one was hurt." He helped Tabatha and me disembark.

Brad frowned as a sporty coupe hurtled past us. "Look, Lucy, do you want to spend time with me or not?"

"Yes, I do, but—"

Brad hailed a cab that screeched to a stop, holding up traffic. Horns blared. "Are you coming?" he asked me.

"No," I said. "Look, I was straight with you from the start. I have a job."

"I told you to quit. I'll take care of you. Like I said, I may get transferred here."

Again, I imagined living in Rome. I had grown to love the city. But my love for Brad was waning. My mind sped with uncertainty until Tabatha yanked on my arm. "Lucia, there's the white horse and carriage."

"That's just an ancient, long-toothed nag," Brad said.

"It is not," Tabatha countered, her hands on her hips. "It's elegant."

The horse was on the old side, but so were the ones I'd seen in photos of New York City.

"I'm out of here." Brad aimed his glare at me. "I'll call you later."

"Wait," I said, wanting to explain to him. But what was the use?

The two drivers exchanged friendly words—nothing I could understand—then the new driver hopped down and proffered his hand to me so I could climb into his buggy. Tabatha jumped in, her limbs agile.

"Welcome," the mustached driver said. "Where am I taking you?"

I brought out my guidebook. "How about going to the Pantheon? That looks interesting." Once perched in the carriage, I read aloud. "It says here, 'Brick stamps on the side of the Pantheon reveal it was built and dedicated between AD 118 and 125.' It's the best-preserved monument in Rome."

"Wow, that's two thousand years old." Tabatha leaned against my arm, gazed up at me. "Can we go?"

The driver turned to us. "*Sì*, I take you. You go in. I wait outside."

"Okay. *Andiamo*." A chance to practice my paltry Italian.

As the carriage moved us at a leisurely pace, the horse's hooves clopping on the cobbled road, I continued to read to Tabatha. "In 609, the Byzantine emperor Phocas gave the building to Pope Boniface IV, who converted it into a Christian church and consecrated it to St. Mary and the Martyrs." I closed the book. "So apparently, it's a church."

"I don't want to go into another church," Tabatha said. "Not unless the Pope is there."

"Let's give it a try," I said.

Twenty minutes later, after zigzagging at a lazy pace, we approached the front of the Pantheon—a building square on the outside but the interior circular and domed with an eye—a round window open to the sky—at the top.

I kept close to Tabatha as we strolled around this fascinating structure. She seemed most intrigued with the fluttering birds. When we exited, we stopped for a few minutes to examine carts crammed with items—sunglasses, scarves, glass bobbles from Venice.

I asked the driver to take us to the hotel. Dollar signs seem to take shape in his eyes when he heard the word *Hassler*. Maybe I should have asked him to take us back to the Piazza Venezia. No, Tabatha and I needed to return and locate her parents.

With voice and arms raised, the hotel's doorman helped me negotiate the price. The driver seemed deflated when I paid him, so I slipped him a tip.

Tabatha and I entered the lobby. I inquired about the Williamses at the front desk. No sign of them. "*Mi dispiace*—I'm sorry," the young woman said.

What on earth was going on?

Minutes after Tabatha and I entered our room I received a call from Mario, who said he'd purchased three opera tickets for this evening. "You're in for a treat. Mozart's *The Marriage of Figaro*. Comic opera at its best. You are both sure to enjoy it. We can eat before or after."

"I don't think I should," I answered. "I still haven't heard from Tabatha's parents." Or from Brad, who would become unhinged. Yet, he could have asked about this evening. I was tired of playing his puppet.

Mario said, "I'm sure they don't want you and their daughter sitting in the hotel all the time. Certainly, they expect you to keep her busy. I can pick you up in an hour."

"Is that Mario?" Tabatha asked. "I knew he'd call."

I held the phone to my ear, but she tugged on my hand. "Give the phone to me," she said, but I grasped it out of her reach.

"He wants to take us to an opera tonight," I said.

"Whatever he wants, I want it too." She sounded ecstatic. I figured she had a crush on Mario; I could understand. There wasn't much not to like about him.

I held the phone out of her reach.

"Are you sure you could sit through a whole opera?" I asked Tabatha.

"How will I know unless I try?" she asked, palms up. "But I need to fix my hair and change clothes first."

"Do people get all dressed up?" I asked Mario.

"Not so much on a weeknight. Anyway, you look charming as you are." Oh, this guy was a smooth talker. Not that I minded.

"Do you want dinner before or after?" he asked.

I relayed the question to Tabatha.

"After," she said. "I'm too excited to eat. I'm not hungry."

Arriving at the fabulous opera house—Il Teatro
dell'Opera di Roma, as Mario called it—a couple hours
later, I felt like a small-town girl who was sadly under-
dressed. Many of the women entering the grand building wore fur jackets or coats and glittering jewelry. But
no one seemed to notice my simple navy-blue Ralph
Lauren dress and a jacket I'd found at an outlet store.
Mama had assured me they accentuated my figure.

Our seats were in a small, partitioned balcony's
first row. Tiers of similar seats encircled the theater's
perimeter. The vast room was resplendent with chan-
deliers and red velvet. A magnificent painting graced
the domed ceiling; in the center hung a dazzling chandelier.

Tabatha stared down to the main floor of the spectacular room as a multitude of people found their seats.
I felt as if I'd been transported to another time, into a
world of grandeur.

"How did you get such good seats?" I asked Mario.

"Sometimes, at the last minute, patrons find they
can't attend." His grinning face told me he'd pulled a
few strings to snag the tickets.

"Why didn't you take us to see *Lucia di Lammermoor*?"
Tabatha asked him.

"It isn't being performed tonight." He leaned closer,
his shoulder brushing mine. "A marvelous opera by
Donizetti, but a sad ending. This will be amusing and
lively." He brought out his cell phone. "Please, both of
you, turn your phones on mute."

We did just as the conductor appeared. A roar of
applause commenced. The conductor gave the audi-

ence a brief nod, then turned to the orchestra, dozens of musicians poised and watching his baton. When it sliced the air, the instruments filled the hall with an overture that seem familiar.

I glanced to Mario, sitting on the other side of Tabatha, and saw he was watching me—my guess was to catch my initial reaction. I grinned as the velvet curtains parted.

The opera delighted me. The marvelous settings, fabulous voices, the whimsical story. And a happy and uplifting ending.

On the drive back to the hotel, Tabatha started singing "Figaro, Figaro, Figaro" from the opera. Mario dove in, his tenor voice brilliant and agile. I joined in, too, thanks to watching Bugs Bunny cartoons as a child.

We all burst into laughter as we neared the hotel's front door.

"We'd better un-silence our phones," I told Tabatha.

"Like my parents are going to call me?" she said. Her cheerful demeanor flattened like a balloon losing air. "I bet they haven't given me a second thought."

"Sure, they have." Although I could show her no proof.

I noticed I'd received a text but ignored it. I figured Brad was trying to track me down. I didn't wish this most lovely evening to end on a sour note.

"I want to take singing lessons," Tabatha said. "To be a voice major in college."

"A marvelous idea," Mario said.

Good, now maybe the subject of her school paper would change. A night at the opera instead of Mussolini. She might forget all about writing a paper on that monster.

"I know a small restaurant nearby. Italian, of course." Mario rounded a corner and found a parking spot. "If the weather was warmer, we could sit outside," Mario said, "but I think we'd better eat indoors."

As Tabatha and I followed him, she raved about the opera.

The host, a tall balding man, greeted Mario in Italian as a friend. "*Buona sera. Come va?*"

"*Bene, grazie,*" Mario said. "I've brought two American young ladies."

"*Perfetto,* a table for three." He seated us in a corner, handed us menus.

A svelte waitress dressed in a white tuxedo shirt and black slacks breezed over to our table. "*Ciao,* Mario." Unless I was mistaken, she was batting her eyes at him.

He stood and gave her a peck on her cheek. "How are you, Barbarella?"

"*Perfetto,* now that you're here." She gave me a cursory glance. "May I bring you a bottle of wine?" she asked him as if I'd turned invisible.

"Sure, that would be fine. You know what I like."

"And a Coke with a couple of maraschino cherries," Tabatha said. "Mario took us to the opera. It was fantastic." Hah, she wasn't going to be ignored.

Barbarella smiled, her lips pressing together, and backed away to fetch the drinks.

When Barbarella opened the bottle, I said, "None for me, thanks," and she shrugged. Mario gave me an inquisitive look but said nothing. I'd fill him in some other time. Maybe.

Mario agreed to order our meal and gave us a lesson. He opened his menu. "First, we have an antipasto plate. *L'antipasto we call it*, which might include prosciutto and other cured meats, crostini and bruschetta, cured vegetables, and little polenta cakes or small fish appetizers. All very, very tasty.

"Then *il primo*, or first course, usually consisting of soups—*zuppe*, risotti, and pastas of all sorts. *Next comes il secondo*, or second course, which consists of fish or meat, served with a side dish—anything from a salad to fried zucchini or braised spinach." He closed his menu, set it aside. *"Finally, il dolce, or dessert, can range from such favorites as tiramisù or torta della nonna—grandma's cake—to cookies."*

I patted my tummy. "How can one person eat all that?"

"I can," Tabatha said. "I bet I can."

CHAPTER 13

BACK IN THE hotel a couple hours later, I asked about the Williamses at the concierge's desk. Still no word nor message from them.

Mario escorted Tabatha and me to our room. Tabatha raced into the powder room, leaving the two of us alone.

"Thank you so much for a fabulous evening," I told him, and his arms slid around my shoulders.

Mario's face neared mine. His lips parted . . . I longed to share a kiss.

Tabatha abruptly opened the door and crooned, "Figaro, Figaro, Figaro."

Mario and I stepped apart.

The sound of my cell phone in my purse shattered the air.

"Lucy, I've been trying to get ahold of you," Gretchen said when I answered.

"Sorry, I had it turned to silent while we were at the opera."

"You got our Tabatha to sit through a whole opera? You're a miracle worker." She chuckled.

"She enjoyed it," I said. "Very much."

Before I could expound, Gretchen said, "We want you to take Tabatha home to Seattle the day after tomorrow."

"The day before Christmas Eve?"

"Yes, we're tied up . . . working on a deal up in Milan. No way to get out of it."

I felt my heart sink as I imagined relaying the message to Tabatha. She'd be crushed, and who could blame her?

"Lucy, are you still there?" Gretchen's voice turned harsh. "Will that be a problem?"

"No." But it was. I glanced at Mario. I wasn't ready to leave Rome.

"Then you can take Tabatha back to Seattle for us and stay with her in our home. We'll reimburse you for any expenses. There's a nice bonus in there for you. Use the guest room on the first floor."

"Okay." My head spun with how I'd most want to spend the next day. I waved Tabatha toward me, figuring her parents would wish to tell her themselves, but Gretchen didn't ask me to pass the phone.

"Your tickets are already purchased," Gretchen said, all business. "You'll receive an email from the airline with necessary information. Get to the airport three hours early." She paused, as if distracted. "I've got to run," she said suddenly and hung up.

"Didn't Mom ask to speak to me?" Tabatha said.

Now what? "I bet she meant to." I tried to sound convincing, when even I didn't believe myself.

Tabatha slumped onto her bed, face down. I moved into the hall, with Mario following.

"The Williamses want me to take Tabatha back to Seattle the day after tomorrow," I told him. "I thought we were spending Christmas here."

"So soon? And I must work all tomorrow. Even a dinner meeting."

I'd planned to spend at least part of the next day with Brad but still felt depleted.

Before I knew what was happening, Mario kissed me on the lips. A brief but potent kiss. Then he spun around, said goodbye, and strode to the elevators as one opened. Was that a final farewell? No "see you tomorrow." He was probably planning to head north to visit his family over the holidays. I never had asked him if he had a girlfriend. He'd kissed the waitress on the cheek. Maybe his brief kiss meant nothing. My head gyrated with questions.

And my lips still tingled from his unexpected show of affection.

Not sure what else to do, I scanned my phone, expecting to see Brad's number. But I saw my mother's instead. I calculated the time in my head and figured it was still early afternoon.

Mama answered immediately. Her voice carried with it a brilliance I hadn't heard in years. "How are you, dear?" she asked.

How was I? Happy. Confused. Disappointed.

"Fine," I said. "It turns out I'm coming home earlier than expected."

"Wonderful. I can't wait to hear all about your trip."

"Yeah, I'll fill you in when I get home."

"Something wrong?" Mama could always read me. With Tabatha in the room, I couldn't speak my mind.

"Lucy? Are you still there?"

"Yes. We just went to an opera and out to dinner. All fun."

"So what's the problem? I can hear it in your voice."

I couldn't tell her the Williamses had deserted Tabatha and me and were sending us packing. I got the feeling Gretchen was lying to me. "Everything is fine," I said and told her about the change in travel plans. "At least we're not spending Christmas Eve on the plane."

"Then you'll be home by then?"

"Yes. Maybe I can bring Tabatha over?"

"Of course you can."

"I'd better run, Mama." She sounded too happy. I told myself it made sense. Her only child would be there for Christmas after all.

BRAD FINALLY CALLED me a few minutes later. "I'm on my way over to take you to dinner," he said. "Somewhere nice."

"I'm sorry, but we already ate," I said.

"I can't wait to see you anyway. I have a surprise."

"But I'm tied up."

"Okay, I hear you," Brad said. "Too late for dinner, but not too late for an after-dinner drink."

I'd heard the hotel's bar was elegant but knew I couldn't bring Tabatha or leave her by herself. She lay in bed in a fetal position sucking her thumb.

"See you in a few minutes," he said. "Trust me, you don't want to miss what I have to show you." Then he hung up.

I checked my face in the mirror. Darn it all, I did care what he thought of me.

TEN MINUTES LATER, a strident knock on the door told me Brad had arrived. That was quick. Had he been drinking downstairs in the hotel's lounge?

As I opened the door, he strode in and swept me into an embrace. He glanced over my shoulder. "She's here?"

"Where else would she be?"

"With her parents."

I figured Tabatha could hear us. Or maybe she really was asleep this time. I put my finger up to my lips to shush him, then beckoned him out in the hall and cracked the door a few inches.

"Let's go down to the bar." His breath smelled of booze. I figured he'd just gulped a bourbon on the rocks, his favorite drink.

I kept my volume subdued. "We'll have to talk out here. I can't leave Tabatha."

"Can't her parents—"

"No, they can't. They're out of town somewhere." Against all logic, I felt myself drawn to him. I knew he wasn't good for me. "Tomorrow's my last day here. I have to go back to Seattle the next day," I said.

His jaw dropped open, but before he could speak, I said, "No, Tabatha can't fly home by herself."

"Then let's make the most of tomorrow," Brad said, his hand stroking my chin. "You're the reason I'm here. To be with you on Christmas. And now you're running out on me."

"I am not leaving because of you. Hey, I didn't even know you'd be in Rome when I got here."

"I thought you'd be delighted." His gaze captured me. "We should spend tomorrow together, okay?" He nuzzled my neck, sending a shiver down my spine. "Like I said, I have a surprise." He leaned back to catch my expression. "Aren't you curious?"

Of course, I was, especially when he patted his jacket pocket. I saw the shape of something the size of a small gift box. But I'd learned to keep my expectations low with this man. I was done pining over him. I couldn't take another disappointment.

"Okay, we're on for tomorrow," I said, leaning away. "The three of us."

He expelled a puff of air. "If you insist."

"I do."

Tabatha wrenched the door open all the way and peered out into the hallway. "What are you two talking about? I heard my name."

"Just making plans for tomorrow," I said. "We need to get out my guidebook."

"Please spare me the churches and art museums," Brad said.

"What about a park?" I asked. "The weather's been so nice. We haven't been to the Borghese Gardens."

"They might have a play area for kids," Brad said.

"Like, I'm not a little kid," Tabatha said, indignant.

"Come on, let's give it a chance," I told her. "Even I like swings."

"Whatever." Tabatha tromped back into our room leaving me alone with Brad, whose arms slid around my shoulders. He attempted to kiss me just as a white-haired couple exited the elevator and advanced our way.

I swerved out of Brad's reach. "Good night, Brad."

"Yeah, right." He marched into the elevator and the doors slid shut.

When I stepped back into the room, I found Tabatha on her iPad. "I'm writing my paper," she said.

"But it's past eleven."

"What time is it in Seattle? Still early, right?"

"That's not fair."

"Do you want me to work on my school paper or not?" She plugged in one of her earbuds. "Maybe my parents will be proud of me for once."

"I'm sure they are already." Although I wondered. What kind of parents would neglect their daughter over Christmas?

She plugged in the other bud, shutting me off.

Tabatha was restless all night, talking in her sleep, keeping me awake. I finally got up to comfort her.

"Mommy?" she said.

"No, it's Lucy."

"I want Mommy."

"I know." I felt like calling my own mother to ask her for advice, but I snuggled into bed. Maybe by tomorrow the jet lag and my mood would have lifted—just in time to fly home.

CHAPTER 14

THE NEXT MORNING after breakfast, Brad arrived all smiles. He directed Tabatha and me to the Villa Borghese Gardens, thanks to an app on his iPhone. But Tabatha seemed depressed and lagged.

"Come on," he told her. "It's not far. And it's a beautiful sunshiny day to the max."

"As long as I don't have to walk too much." She plodded along as if she were scaling the Spanish Steps again. "Otherwise I'll never make it."

"Sure we will," I said. "One step at a time." My words reminded me of an NA meeting, which I could use right now. I felt stressed—in need of a crutch. No, never again, I promised myself.

Finally, we entered the elaborate gardens that seemed to stretch for miles, crisscrossed with paths and dotted with pools and statues. Even with bare trees and leaves on the ground, the sun's brilliance felt comforting. No honking cars or Rome's usual street hustle—an oasis in the center of the city. A couple of bicyclists rolled by at a languid speed. In the distance, I spotted a boy with a kite.

"Look, there's a swing set," Brad said to Tabatha.

"I'm not a five-year-old." Tabatha crossed her arms.

"Come on, I'll push you," I said. "It'll be fun."

With reluctance, Tabatha sat on a swing, and I propelled her.

"Oh, I have a cool idea," Tabatha said, pumping her legs. "For my paper."

"What is it?" I asked. "About the Pantheon?"

She grinned. "You'll have to wait and see."

I gave her another push.

"Stop, I can do it myself." She laughed and continued pumping with vigor.

As the sun warmed the air, Brad seemed content to sit and watch us. Maybe he had matured. He patted the seat next to him, and I lowered myself on the bench.

"Finally," he said, his hand dipping into his jacket pocket. "I realized what I'd be missing. I don't want to lose you."

I felt Brad's charisma pulling me into his orbit. We shared a quick kiss, but the magic was gone. Or maybe just temporarily. I reasoned with myself not to make a hasty decision.

"Please stay and spend Christmas with me," he said.

"I can't. I wish I could stay. I'm not ready to leave Rome yet."

"In that case, I have something for you. An early Christmas present." He extracted a small box wrapped in silver paper from his jacket pocket. An engagement ring? Brad beamed as he gave it to me. "Open it," he said.

My hands trembled as I tore off the wrapping and opened a box to find a small silver airplane.

"For your charm bracelet," he said.

"Thank you." I didn't own a charm bracelet, and the last thing I'd want on one would be an airplane, which even looked like my father's. A thoughtful gift, I told myself, but not an engagement ring. I reprimanded myself for getting my hopes up, then reminded myself I wasn't sure I'd accept his proposal anyway.

Brad did work for Boeing and had his pilot's license, so that component made sense.

Looking into his striking face, I wondered how many women would turn him down. Which one of his former girlfriends owned a charm bracelet?

"Don't you like it?" he asked.

"Sure, I do. Thank you. It's very pretty."

"Why don't you take it out of the box?"

I struggled to remove it, but it was attached with a plastic-covered wire to the bottom.

"Here, I'll do it. He grappled with the box so hard the plane fell to the ground. His hand swiped out, but he missed catching it. "Now look what you made me do." His voice turned crabby. "Get it," he said.

"No, you get it yourself." I'd never used that tone with him. He stared at me with disbelief in his eyes. The veins on his neck coiled like snakes.

"Never mind, I'll do it," he said with a snap. His hand swiped down to retrieve the charm.

"I'm sorry," I said. "I don't have anything for you yet."

His face transformed from one of anger to kindness, his mouth softening. "No worries, Lucy, plenty of shopping in Japan."

"What do you mean?"

"It's just as well you're not staying here." His elbow rested on the back of the bench. "I've decided I like Japan better than Rome. I visited the facility south of here yesterday and didn't like it all that much. You'll adore Japan."

"Huh?"

"Wait until you see it."

"Japan? You want me to move there and live with you?"

"I do, Lucy." He inched closer to kiss me again, but I drew back. "We'll spend Christmas together."

"But I don't want to live in Japan." As a single woman.

"Why not? It's a wonderful place. Orderly and clean. You'll love it."

"But what would I do with myself?"

"Get a job?"

No mention of marriage or raising a family.

"I don't think so."

"You wouldn't need to work. You could shop or lounge around waiting for me to come home every day."

"No, thanks."

The corners of his mouth drew back. "Suddenly I'm not good enough for you?"

"I didn't say that."

"You didn't have to." His fingers straightened; his hand shoved out, toppling me off the bench. I landed on my rear end with a thud.

"Ouch!"

"Lucia!" Tabatha jumped to the ground from the swing at what seemed a dangerous height. She stormed over to us. "Are you okay, Lucia?"

"I think so." My head spun as I recalled the time Brad bumped into me on the stairs of his apartment in Seattle, sending me flying and bruised, then claimed it was an accident. He'd apologized profusely and brought me flowers and Fran's chocolate after.

A gaggle of giggling children neared us, each claiming a swing, speaking in rapid-fire Italian.

Brad got down on his knees to help me up. "I'm so sorry, Lucy. I don't know what got into me." His fingers under my armpits, he sat me on the bench as if I were a rag doll. "It will never happen again. I promise." He stroked my hair. "I'll make it up to you."

"I saw him push you," Tabatha said. "Why would you let him treat you like that?"

My first reaction was to defend Brad. Until he spoke to her.

"Shut up, you spoiled little brat." He grabbed her forearm.

"Hey, let go of me." Tabatha threw a punch, hit him in the chest.

Brad retaliated with a slap to her face. She cried out. "Ow!" Her hand flew up to her cheek.

"How dare you?" I screamed. "Get out of here before I call the police."

His face twisted with rage. "Okay, Miss Goody-goody." He barked a laugh as he stood. "You have no business taking care of a child."

All heads around us turned our way. Playing kids and laughing voices came to a standstill. Even the birds stopped chirping.

"Hey, Lucy," Brad said. "Merry Christmas." He spun on his heel and marched off.

Tabatha took my hand. "Come on, Lucia, let's get out of here."

CHAPTER 15

CHIN LIFTED, I tried to appear dignified and
confident as I watched Brad stomp off in a huff.
A moment later, he was out of sight, and I assumed
out of my life.

"Let's visit Maria," Tabatha said. "I want to say
goodbye to the puppies before we leave."

"Sure." I had nothing else planned until tomorrow. I
summoned an Uber to take us to Piazza Venezia. Leonardo welcomed us when we disembarked.

"Come have a seat," he said. "What can I get you?"

"Nothing to eat, we've come to see Maria," Tabatha
said. "And the puppies."

"I'm so sorry, but they're gone." He pulled chairs out
for us, but we remained standing. "Our parents came
to get her last night." He steepled his fingers. "Christmas is the time for forgiveness, they said. They forgave
her as God forgives us."

"But what about the puppies?" Tabatha said, desperation in her voice.

"My parents, they put them in the back of their truck. They have a small farm south of here, near Naples. Much better for dogs than the city." He glanced up to a window. "Miss, if you want, you can move into Maria's apartment. A very low rent."

"That's a cool idea," Tabatha said. "You and I could live there together, Lucia."

"Fun as it sounds, your parents would say no way." Things were moving too quickly.

"Where are my so-called parents?" Tabatha asked. "They'd never miss us. We should go back to the hotel, pack our things, and bring them over here immediately."

As I admired the stately Christmas tree and the Victor Emmanuel, I imagined beginning my day right here— the aroma of Leonardo's coffee wafting up, the smells of pastry. I sighed. It seemed like heaven.

"I could help you move in," Leonardo said. "My friend owns a van."

"Thanks," I said, "but Tabatha and I better pack our suitcases tonight to catch an early flight in the morning."

"And leave before Christmas? Not even visit St. Peter's first?"

"I must say goodbye to the Pope before we leave," Tabatha said. "I promised him I would."

Leonardo gave her a double take, the corner of his mouth tipping up. "The most spectacular Christmas tree in all of Rome is at the Vatican in Saint Peter's Square."

"I want to see it," Tabatha said.

"You already did." I clasped her shoulder to keep her from spinning away. "Twice," I said.

"A life-size nativity scene will be unveiled on Christmas Eve," Leonardo said. "It would be a pity to miss it."

"The Pope mentioned it to me," Tabatha said. "He told me so, himself."

"We'll drive by on the way back to the hotel," I told her.

"And tour St. Peter's one more time?"

Much as I wanted to wander the magnificent church again, I said, "No. I'm sorry. Not enough time."

"Then I will never see you again?" Leonardo gazed into my eyes as only an Italian man could. But there was only one man I really wanted to see.

As our Uber driver zigzagged the city at a leisurely speed as I'd instructed, Tabatha and I oohed and aahed over the splendid Christmas decor, especially at St. Peter's Square.

"My favorite tree awaits us at the top of the Spanish Steps," I told her.

"You're just trying to trick me into going back to the hotel," she said.

"Partly." I was already planning the itinerary for my next trip to Rome. I couldn't afford a luxurious suite, but I'd find a way to return.

THE NEXT MORNING, as the sun rose to reveal peach-colored clouds, Tabatha and I sat in first class in a massive Boeing 767. So this is how the other half lives,

I thought as I eased into my cushy seat, with Tabatha by the window.

"Christmas is only one day away," Tabatha said. "I hope Santa will be able to find me after all this traveling." At fifteen, did she really think Santa Claus would arrive steering his sleigh of reindeer? Maybe her parents had kept that fable going. If so, I wished they'd warned me. Well, I wished they'd done a lot of things.

"I'm sure he'll find you." I was thankful for the shopping I'd done, especially in the Jewish Ghetto. A scarf and a purse for my mother, a bracelet and sunglasses for Tabatha. Without siblings, I didn't do much shopping at Christmas, but I'd bought a couple broaches made in Venice and a glass paperweight I wouldn't mind getting saddled with.

"Can't wait to see you," Mama said when I called to tell her we were on our way. "Expect something new," she'd added before she rang off.

Huh? What was up with her? She was probably wondering the same thing about me.

Peering past Tabatha out the aircraft's window, I regretted leaving Rome, but not Brad—meaning not living with an abusive bully on the other side of the world as a single woman.

Tabatha slumped in her seat. "When we get home, let's put up the Christmas tree."

"Okay." Surely, she would have heard from her parents by Christmas. "You know where everything is?"

"In boxes in the basement."

"I'll bet we can figure it out if your folks don't mind."

She turned to me, bulged her eyes like a goldfish. "Like they care about me?"

I couldn't argue with her.

"They probably forgot to buy me a Christmas present." Her face melted into a mask of despondency.

"Don't give up on them," I said. Even though I had.

A flight attendant came by offering champagne for me or soda pop for Tabatha.

I could use a drink. Oh, yes. Just a sip. My hand reached out. But before I could snag the glass, the flight attendant said, "Hello, sir," in a cooing voice. "May I offer you champagne? I saw movement as someone opened the overhead bin across the aisle.

"Maybe later."

My eyes widened, and my jaw dropped when I spotted Mario seating himself across the aisle from us.

CHAPTER 16

"I GOT AN UPGRADE," he said when he noticed my gawking face.

"*Buongiorno*, Mario," Tabatha said, elevating off her chair, as if he were a celebrity. "What are you doing here?"

He sent her a benevolent smile. "Hi, Tabatha. How are you?"

"You're flying to Seattle?" I asked him.

"Yes. The Amazon bigwigs called and summoned me back, right before Christmas." He shrugged. "Not that I'm unhappy to see you. A lovely surprise."

I arched an eyebrow. "And you just happened to get a seat near us?" I didn't believe in coincidences.

"Not really." His smile stretched into a grin. "I asked a gentleman to swap seats. He wanted to sit on the bulkhead, where I was assigned. So now we're both happy."

I was delighted to see Mario. But when it came to men, I didn't trust myself. Take Brad, that creep. Why was I such a sucker? If only my father were still alive to give me advice. No, I needed to give up that dream of a perfect papa and knock him off his pedestal. He'd bailed out on us, leaving unpaid bills that had forced Mama to work overtime.

With Mario on board, Tabatha didn't want the window seat anymore, so I traded seats with her and gazed toward the North Pole. I banished the negative thoughts from my brain and focused my vision on the stark white mountaintops that seemed to stretch forever.

When we landed at Chicago O'Hare, Mario helped us get through customs with our luggage. Finally, in Seattle, Mario assisted in retrieving our suitcases and summoning an Uber. "We can share it," he said. "If you don't mind."

"Sure, that would be fine," Tabatha said. "Won't it, Lucia?"

I couldn't think of a reason why not. And yet I felt wary.

"Well?" Tabatha said. "Are you going to answer him?"

I couldn't come up with a logical reason why not. "Sure. Okay. Thanks, Mario."

"The pleasure is all mine."

Soon we three sat in the back seat of an Uber—a wide black Escalade.

On the way to the Williamses' home, Tabatha fell asleep, her head on my shoulder. I felt myself dozing off, too, until I heard Mario speaking to the driver. I woke up with a jolt as the vehicle pulled into the Williamses' circular driveway.

I nudged Tabatha. "Wake up, sweetie. You're home."

"Too tired," she murmured, her head still on my shoulder.

"I'll carry her in," Mario said. He asked the driver to bring the bags to the front door. "Has the house been vacant since you left?" Mario asked me as he lifted Tabatha.

"Yes. As far as I know. The cleaning service might have come, not that anyone's been home."

I was glad for the Williamses' security cameras as I unlocked the front door and disarmed the alarm system.

"I'd feel better if I came in to check the house for intruders." He placed Tabatha on the living room couch. She let out a whimper.

"This is a splendid home." He scanned the walls, took in the paintings and sculptures.

"Are you all right?" I asked her. "Want to go upstairs to bed?"

"Too far away. I'll sleep here." She went limp, and her eyes closed as she sank into the leather cushions.

I led Mario into the kitchen and offered him a drink.

"I have some explaining to do," he said.

"What are you talking about?" I steeled myself. After the incident with Brad, I was prepared for the worst from all men.

"The Williamses asked me to look after Tabatha and you in Rome."

"They hired you to be our bodyguard without telling me?"

"No, just to keep an eye out, which I was happy to do."

"But how? When?"

"Stan and I exchanged contact information after I drove you home from St. Peter's." Mario glanced to the floor. "The next day he called and asked me to keep an eye on Tabatha and you, if I happened to run into you two. Which I did."

"What?" I could feel my blood pressure elevating, pounding in my ears. "Why didn't you mention it?"

"I should have. Exchanging numbers is such a common occurrence in my business that I didn't give it much thought. I'm terribly sorry. And I wanted to see you."

What else had he neglected to tell me? I was ready to boot him out the door but realized he might have more to say. "Do you know where they are now?" I asked. From his grave expression, I surmised he had bad news. "Please tell me they're not in the hospital."

He moved closer and spoke in my ear. "I did some digging," he said, his voice a skosh above a whisper. "The Williamses appear to be in jail."

Had I heard him correctly? "Tell me you're kidding."

"I wish I were. The good news is they are not being officially held. Yet."

"Held for what?"

"That bit of information I was unable to obtain for sure." Mario kept his volume low. "My best guess is art theft, something of that nature. Which would be considered a serious crime in Italy."

"But why didn't you tell me?" My confidence in Mario was wavering.

"I was waiting until I had something concrete. I didn't want to scare Tabatha."

"Poor girl." I thought about how much she was counting on her parents showing up for Christmas. "I think you'd better leave before Tabatha gets wind of this." She'd come unglued.

"But, please—" He moved closer to embrace me, but I pushed him away. I had too much to think about.

"Don't forget your suitcase." I ushered him out the front door and closed it quietly so as not to wake Tabatha.

As soon as he was gone, a cloud of gloom enveloped me as I headed for the guest room to unpack. I opened my suitcase and removed my toiletries and clothing—mostly wrinkled. Then I unzipped the lid, where I'd stuffed my soiled clothes. My fingertips touched something hard, covered with paper and in a plastic bag, and unfamiliar. I dug further until I reached a rectangular flat package taped together. What on earth?

I unwrapped it and was stunned to find an unframed sepia-and-white-on-canvas painting of a young angel, a halo floating above its head, that looked like a seventeenth century Rembrandt. I'd studied his work at length in college. No signature at the bottom, but the master had created hundreds of paintings and etchings without signing them. Or was it a forgery? Some kind of prank? Who would hide the painting there?

The Williamses were the obvious culprits. They must have come into our hotel room in Rome while Tabatha and I were out. But I had no way to prove my theory. In any case, I was furious. Fuming. What if I'd been stopped in customs in Chicago? I could be in jail. I pictured a bleak windowless room in a prison that smelled of urine.

Thankfully, Tabatha's whining had distracted the guards at security.

CHAPTER 17

I NEEDED TO GET my act together. I had to get rid of this painting.

Yet I admitted I wanted the masterpiece myself if it really was a genuine Rembrandt. The painting's surface looked old enough.

"Lucia?" Tabatha's voice jolted me back to this room. "Whatcha got there?" She stood looking over my shoulder.

A blanket of shame and guilt washed over me. Not that I'd done anything wrong.

I straightened my spine. "Tabatha, did you put this painting in my suitcase?"

"Huh? I've never seen it before in my life. I swear."

"Well, someone stashed it there."

She screwed up her face. "My parents?"

I saw nothing to laugh about but felt the corners of my mouth curving up because I was imagining that exact scenario.

I extracted my remaining clothing—except for a sweater—and zipped the painting back in the suitcase's lid.

Tabatha planted her hands on her hips. "So where did it come from, Lucia? Did you steal it?"

I stared into her eyes, trying to see behind them to where the truth dwelled. "Absolutely not," I said. "Are you sure you know nothing about this painting?" I didn't trust her.

"Like I said, I've never seen it before." She yawned. "I need to sleep before I conk over."

"All right, sweetie."

I helped her scale the stairs to the second floor, where she dove into her bed. I tucked the covers up around her chin. She shut her eyes and inserted her thumb in her mouth.

WHEN I WAS down on the first floor, I pulled out my iPad. On a whim—or was it a premonition—I Googled "art missing since WWII." A plethora of paintings filled the screen. I noticed a description of a painting by Rembrandt that sounded much like the one in my suitcase, cataloged by the Art Loss Register as missing due to the Nazi invasion of France.

Little was known about the painting even before World War II. Apparently, the small painting was kept in a French countryside château that was plundered by Nazis, who took the painting to Paris sometime in the early 1940s to become part of Hitler's museum, along with more than three hundred other pieces of art that

Hitler coveted. Even though 162 of the pieces chosen for Hitler's museum were recovered, there had been no sign of the others, including a painting of an angel by Rembrandt.

A château? Mama rarely mentioned anything about her French ancestors. Nothing about a Rembrandt being in my great-grandfather's collection. I wondered if someone had cataloged his compilation. But who would know? Mama had been searching for his paintings most of her adult life and had come up empty except for the one in her bedroom, which she wouldn't insure for fear someone from the insurance company would recognize it. I surmised Mama's sister, Anna, would lay claim on the painting if she caught wind of its existence.

Hold everything, my imagination was taking me on an illogical roller-coaster ride.

"Lucia. Lucia." Tabatha tapped my arm, causing me to jolt.

I closed my iPad. "How long have you been in the kitchen?"

"Uh, not long. I can't sleep. And I'm hungry."

In a stupor, I hadn't gone to bed myself. My mind buzzed with questions about the Williamses and about the painting in my suitcase. I shivered when I considered the consequences if it had been detected at the airport.

"Lucia, wake up," Tabatha persisted.

What time was it in Rome? No matter. I needed to readjust my inner clock and figure out what to do with the painting. Bottom line: I possessed a possibly valu-able work of art that wasn't mine.

Ugh, I should consult my bossy cousin, Maureen, the family historian, whom I hadn't seen for years. We were like oil and water. We'd never mixed well. But she kept a website to assist Jews searching for missing pieces of art that might come in handy.

I sat up and swung my legs around. I was ready for breakfast too. I did the math. It would be morning in Rome. I'd worry about the time change when Tabatha needed to get ready for school in a couple of weeks.

"Let's do it," I said. "What would you like?"

"Hot chocolate and those yummy pastries they have in Rome."

"Sounds divine. Hot chocolate coming up for both of us, but those fruit-filled croissants will have to wait for your next trip."

"Maybe Mom and Dad will bring some home for me."

"I'll try calling them again." I didn't buy Mario's story.

"Hey, Lucia, want to read my school paper? Since I was awake, I got on the computer and printed it off."

"Okay, if you like." I prepared the cocoa and poured two cups, set the mugs on the table.

She scampered upstairs and returned with a page of white paper. "Here, read it." Her eyes came alive with expectation. "Never mind, I will."

GIRL ON A SWING
By Tabatha Williams

Rome, Italy, 1939

Claretta Petacci gripped the package. She'd rather it was small, the size of a bobble of jewelry, but realized she was holding a painting. There was no use trying to hide it from Benito Mussolini—Il Duce—so she said, "Look, Ben, a gift from Adolfo Hitler himself."

Il Duce's mouth twisted. "It must be for me."

"No, it has my name on it."

He grabbed the package. If only she'd hidden it, but too late. Benito ripped it open to expose a smallish painting of a flirtatious girl on a swing. The kind of frivolous rendition he despised and was trying to eradicate from his new, improved Italy.

"Please, let me see it for just one moment." She peeked around him to admire the delicate brushstrokes and bright colors, framed in ornate gold. She saw the signature: Fragonard, a French painter who'd died over a century earlier.

"Why would he insult you with such a hideous gift?" Benito tossed it into the corner of the room. "Hitler studied painting and considers himself an artist. What a laugh."

Benito's mistress since age nineteen, Claretta knew better than to argue with him. He was a jealous and cruel man who must be treated with care. Later, when he was entertaining another woman, she'd retrieve the painting and stash it away with the collection only her brother knew about. Much as she adored Ben, he owed her that. After all, she tolerated his never-ending stream of women and

*turned a blind eye on his brutality. She wouldn't enter it
in her diary this time.*

"Well, what do you think?" Tabatha asked the moment Lucy finished reading.

"It's excellent. Wow, I'm impressed by your writing skills and vocabulary. But I doubt if any of Fragonard's paintings were stolen during WWII, let alone his famous *The Swing*." I recalled the painting from college art history classes.

"My teacher will probably hate it too."

"No, she won't. I shouldn't have said anything." I wished I could retract my declaration.

"You were just being honest. My paper stinks."

"No, it doesn't. I'm the blabbermouth stinker."

"That's not funny. Why are you trying to ruin things for me?" Her voice shaky, Tabatha sounded on the verge of crying.

"That was thoughtless of me, sweetie." I took her hand and said, "What do I know? Fragonard could have painted dozens of similar works. Sorry." Why stifle Tabatha's enthusiasm? "You're a fine writer with an active imagination. I'm impressed. And the truth is the Nazis plundered hundreds of paintings from France."

"How do you know?" she asked.

"It was my favorite professor's particular area of interest. He spoke of it often." I scanned her paper. "Tabatha, I meant what I said about your excellent writing ability. And good for you for getting your homework done before the last minute." I sipped my hot chocolate; it couldn't compare to what I'd enjoyed in Italy.

Tabatha swigged a gulp, then licked the froth off her upper lip. "I have a cool idea," she said, leaving her paper on the counter. "Let's look down in the basement before my parents get home."

"You mean bring up the Christmas tree?"

"Not exactly." She smirked. "There's a closet . . ."

"No, your mother indicated that was off limits." Yet I was dying of curiosity. I'd noticed the locked door while doing laundry in the basement.

"We could ask Mommy, but like where is she?" Tabatha flicked a switch, illuminating the lights, and began her descent to the basement. "Are you coming or not?"

The story of Pandora's box snaked through my mind. Pandora opened a forbidden container and out flew a multitude of miseries. Just an ancient myth, I told myself. Yet I wondered if an evil demon lay hidden in that closet.

"We'd need the key," I said, glad that I didn't know where it was. I harbored enough troubles.

"No worries. I know where they keep it," She tittered. "I know a lot more than they think I do, including how to turn off the camera surveillance system, which I disarmed five minutes ago."

Tabatha disappeared then returned brandishing a set of keys.

"I don't think this is a good idea," I said, but she slipped past me.

"Come on, scaredy-cat." Her voice echoed in the stairwell.

As she and I pattered down into the basement, my mind raced with uncertainties, and my heartbeat increased. What if the Williamses suddenly showed up? Could I trust Tabatha to say this was her idea? Even so, they were paying me to look after her, not the other way around.

At the bottom of the carpeted staircase, Tabatha jimmied a key into the door's lock, then pulled it open. Ahead lay blackness. She pulled a string and turned on a dim overhead light. Another door stood several yards ahead, but it was made of metal and housed a combination lock, like a huge bank vault.

"I know how this works," Tabatha said, her voice buoyant.

"Oh no, I don't think we should." My heart sped up further with trepidation.

Tabatha was already rotating the dial back and forth. "Got it." She wrenched a bar down, then tugged at the handle without success. "Lucia, help me open this. I'm not strong enough."

CHAPTER 18

I FELT AS IF we were entering a secret museum. The air smelled like my grandmother's attic on a summer's day. Ahead, framed paintings leaned against each other, gathering dust. Tabatha and I rifled through the dozens of signed paintings I'd never seen in art history classes. Monet, Degas, Toulouse-Lautrec. Dust motes floated into my nostrils making me sneeze.

"These paintings are all stolen," Tabatha said, cocking her hip.

"How do you know?"

She turned to catch my expression. "For someone your age, you sure are dumb," she said.

"Hey, I resent that." I could hear a surge of anger inflate my voice. "Who do you think you are, an art historian?"

"Fine. Let's just say my parents bought some of these paintings knowing they've been missing for decades." She exited the vault and sat on the stairs. "I've seen them sneaking them into the house, overheard their conversations." She let out a girlish chortle. "Sometimes they forget I live here too."

I was conflicted, as if my world were swirling into another universe. Half of me wanted to call the police, but would they believe me? Could I prove these were missing masterpieces?

"I'm so tired," Tabatha said. Still perched on the stairs, her eyelids sagged. I was tempted to keep rummaging through the paintings but decided I needed Tabatha as a witness. If I was lucky, the Williamses would never know we'd been down here. But if not . . .

"Help me lock this up the way it was," I said.

"Okay, but then I'm taking a nap."

"Good idea."

LATER, WITH TABATHA sacked out on the couch, I got back online and looked again at the paintings stolen during World War II and never recovered. Unless my imagination had spun out of control into the land of make-believe, several were in the basement room.

Back in the guest room, I checked the clock to see it was seven in the morning. In spite of my troubled thoughts, I flopped into bed and submerged into comatose slumber. I woke unrested at ten o'clock and felt dizzy when I got to my feet. Sunlight illuminated my room.

I toddled into the living room. Tabatha was still snoozing.

Back in the guest room, I sat on the bed and called my mother, a woman who'd birthed but one child. Me.

"Wonderful to hear your voice," she said. "Where are you? When are you coming home?"

"If you mean Seattle, I'm here."

"That's a relief, darling. Did you have fun?"

"Yes and no." I'd fill her in later. "After I shower, maybe I could stop by and tell you all about it. And return my suitcase." I yawned, trying to shake off my jet lag. "When do you get home from work?"

"I have the day off—have you forgotten it's Christmas Eve?"

I had. "Oops. Must be the jet lag." I was still dazzled by the paintings in the basement and by Tabatha's school paper. She'd told me it was fiction. Of course, it was.

"Sorry, Mama, my brain's back in Rome."

"I have lots to do and prepare. Can't wait to see you, dear."

"Going shopping today?"

Usually she spent Christmas Eve day last-minute shopping. Maybe she was waiting for the after-Christmas sales. "No, all done."

"Perfect," I said. "After I feed Tabatha, we'll stop by."

"Her parents still aren't home?"

"Not yet."

"That's odd."

"I couldn't agree more."

"In that case, you both should come over for dinner and then spend the night here."

"Sounds like a better plan than eating pizza out of their freezer. See you in a couple of hours."

"Wait," she said. "There's something important I need to tell you first."

I held my breath, listening to the hallow silence. "Yes? Is something wrong?" As I waited, worst-case scenarios flashed through my mind. Cancer? I knew this was her worst fear. Because her mother, my grandmother, and her aunt had died of ovarian cancer, Mama had recently taken DNA genetic testing.

"Mama, is there a problem?"

"Quite the contrary." Her voice slid up an octave. "Something's right. There's a new man in my life."

My throat tightened. "Uh—that's wonderful." My declaration sounded false even to me. Of course, I wanted her to have a man to love—and vice-versa. I needed to get over my problem, whatever it was. No use speculating about my mother now. I'd no doubt meet this guy in the near future. It wasn't as if she never dated. She had had several male friends over the last few years, but nothing serious. Which is how I liked it. I mean, if she fell in love and got married, where would they live? Would I be booted out?

"I can't wait for you to meet him," she said. "In fact, he's here right now reading the paper."

"Aren't you afraid after what happened to Papa?"

"I guess so. But I can't remember when I've been happier." Her voice sounded light and breezy—unnerving me for no logical reason.

I hung up and tossed my dirty clothes in the corner. I'd wait and wash Tabatha's first. Where on earth were her parents? I hoped they'd called an attorney to help them with any legal problems.

My cell phone jarred me when it rang. How ridiculous to feel butterflies when I recognized Mario's number. I needed to get over feeling like a gullible teenager. I convinced myself he could help me detangle this gnarled mess. Maybe he knew by now where the Williamses were.

I kept myself from saying "Hello?" like a teenager. Instead, I took a calming breath and said, "Hey, Mario, what's up?"

"Just checking to see if everything's okay."

"You tell me." Mario's handsome face swam in the back of my mind. His charming personality was nothing like American men. When was the last time a guy opened the car door for me? But I wouldn't be hoodwinked by suave manners. "Did the Williamses ask you to call?" I asked, though I knew it sounded petty.

"No, I haven't spoken to either one of them."

"Then, to what do I owe this call?"

"Lucia, I'm missing you. I was thinking you and I might have dinner together once the Williamses are home."

"I haven't heard from them yet." I paused, thinking. "How do you know they're in jail? Are you sure?"

"I have a cousin who works for the police department as a detective in Florence." His voice was as creamy as butter. "But I've learned nothing new since then. Would you like me to call him?"

I felt like a hooked trout being reeled in, irritating me no end. "If it wouldn't be too much trouble." I tried to keep distress out of my voice. "I'd appreciate that."

Was he just a smooth talker?

CHAPTER 19

MIXED RAIN AND snow splattered down as I drove Tabatha to my mother's house in my ten-year-old Toyota Camry. I flipped on the windshield wipers and made sure to keep below the speed limit as I wended my way up Capitol Hill to the home I'd grown up in. Tabatha slumped in the passenger seat.

"Why couldn't we just stay in Rome for Christmas?" she asked. "It always rains in Seattle."

"Staying in Rome would have suited me fine."

"Then let's go back to the airport and hop on a jet." Her words sprayed out like water from a hose. "You still have my mother's credit card."

"But not her permission to fly you back to Rome."

"Why not? Is she going to fire you?"

"Maybe worse. Your parents could charge me with kidnapping."

"They'd never do that."

"I'm not so sure." The car's tires slid when I slowed for a stop light. "We're almost there." I hung a right onto the familiar street and pulled up front of the two-story craftsman home I'd grown up in. Why hadn't I worn my waterproof L.L. Bean fleece-lined coat? I lugged the suitcase out of the trunk, then opened Tabatha's door. "Come on, sweetie."

"Can't I just wait here and take a nap?" Her head flopped against the back of the seat.

"No, it's too cold. This rain looks to be turning into snow."

"Snow?" She sat up straight. "Real snow?"

"Yes. Come on, sweetie."

"Goodie." Tabatha jumped out and gazed into the sky, tried to lick the snowflakes. I carried the suitcase up the front porch staircase as the snow increased. I hoped the painting wouldn't get damaged.

"Come on, Tabatha." I heard our boisterous cairn terrier, Sassy, yipping inside.

"You have a dog?" Tabatha asked, perking up. "I love dogs. Oh, I miss my puppy in Rome. You should have let me bring her home."

"It's safe and sound with its mother and Maria," I said.

Mama opened the door before I could ring the bell. Good, I had so much to ask her. She was my moral compass.

Sassy was beyond happy. She frolicked between my legs and licked my fingertips. Music floated throughout the house. Bing Crosby crooned, "I'm dreaming of a white Christmas."

"Darling daughter, wonderful to see you." Mama hugged me. "Come in. And who's this young lady?"

"Tabatha, come on in and meet my mother, Gladys Goff."

"Hello, dear," Mama said, taking Tabatha's drenched jacket. My mother's lips stretched wide into a grin. "And I have someone I'd like to introduce to you, Lucy."

"Oh?" I handed her my jacket. She hung both on the back of the closet door.

I took in the living room, decorated for Christmas. The tree was taller than usual. New white lights and pink and silver-colored ornaments hung on it. It looked beautiful, I suppose, but too modern and sophisticated. I felt off-kilter, as though I'd stepped into the wrong house. So much had changed.

A burley man in his sixties stepped into view. My mother slipped her arm into the crook of his elbow. "Lucy, this is Tom Baker." She sounded as if she were introducing me to royalty. "Tom, this is my daughter, Lucy, and her friend Tabatha."

"Hi," I said. "Nice to meet you." Was he planning to spend Christmas night with my mother? He certainly looked at ease and at home.

He put out his hand to shake mine. He was quite a looker, his hair short, in a crew cut. Ex-military?

"My pleasure." His drawl sounded as though he were from Texas. Oklahoma? Definitely not Northwest local.

I wiped my damp hand on my jeans. "Sorry my hand's wet."

"That's okay." He shook Tabatha's too.

My mother said, "Tom, honey, would you carry Lucy's suitcase down into the basement?"

"Stop, I can do it," I blurted out. What if he opened it?

My mother sent me a quizzical look.

"I'd rather," I said, but he took hold of the handle.

"No offense meant, but where I'm from gentlemen do the carrying." He hefted up the suitcase and headed for the door to the basement, lumbering down the wooden stairs.

Mama beamed, her green eyes sparkling. "Isn't he wonderful?"

"He seems very nice."

I wanted to speak to her in private. My plan was to park Tabatha in front of the TV or find her a book. I had a zillion books left over from middle and high school. But I didn't dare speak openly in front of Tom. Or would Mama tell him everything the minute I left anyway?

"Hey, Tabatha, you're welcome to look through the books in my bedroom. It's on the second floor. First door on the right."

"I'm too sleepy."

"You need to reset your inner clock, sweetie. Go on up."

"Okay, if I have to." As Tabatha plodded up the stairs, I took hold of my mother's elbow and spoke in her ear. "I need to talk to you sometime today about your grandfather's art collection."

She worried her lips. "You sound like your cousin Maureen." Mama rarely spoke of her sister Anna's family. Some sort of riff. "Why this sudden interest?"

"Just an inkling . . . to help Tabatha with her home-work," I lied. "Probably a wild goose chase." I pulled out my phone. "Maureen might be just the person I need. I'm going to call her. What's her number?"

"It's in my phone book. But I'd better warn you, she's miffed that I have one of your great-grandfather's paintings. My mother gave it to me, and I'm keeping it." She pressed her lips together and hesitated. "Not only that, but Anna holds me partially responsible for your father's death."

"Huh? Why would she?" I assessed her expression. Was Mama teasing?

She gave her head a small shake.

"But Papa's death was an accident. Right?"

She ran her fingers through her short hair.

"Mama?"

"Most likely."

"What do you mean, most likely. Is that code for pilot error?"

Her hands wrapped her throat. "I always told you his plane's engine malfunctioned, but we don't know for sure. It had just gotten its required annual main-tenance."

"Didn't he call Mayday or SOS or something to ground control?"

"No."

"I need to know the truth. Do you think I'm still too young? I'm a grown woman."

Her usually placid face turned severe. "He flew straight into a foothill in the Cascades near Mount Baker."

I waited for her to smile and tell me she was joking. "Was there a storm or something?" I asked.

"No, a perfectly clear day."

"What are you trying to tell me?" My mind flipped through the worst-case scenarios. "He ran out of fuel? Forgot to check the oil?"

She shook her head.

Deep in the crevices of my memories, I recalled my father taking me up in his Cessna 172. Sitting in the hangar, he walked around the plane, meticulously surveying the fuel level, the oil, then once inside checking and rechecking every gauge.

"Hurry up," I'd begged him. "Let's go, Papa."

"Hold your horses. Your mother would kill me if anything happened to you," he said with a chuckle, always the jokester. How I missed his sense of humor.

White noise flooded my ears. In my mind's eye I could see him clutching the yoke. I heard the propellers beating . . . then a deafening crash of metal against a rocky cliff, followed by nothing but wind whistling sounding like shards of broken glass in my ears.

"Surely a team of first responders went over the accident," I said.

"It took them days to find the Cessna."

"Had Papa been drinking? A heart attack or stroke?"

"No, nothing like that. Worse."

CHAPTER 20

"**W**HAT COULD BE worse?" I asked. Like a sieve, my mind sorted through the possibilities until it hit a cement wall. My voice squeaked as my windpipe constricted. "Mama, please tell me."

"The authorities pronounced it suicide." Her face took on a chalky mask. "Death on impact."

My world flailed out of control as I pictured Papa aiming his plane into the side of a mountain. "I don't believe it. Did he leave you a note?" I asked. "Was he depressed?" Was I in some way responsible?

"I'm sorry, I should have told you years ago," she said, a tear escaping her eye. "I was trying to spare you the pain. There was no good time."

My insides felt as though they were shredding apart. I'd always relied on Mama to be honest. "By fibbing to me?" I asked.

"I wasn't really deceiving you . . . I still don't know what happened or why he was so troubled."

"You knew he was depressed?" Which could mean anything. "You were leaving him for another man?"

"No, just the opposite." She pursed her lips for a moment. "He had other women, since you've asked. Many."

I couldn't believe my perfect father was cheating on Mama. "Was he alone on the plane?" Was I asking for more information than I wanted?

"Apparently. But I shouldn't have let him go out flying that day." She gave her head a small shake. "Not that I had any control over him in any way."

Tabatha trotted down the stairs. "Hey, Lucia, my mom just called." Her feet landed hard on the wooden floor.

"Your parents are back in Seattle?" I lowered myself onto the couch. I tried to appear relaxed when in fact I was terrified. I'd have to confront them about the painting in my suitcase. Or they might forcefully take it. I needed to have a plan, but nothing came to mind.

Tabatha plopped down next to me. "Not yet, but tomorrow. As soon as they land, they'll come fetch me." She screwed up her face. "Bummer, huh?"

To put it mildly. "How will they know where to go?"

"Duh. You gave them your address when they hired you, didn't you?"

"Oh, yeah."

"I look forward to meeting them." Mama must have caught my look of angst.

Tabatha whispered in my ear. "Don't worry, I won't tell them a thing." Sassy jumped up on the couch next to Tabatha, who scratched behind the dog's ears.

"Is there a problem?" Mama asked.

"Not at all," Tabatha said, saving me from lying.

Tom emerged from the basement and closed the door behind himself. He spoke to me. "I figured you'd have dirty laundry, so I left the suitcase near the washing machine."

"Thanks," I said. "Actually, there are some Christmas presents in there, so no peeking, anyone." I scanned the tree with distaste. Why not use our usual ornaments that I adored? Some of the new monochromatic orbs still lay in their boxes.

Tabatha aimed her words at my mother. "I can finish decorating the tree and help with anything you need."

"Thank you, dear." Mama smiled. "Many hands make light work."

"The more the merrier," Tom said.

"Do you have somewhere you're supposed to be?" I asked him.

"Lucy, don't be rude." My mother's stern voice dipped an octave. Even little Sassy noticed and lowered her head, her triangle ears pinned back. "Tom is my guest," Mama said. "I expect you to treat him with respect."

"I'm so sorry," I said. "Please forgive me." Apparently, hearing the details of my father's demise had sent me into a sea of self-pity. My body ached to its core. If only I had one little white pill to salve my newly opened wound. I was tempted to check Mama's medicine chest up in the bathroom.

"Not a problem." Tom noticed Tabatha again. "And who did you say this lovely young lady is? A relative or family friend?" he asked.

"I'm Tabatha Williams. Lucia's—er, friend." She smiled up at him.

"A special Christmas visitor," Mama said.

Maybe, with Tom here, Tabatha and I should return to her mausoleum of a house. I bet their medicine cabinet held a plethora of opioids. And in the wine cellar and liquor cabinet, booze galore. Scotch, gin, and wines. They'd never notice . . .

What was I thinking? The Williamses' was the worst place for me to be. No matter what transpired, I must stay here.

"I can cook as well as most chefs," Tabatha told Mama. "I know Rachael Ray personally."

"The real Rachael Ray, who's on TV?"

"Yup. The one and only."

Mama shot me a look of disbelief. "Sure, honey, I'll take all the help I can get."

Tabatha spun around and pressed her nose to the window. "Look, it's snowing harder."

"It sure is," Tom said. "I love snow. But it can bring this city to a standstill."

"Glad you're all spending the night right here." Mama grinned at him in a way that told me that was their plan all along. Which shouldn't rattle me. They were entitled, especially now that I knew my father had cheated on her, and in the end left her. Well, he left both of us.

I gazed out the window. It rarely snowed this much in Seattle, let alone on Christmas. Across the street, our neighbors had gone all out with the colored lights. Snowflakes wafted down like feathers.

"If only Mario was here," Tabatha said to me. "He's all by himself tonight."

"Oh?" Mama's brows lifted as she scanned my face. "We have plenty of room at the table and enough pot roast to feed an army."

"Call him," Tabatha said to me. "You know you want to."

"No." Yet I did wish to see him. Needy is what I was. Otherwise why did I crave painkillers?

"If you don't call him, I will," Tabatha said.

As Tom turned on a medley of Christmas music, my phone blared. Everyone stood like statues, staring at my handbag.

I scooped the phone out of my purse and saw Brad's name. I froze. He could twist my mind into a pretzel, but I answered.

"Lucy, baby."

"Hi, Brad. Where are you?"

"I'd rather not say."

What kind of a game was he playing?

I watched snowflakes blanket my car, transforming everything to white and smooth. I listened to an SUV on the street, slowly rolling by. I wasn't going anywhere, so most likely he couldn't make it here.

"Whoever it is, invite them over," my mother called from the dining room. "Come on, Tabatha. You and I can set the table together."

"Okay, as long as there's a spot for Mario."

"Who's that?" Mama asked her.

"He's in love with Lucia." Tabatha sent me a Cheshire cat grin. "And she has a big-time crush on him."

CHAPTER 21

"**D**ID I HEAR that right?" Brad asked, incredulous. "You have your Italian stallion coming over?" Then his voice turned creamy. "Just when I have a surprise Christmas present for you. An engagement ring." He waited so long for my response I thought he'd hung up. "Lucy, I realized I can't live without you. If that means tying the knot, so be it."

"How romantic."

"Come on and give me a break. It's what we both want, isn't it?"

At one time, I would have said yes, but not anymore.

"Where are you?" he asked. "At your mother's? I checked the hotel and then the airline. I know you flew to Seattle."

Would they really divulge that kind of information?

"I have friends in high places," he said, as if reading my mind. "The hotel was a cinch. And a former girlfriend works for the airline."

Former, I wondered. Or had she and I shared him over the last six months? No, that wasn't fair; I had no way to confirm my fears.

"Tell whoever it is to come on over," Mama said.

"No, not if that's Brad," Tabatha piped in. "He hates me."

"That little—" Brad stifled his rant. "Please thank your mother. I accept her generous invitation. Don't worry, I remember where you live."

Imagining him in Rome, I breathed a sigh of relief, but he shattered my tranquility.

"I'd better dash," he said. "Got a plane to catch."

He was probably in Chicago. Halfway across the country. I did the math and convinced myself he couldn't make it here in under four hours. Most likely longer.

I moved into the kitchen to help Mama and overheard Tabatha say, "He has no family in the area and nowhere to go other than a restaurant."

"That's not true," I said. "Brad's parents live nearby."

"Brad? I thought someone named Mario was on his way." Mama tilted her head and grinned at me. "It seems I have a popular daughter."

"Mario called?" I asked. My heart filled with unexpected warmth.

"No," Tabatha said, "I called him. Your mom gave me the address. He said he'll be here in twenty minutes."

"What?" I lowered my eyebrows at Mama. "Without asking me first?"

"I thought you'd be pleased. Tabatha told me what a help he'd been to both of you."

"But—"

"Want me to set the table?" Tom asked Mama. Our oval-shaped pedestal table could seat a dozen, but Mama and I usually ate in the kitchen, a nice, cozy spot overlooking the backyard, where I played with my friends as a child. My father had built me a tree house that still stood waiting for my own children. Which meant I needed to get married.

"Sure," she said, "but maybe not wine glasses." She must have sensed my cravings.

"Go ahead and have wine," I said, "but none for me." I turned to Tom and said, "I don't drink." Although I could easily be persuaded.

"We have eggnog and sparkling cider." Mama brought out glasses and set them on the table. She directed Tom to the hutch. "Please help me bring out the good china. We rarely use it."

She reached down to extract a half dozen plates, handed them to him. He placed them on the table.

"Isn't that a wedding present from your parents?" I asked, admiring the Royal Doulton pattern.

"Yes, but why not use it? What am I waiting for? We don't entertain often enough." She and Tom exchanged a look that told me he was the honored guest she'd been waiting for. I should be happy for her, but I wasn't. I felt like a child as I recalled the Christmas mornings I'd spent with both of my parents. My father was overly generous. Presents from Santa stacked high under the tree for Mama and me. They'd seemed happy. As their only child, I'd been spoiled. Maybe I still was.

Minutes later, the table was taking shape with our good silver-plated flatware, salt and pepper, butter, and napkins.

My skin felt itchy. This would be the perfect time to call my NA sponsor, but I didn't want to bother her on Christmas Eve. What would I tell her? That I just found out my father committed suicide? That I was going to sit down to eat with a man I yearned for against my better judgement and one who said he was bringing me an engagement ring? Maybe neither Mario nor Brad would show up.

"Tabatha and I are leaving," I said.

"No-no-no." Tabatha stomped her feet. "I want to stay. You can't make me leave."

"Did I do or say something wrong?" Tom asked.

"Not at all," Mama said.

"I'm staying here or flying back to Rome." Tabatha picked up a dinner plate and hurled it into the living room where it landed with a crash. Mama's jaw dropped, but she didn't survey the damage.

"How dare you?" I wanted to strangle Tabatha. Or toss a plate myself. If I couldn't have a drug, I needed a release. I picked a up a butter plate.

As I considered my next move, Tabatha swiped a crystal saltshaker and hurled it at me, hitting me in the chest. Incensed, I tossed the butter plate at her but missed my target. Instead, I knocked an antique clock off the hutch. It landed with a thud.

"Have you lost your mind?" Mama asked me.

"You saw her. First, a broken plate, then she used me as a target."

"She's a teenager who needs her parents."

"She needs something, all right." My words blasted into Tabatha. She looked like a wounded bird, its wings folding in.

"Please, everyone, calm down," Mama said.

"Are your Christmas Eves always like this?" Tom asked her.

"No, I can't imagine what's gotten into my daughter."

Tom picked up the clock. I was relieved to see it in one piece, but the butter plate was not so fortunate.

"She started it," I said.

Mama shot me a look that told me I was acting like an immature fool. "Which means you have to revert to childhood?" she said. "You never behaved like this when you were a teen. What in the world is going on with you?"

I wanted to run away. I wanted my opioid crutch. I scoped out the window at the accumulating snow. Beyond pretty, but it didn't cover my shame and fear. A white Christmas was a rarity in Seattle. I knew the streets would be a mess. I wasn't going anywhere. Where would I go, anyway? Not to the Williamses'.

"You'd better watch your step," Tabatha said to me, snagging me back to the dining room. "I know your little secret that could land you in prison."

"What is she talking about?" Mama asked.

I had no way of explaining. "It's nothing."

"Liar, liar, pants on fire." Tabatha seemed to grow in stature.

THE FRONT DOORBELL chimed.

"That must be Mario," Tabatha said. Like a chameleon, her voice suddenly rang with gaiety. "Let me answer." She skipped to the front door, opened it, then slammed it.

A drumroll of heavy knocking followed.

Tom strode to the door and opened it. "Hello, and Merry Christmas."

"Hey." Brad shook himself off and stomped his feet. "Lucy's expecting me."

"Please come in," Tom said.

Mama nudged me toward Brad as he stepped into the front hall. He was oh-so handsome and charm- ing—when he wanted to be.

"Hi, Brad," I said. "This is a surprise."

"Merry Christmas, sugar." He shed his jacket. "And hello, Mrs. Goff."

"Please call me Gladys. Good to see you again. It's been too long."

We'd dated for several years, but this was only the fourth or so time they'd met face-to-face. Brad and I usually met somewhere, or I dashed out when I saw his car swerve to a halt at the sidewalk out front.

"Your Christmas tree looks outstanding, Mrs. Goff—I mean Gladys." He looked down at the broken dish. "What happened here?"

"An accident." Mama picked up a couple pieces and deposited them on the coffee table.

His gaze traveled around the room, resting for a moment on the menorah, then continuing back to me. I wondered what he thought. Surely, he knew my mother was of Jewish roots. Or had I neglected to tell him because I figured he wouldn't approve? It's not as if Mama and I attended synagogue when I was young. And there was also a magnificent Christmas tree.

"Tom, may I introduce you to Lucy's friend Brad?" Mama said.

"Hi there." Tom shook Brad's hand.

"Good to meet you, sir," Brad said.

"What gives?" I asked Brad as Mama hung up his jacket. "I thought you were in Chicago."

He chuckled, as if enjoying my confusion. Of course he was.

"An early Christmas present, Lucy. I actually called you from the Sea-Tac tarmac." He moved over to me, wrapped me in his arms, and kissed my cheek. "Happy to see me?"

"No," Tabatha said. "She's not."

"Hello, Tabatha," he said through a forced smile. "Merry Christmas. I brought you a present too."

"You did?"

"Yep." He turned to Mama. "Say, I hope I'm not intruding."

"Not at all." Mama waited with expectation in her eyes. Not that I blamed her. Brad was a master of manipulation. I felt myself being sucked in. Darn it all, I did still have feelings for him.

Brad's facial features turned serious. "Gladys, I've come on an important mission: to ask you for your daughter's hand in marriage."

"How exciting," Mama gushed.

"Wait, how about me?" My hands clasped my hips. "Don't I have any say?"

"Of course you do. I'm trying to use proper decorum."

"The answer is N-O—no," Tabatha said.

Brad chuckled. I could tell he was containing his anger. "I don't think Lucy and I need your approval. You're just a little girl."

"I am not a little girl." Her cheeks flushed beet-red.

"Yes, you are," he said. "A spoiled little brat is a better description."

She stomped her foot. I hoped she wouldn't throw anything at him.

"Where are your parents?" he asked. "Why aren't you with them?"

"Brad, please." I had to de-escalate his hurtful rhetoric. "We're not exactly sure where they are."

"You don't know where her parents are on Christmas Eve? That's a hoot."

Tabatha melted to her knees and burst into blubbering tears. "They don't love me. Nobody does."

My mother and I whisked over to her, but she was inconsolable for several minutes.

"I love you, Tabatha," I said.

"You're just saying that so I don't reveal your secret."

"What's she talking about?" Brad asked with a sense of urgency. "Is there something I should know before we get married?"

"I haven't agreed to marry you. In fact, I haven't heard a marriage proposal."

Brad reached into his pocket and whipped out a small eggshell-blue box. The room fell silent.

He got down on one knee and opened the box to expose a magnificent pear-shaped diamond ring surrounded with sparkling diamond baguettes. "This baby's two carats," he said.

Mama looked over my shoulder. "Oh my, that's— exquisite."

I had to give it to him, he'd gone all out. But I couldn't imagine wearing such a showy ring. I'd have to remove it when I worked in the garden, when I cleaned house, or most any time.

He lifted the ring out of the box, poised to slip it on my ring finger. But I pulled my hand away.

"What's wrong, sugar?" he asked. "Don't you like it?

The doorbell rang.

CHAPTER 22

WHEN TOM TURNED the knob and tugged the front door open, I recognized Mario's voice. Warm and smooth as caramel.

"Mario!" Tabatha sprang to her feet like a cat. "I knew you'd come." She raced over to hug him.

"My Uber driver couldn't make it up that last hill, so I walked." Carrying a large paper bag, he draped an arm around her. "Good to see you, *bella ragazza*." He glanced to me and Brad. "Am I interrupting something?"

"Yes," Brad said. "Are you blind? Get out of here."

"Wait just a minute," Tom said. "This isn't your home."

Snowflakes melted on the tips of Mario's hair, making it curl in the nicest way. "Maybe I should leave," he said.

"No," Tabatha screeched.

Mama looked to me. "What say you?" she asked.

"I want him to stay," Tabatha said. "Please don't go, Mario."

Brad stood tall and puffed out his chest. "Doesn't her fiancé have any say?"

"We're not engaged yet," I said.

"That's good news," Mario said.

I wished he'd come over to me and give me a Gone-with-the-Wind embrace, the way Rhett Butler had swept Scarlett off her feet. But he stood staring at me, his lips parted as if he had something important to say. But he remained mute.

"I'm Lucy's mother, Gladys." Mama took Mario's bomber-style jacket and gave it a shake out the front porch. Through the open door, I saw snow plummeting from the sky. A whiteout. No one was going anywhere tonight.

"A pleasure to meet you, Gladys," Mario said, coming alive.

I wanted to speak to Mario in private but knew I couldn't with this room full of people. Maybe I could sit next to him at dinner, but Brad would no doubt claim that seat.

The aroma of Mama's pot roast floated from the kitchen. "I've got to check the food," my mother said.

"I'll help you." Anything to give me time to think. If the two men got in an argument, I hoped Tom would play the peacemaker. He seemed calm and easygoing.

Minutes later, in the kitchen, Mama chuckled. "Looks as though you have two suitors. Why didn't you tell me?" She drained the boiled potatoes.

"I didn't know. Mario may view me as a friend. He's never said anything about a relationship." I mashed the potatoes, adding a stick of butter, milk, and a dollop of sour cream.

"I saw the way he looked at you." Mama sprinkled salt on my potatoes, then a dash of pepper.

"I don't really know much about him." And he didn't know the real me. I might never be free from my addictions. Not completely. I needed to start attending meetings again and chat with my sponsor.

"How do you feel about him?" she asked.

I recalled how gently he'd treated me when I hurt my wrist and how kind he'd been to Tabatha. Not to mention taking us to the opera and chauffeuring us around Rome.

"What if he wants me to move to Italy with him?" I asked, recalling the aromas of cooking pizza and the sounds of the traffic and the splashing water in the Trevi Fountain. "He could grow tired of Amazon and decide to go back."

"Would that be so bad?" She cracked the oven door and checked her pot roast.

"Are you trying to get rid of me?" I asked.

"Absolutely not. But you are an adult."

"With a monkey on her back. Mama, I'm afraid." I thought of my suitcase but decided not to divulge its contents. Why burden her further?

She wrapped her arms around me. "I wish there was something I could do to help you."

"Your support means everything to me." I sniffed. "And seeing the Christmas tree all decorated filled me with happiness." Not that I was crazy about the new sophisticated decorations. What was wrong with our old ones? "And the snow was an unexpected gift."

"I know, can you believe it? It's been years since we've had a white Christmas."

"Tell me about Tom," I said.

Her cheeks filled with color. "We met online of all things. He's retired from the navy—an admiral—so I figured I could trust him."

"I take it you like him."

"I do. We have much in common, and he's reliable."

"Not like Papa."

"I loved your father with all my heart. But you're right. I didn't trust him, for a multitude of reasons."

"And Tom? Are you two committed . . . to anything?"

"Yes."

"Why didn't you tell me before?"

"I wanted to be sure."

"Sure enough to marry him?"

"Yes."

"But no ring and a date?"

"We've been looking at rings . . . and pondering dates."

I was happy for her but felt like doing some digging. I knew all too well how easily women could get suckered. "What does he do all day?" I asked.

"He's retired, but he works part-time as a consultant for a security company."

"Where does he live when he's not here?"

She sent me what seemed like a condescending smile. "He owns a beautiful waterfront home on Mercer Island."

"Nice. Hard to beat living on Lake Washington."

Men's voices flared in volume in the living room, sounding like a dog fight. Then Tabatha screamed. Mama and I raced into the living room just in time to see the tree topple over, the ornaments flying to the carpet, crashing and breaking.

My mouth gaped open.

"Tom," Mama said, "couldn't you have stopped this catastrophe?"

"I tried, but they—"

"It was Mario's fault," Brad said.

"It was not," Tabatha said. "You grabbed Mario by the shirt collar and kept pushing him until you tripped on that present and hit the tree full force."

"Not true." Brad raised his hands. "I'm innocent. I wouldn't waste my time with that Italian lowlife."

Mama and I turned to Tom, who shrugged with a sheepish expression. "I was bending down to see if the tree needed water when those two got into an argument about Lucy."

I waited for Mario to defend himself, but he didn't. Why on earth not?

"My new ornaments." Mama sobbed. Bits and pieces lay across the carpet and sofa.

"I'm so sorry, Gladys," Tom said.

"It wasn't your fault." Mama nudged the shards into a heap. "Ouch." She sucked on a fresh cut and glared at Brad, then at Mario. "What were you two thinking? Acting like a couple of teenagers."

"It wasn't Mario's fault," Tabatha said. "Brad was goading him. Shoving him in the chest."

"I didn't know what to think." Mario closed in on me. "Are you engaged to Brad?"

"No, and I'm not making any decisions tonight. Not after this calamity."

Tom righted the tree. "This stand isn't very stable, Gladys, but it should work. My SUV can make it if you want me to go out and buy a new one."

"No, thanks, let's just get it up again and save the few remaining ornaments."

"I don't mind if you want me to go out and purchase more decorations."

"On Christmas Eve in a snowstorm?" She tossed Tom a wry grin. "Actually, we still have our old decorations in the basement. I'm afraid I'm a regular little pack rat."

"And here I thought you were perfect." He sent her a smile.

I felt relieved. "You kept them?"

"The ones I thought you might like someday when you have your own tree."

In other words, she expected me to live somewhere else next Christmas, I assumed.

"Can I trim the tree?" Tabatha's voice was all aflutter. "At home, a professional decorator does it. Most years, we don't even have a tree at all." She looked on the verge of tears again. No doubt she missed her parents. I didn't understand why they hadn't contacted her.

"Of course, you can decorate, honey," Mama told her. "Once we get the tree upright again."

"Maybe we can make our own decorations out of ribbons," Tabatha said. "Do you have any pine cones?

We could dip them in glue and glitter the way Martha Stewart showed me."

"I'll help clean up." Mario's face was grim as he gathered shards, and then turned on the vacuum cleaner Mama had lugged out of a closet.

I was irked when I noticed Brad sitting by the fireplace idle.

"You should help," I said to him.

"Why? This was all his fault." Brad folded one leg over his knee. "He's lucky I didn't deck him. Boxing was my college sport."

The vacuum cleaner's whirring motor drowned out the rest of Brad's hostile diatribe. I didn't know what to think. Why didn't Mario defend himself if he was innocent? How come he didn't speak to me?

Tabatha trotted down into the basement with Mama and returned with a couple of worn brown cardboard boxes that catapulted me back to my childhood. I recalled my father carrying up the boxes each Christmas. A zillion memories of my youth inundated my mind: from getting my picture taken with Santa to shopping with Mama to find the consummate gift for my father, who always made a fuss when he opened it. "Just what I wanted," he'd said. And he'd hugged me as if he loved me more than anything. Then why had he left me? Why would he kill himself? I couldn't let myself believe it.

"How come you bought new ornaments?" I asked Mama. "I thought you loved our old ones."

"A new beginning?" She glanced to Tom, and it all made sense. She was in love with him and wanted to leave her past behind. "But it looks like we'll be using the old ones again this year," she said.

With Brad hunkered on the couch, Mario and Tom stood up the tree and watered it. Tabatha exhumed our old ornaments.

"Ooh, this is so pretty." Tabatha held up the tree topper, an angel. "We absolutely must use this."

Time seemed to roll in on itself as she admired the decorative angel. My papa had brought it home for me several years before his death. "You're my special angel," he'd said. Words I hadn't recalled for many years. Why would a man who thought of me as his angel bail out on his daughter?

With the tree resurrected, Mario took the angel from Tabatha and placed it on top.

"Thank you," I said, and he finally looked me in the eye.

"Should I leave?" he asked.

"Before dinner?" I felt my mouth curve into a smile.

Still, he looked solemn. "Are you betrothed to another man?"

"What's it to you?" Brad asked, his voice booming. He got to his feet. The floorboards creaked.

I maintained eye contact with Mario. "Do you mean am I engaged to be married?" I took Mario's hand and said, "No, I'm not."

CHAPTER 23

TABATHA PULLED HER gaze away from the angel and surveyed under the tree. "I don't see any presents for me."

I dropped Mario's hand.

"Santa isn't due to arrive for hours," I said.

"And my presents are in that bag by the front door," Mario said.

"You brought me a present?" Tabatha's countenance became animated.

"Yes, and one for Lucia."

"You didn't have to." I wished I had something for him.

"I wanted to bring you a token, Lucia."

"Aren't you the generous one?" Brad folded his arms. "Whatever it is can't compare to the ring in my pocket."

"But she has apparently turned you down. No?"

Brad scowled.

Tom moved in on him and clamped his shoulder. "Hey, fellas, let's not knock over this tree again."

"Yes, sir," Brad said, sounding smarmy. As if he weren't provoking Mario. Brad checked his wristwatch. "I'd better head over to my parents' for a while," he said to me. "Wanna come, Lucy? My Jeep can make it, no problem. My folks will be thrilled to hear we're engaged."

"But we're not." I felt doubt worming into me. Brad was not the kind of man who would take rejection lightly. He might never ask me again.

"You won't be sorry," he said. "I can drop you off later, whenever you like."

"No, thanks." I wouldn't leave Tabatha if nothing else.

Brad latched his gaze onto me. "In that case, I'll come back later for dessert, if that's okay," he said. "Remember what I brought you. My proposal still stands." Before I could speak, he bestowed a quick kiss on my lips.

Feeling my cheeks flood, I backed away.

When he opened the door and stepped outside, a gust of arctic air blew into the house. The snow obscured the neighbor's multicolored lights like a dust storm. I couldn't see, but I heard his Jeep's engine ignite, then the vehicle jerked and skidded away. I felt as if I was in a tug-of-war between my heart and my brain. The logical side said I should go visit his folks.

Tom closed the door. "Hope he knows how to drive in that white stuff."

"I hope he drives off a cliff," Tabatha said. "That creep."

We all chuckled.

"Please go trim the tree," Mama told me. "Tom wants to help me in the kitchen."

So I'd been replaced. "Okay."

"Lucia, Mario and I need you in the living room," Tabatha said.

Mario's hand brushed mine as I passed by him. I felt a spark of happiness mixed with anxiety. "I wish I had you to myself," he said in my ear.

"I'm glad Brad's gone," Tabatha said. "We can get back to having fun."

My phone rang. "Don't answer it," Tabatha said.

I glanced at the screen and saw my NA sponsor's name. "I need to get this. It's a close friend, no doubt wanting to wish me Merry Christmas." I stepped into the hallway "Hi, Sharon. Merry Christmas."

"And to you. Are you still in Rome?"

"No, I just got home yesterday."

"You're back so quickly and didn't tell me?"

"Uh, I was working. Looking after Tabatha." I gave her a quick rundown of what had happened.

"And now? Are you clean?" she asked, no nonsense.

No need to lie to her. "The short answer is I loved being in Rome, but I've been struggling. I'd go to an NA meeting tonight if I thought I could drive to it."

"There's a meeting every night, even Christmas Eve. This is one of the hardest nights of the year, and you know it."

"I just learned my father committed suicide," I blurted out. "And the guy I thought I was in love with finally asked me to marry him, but I panicked. He's no good for me."

"Is there anyone there who can help you? Honesty is essential, right?"

You're only as sick as your secrets, I'd heard in NA meetings. An excellent bit of advice I'd been choosing to ignore. "Yes." I needed to admit I was powerless over drugs and alcohol. I needed a Higher Power greater than myself to help restore me to sanity every day of my life. "Not that I'm coming unglued."

"Lucy, do you want me to come over there? I will."

"No, the snow's too bad." I looked out the window and saw nothing but pristine white. "My mother already knows, but she has a new boyfriend who's in the kitchen helping her."

"No secrets, Lucy."

"Yeah, I know."

I watched Mario help Tabatha trim the tree with the ornaments of my youth. Tabatha turned to enter the kitchen. I heard her speaking to Mama and Tom, leaving Mario alone.

"There is someone," I told Sharon.

"What's keeping you?" Guess I didn't answer her fast enough because she said, "There's a big AA and NA get-together tonight. It's a tough night for many folks. I can ask a friend to swing by and fetch you."

"No, but thanks for the offer. I have someone here." Did I?

I hung up and returned to the living room to see Mario putting the finishing touches on the tree. I'd tell him the truth about me. Most of it anyway.

"I want to speak to you, Mario," I said, patting the couch. "Something personal. If you don't mind." Indecision swam through me.

He surprised me by sitting on the couch close by. "What are you thinking about, Lucia? Are you worried about Brad?"

I filled my lungs with the aroma of the noble fir, then let out a sigh. "I don't know what to think about him. But that's not my biggest problem."

He tilted his head. "Can I help? I'd do anything for you."

"You would?" Had I heard him right? Was he pulling my leg? "Anything?"

"Since the moment we met." He draped an arm over the back of the couch.

"You mean on the plane?" I sputtered a laugh. "I must have looked like a stray cat."

"No, no, you looked charming. And I've found you to be a very special woman. So kind to Tabatha. She adores you."

"Not as much as she likes you," I said. His agreement with the Williamses snaked through the back of my mind. Did I really trust Mario?

No more secrets, I admonished myself. "There's something I need to tell you."

"That you're going to marry Brad? I was afraid of that."

"It's not him." I'd divulged my story to many strangers at meetings, but the words seemed lodged in my throat. "I have a problem. With drugs."

"Seriously?"

"Yes. But I'm clean. Tonight anyway. And I have been for years. But the desire keeps gnawing at me. That pain medication . . ."

"I'm so sorry for insisting you take it for your wrist."

I was thankful I'd resisted. "Not your fault. If I'd been honest, the doctor wouldn't have prescribed it."

"Where is the medication now?"

"In my purse. I need to get rid of it. Take it to a disposal center at the pharmacy."

"I'll take it for you if that would help."

"Yes, that would be very helpful. Or I could ask my mother."

"Have you taken any?"

"No, but I've come close. And Christmas Eve is a hard night for me." I stood and reached into my purse. At the bottom of the jumble lay the pill vial. "Here, would you take this from me?" I hesitated then gave it to him.

"Of course."

"Am I putting you in any kind of danger?" I asked him.

"No, I have no desire for anything but you." His proclamation sounded like something out of a movie. Could I believe him?

As I handed him the vial, Tabatha stepped into the room. She'd clearly been listening to our whole conversation.

CHAPTER 24

TABATHA STEPPED INTO the room. "You're a druggie?" she asked, her voice turning gritty. "No wonder my parents had hesitations about hiring you."

"They don't know about it." I was a master at hiding my addiction. At least I thought I was.

She planted her hands on her hips. "It all makes sense why you'd steal a priceless painting. To pay for drugs." She edged closer. "I've heard addicts will do anything to feed their cravings. We learned about it at school."

"Look, I still don't know where the painting came from." Not entirely true. Her parents must have put it in my suitcase—the only logical possibility. Yet I had no evidence.

"A painting?" Mario said. "What are you talking about?"

"Uh . . . I found a painting zipped in the lid of my suitcase when I got back to the States," I said. "I don't know what I would have done if the customs officers had found it." I tried to read his expression. Did my story sound like a fabrication? Or was he in on the charade?

"I did not put it there," I said. "I swear."

"As if your word means anything," Tabatha shot back. "You're a druggie."

I cringed. But there was no use in denying the truth.

"Where is this painting now?" Mario asked.

I didn't want to show him, or anyone, until I'd had more time to evaluate my next move.

"Is it valuable?" he asked.

"Yup, and I know where it is," Tabatha said. "At least I have a good guess."

Mario got to his feet.

I stayed put on the couch. "Are you a part of the Williamses' scheme?" I asked him. I recalled the treasure trove of paintings in their basement. Few could resist. "Do you work for them?"

"No, not at all." His brows lowered, telling me he was troubled or angry.

"But you did tell them you'd keep an eye on us," I shot back.

"As a courtesy. They paid me nothing. I wanted to see you again, Lucia."

"And how about me?" Tabatha asked. "Did you want to see me too?"

"Yes, I also wanted to see you," he said, his gaze not leaving me.

Scrumptious aromas wafted from the kitchen. With all that was happening, I was amazed to find myself hungry. "I wonder what time it is in Rome."

Mario's eyes flashed with amusement. "You're ready to go back to Rome so soon? Maybe for New Year's Eve?"

"Sure." I did want to go back for New Year's Eve. I imagined what fun it would be if Mario were there—unless I was incarcerated in the slammer. Mama and Tom would no doubt be celebrating that night with flutes of champagne and didn't need a fifth wheel. And why ruin her Christmas by telling her about the painting? I felt as if I were being crushed in a vise.

Moments later, laughter fluttered and voices mingled as Mama and Tom exited the kitchen and came through the dining room into the living room. Mama walked with a bounce in her step. No doubt about it, she was the happiest I'd seen her in many years. I remembered when I'd first told her of my opioid addiction. She'd been crushed with worry and probably still wondered if I'd end up living under the freeway. Ugh. A dingy, ugly thought. But I needed to admit it could happen to me. More than anything I must stay off narcotics and booze.

"What's going on?" Mama asked.

"We heard raised voices," Tom said.

"It was nothing," I said.

"She's lying," Tabatha drilled her glare into me. "She's hooked on narcotics."

"Your mother told me about your struggle," Tom said.

I felt all eyes on me. "I've been clean for five years," I said to the tree.

"That's wonderful," Mama said. She'd seen me at my worst, paid for my rehab. "Keep it up. I'm proud of you, daughter."

"Would you still be proud if you knew she was a smuggler?" Tabatha asked her.

"What are you talking about?" Mama turned snarly. "She is nothing of the sort."

"Oh yeah? Look in her suitcase."

Mama turned to Tom. "Now what?" she asked him.

"Go down in the basement and check it out?" He turned to me. "You have a problem with that?"

"I do." Mario rubbed his palms together. "Let Lucia have her say first."

My hero, I thought. But I figured his already tarnished opinion of me was about to plunge down to Earth in flames the way my whole life was spiraling out of control.

While attaching a glass ornament shaped like a pine cone to the tree, I rehearsed my speech. Did I even believe a masterpiece happened to show up in my suitcase's lid? I would have to implicate the Williamses if I spoke my mind. Unless the culprit was someone else. Worst-case scenario would be Mario, who had seemed too eager to spend time with me from the moment we met.

"Tom?" I said. "If you wouldn't mind, would you bring my suitcase back upstairs?" I might as well get this over with.

"That okay with you?" Tom asked my mother.

"Sure, we have nothing to hide." She turned to me. "Do we? Please tell me it's not full of drugs."

"No, Mama, but there is something . . ."

Tom strolled to the staircase, descended to the basement. My heart sped up to triple-time as I waited.

Someone stabbed the front doorbell in rapid succession. Followed by a womp-womp-womp of a heavy hand.

CHAPTER 25

"LET ME IN," Brad hollered from out in the blizzard. "I'm freezing."

"I'm tempted to leave him there," Mario said, and Tabatha giggled.

As Mario turned the knob, Brad rammed against the door and flew into the house. He stumbled and fell at Mario's feet, leaving a snowy heap on the carpet.

"Why you little—" Brad's face was so contorted with rage I thought he'd take a swing at Mario, but Brad soothed his back instead. "I should sue you."

Mario reached out a hand and helped Brad to his feet. "No offense meant," Mario told him.

"Like I'm going to believe anything you say. You're trying to steal my girl away."

"I'd be lying if I said I didn't care for Lucia. But I don't see an engagement ring on her finger." Mario helped Brad steady himself. "What are you doing here anyway?"

"Some FedEx idiot in his delivery truck skidded into me. My Jeep's totaled." Brad dropped Mario's hand, as if Mario carried a disease.

"Last minute deliveries," Mama said. "They're always in a hurry."

"I called my folks and told them I'd be eating here. If that's okay with you, Gladys." Brad shed his jacket and shucked off his soaked shoes.

"I've got a spare pair of slippers in the closet," Tom said. A spare pair? I was only gone for a few days.

"That would be great." Brad rubbed the small of his back.

"You need to see a doctor or a chiropractor?" Mama asked, steering him to the easy chair. "Although I'm not sure how we'd get you there."

"I could drive him," Tom said.

"Nah, a little bruise won't bother me. I played football in college." He winced when he put weight on his legs, then hobbled to the chair.

Tom lugged my suitcase to the first floor and lay it on its side.

"Let me do it." I opened the main compartment, avoiding the front pocket and the painting for as long as I could. Inside lay a clutter of paper and boxes.

"Presents! Is there something for me?" Tabatha suddenly sounded like a little girl. "All I really want is a puppy, like the one we saw."

"You know I couldn't bring a dog into the country," I said. Sassy wandered at my feet and sniffed the suitcase.

"But you snuck in something else," Tabatha said, her childish curiosity gone as quickly as it came. "Right?"

"Hush," I said, my finger to my lips. I didn't want Brad to see its contents.

"You brought something . . ." Mama wrung her hands.

"What's she so worried about?" Brad asked the room. No one answered. "Someone open the suitcase already, or I'll do it myself."

Mario stood behind me. "You don't need to open it," he said in my ear, his hand on my shoulder.

"Open it, please," Tabatha said. "I want to see what Santa brought me."

"Too early for Santa," Mama said, smoothly shifting the conversation to safer subjects. "We'll have to wait until midnight. But perhaps we can wrap and put the presents under the tree."

I pivoted to Mario. "Sorry, I don't have anything for you. I didn't know if I'd be seeing you again." Ever.

His gaze devoured me. "I wouldn't let that happen."

"I'll help you wrap." Tabatha's voice rose in pitch. "Where's the paper, Mrs. Goff? And ribbon." She opened the suitcase wider in front of my audience and reached in.

"Wait," I told Tabatha, louder than I intended. "I'll do it."

AN HOUR LATER, most of my presents were wrapped, thanks to Mama and Tabatha's eager fingers. Using the coffee table as an assembly area, Tabatha wrapped Mamma's gifts and Mama wrapped Tabatha's. I wrote out the gift tags to keep things straight and made sure no one opened the suitcase lid. Tabatha was proficient with the ribbon and pleased with herself.

"Sorry I have nothing for you, Tom," I said, turning to see him watching us.

"Well, of course not," Tom said. "You didn't even know I existed."

"And you, Brad, I didn't think I'd be seeing you tonight."

"All I want for Christmas is the word *yes*," Brad said, reaching over to take my hand. He lowered his voice as he glanced out the window. "I'll never make it home tonight. Maybe you could share your bed, so I don't have to sleep in this chair. My aching back—"

"No, Brad." I backstepped out of his reach. "You and Mario can sleep on the first floor. One on this couch and one on the couch in the TV room."

"You have a TV?" Tabatha sounded giddy. "We can watch Christmas movies later. My parents always do. Wherever they are . . ." She got to her feet, then stopped and looked into the gaping suitcase. Her expression changed again. "But first you need to show everyone what's in the suitcase's lid, Lucia. They all want to see what's in there."

"What's she talking about?" Brad asked.

The world stopped revolving. Or had I just stop breathing?

"There's another present in the lid?" Mama asked.

My hands trembled. "Someone put something in there without my knowledge, Mama. You've got to believe me."

"I believe whatever you tell me," she said.

"Well, I don't." Brad's voice blasted. "What's going on?"

I took hold of the zipper's metal pull, all the time telling myself divulging the painting was inevitable.

"Open the damn lid," Brad said.

"You don't have to do anything you don't want to," Mario said. "Ignore this bully."

"I'll open it," Tabatha said with a giggle. Like a sprite, she unzipped the lid to reveal a gaping empty space.

My heart dropped. "Where is it?" I asked her.

"Where's what?" Mama said. "What are you all talking about?"

Tabatha danced in delight. She ran over to me and whispered in my ear. "I hid it in the washing machine."

"Oh no, that's a terrible hiding place. You had no right." I turned to my mother. "Mama, please tell me you're not doing a load of wash."

"Not yet. But I will eventually. Do you have something you want to launder?"

"No." No more lying, I told myself. "Apparently, Tabatha is using the washing machine to hide something valuable." I turned to Tabatha. "Not a good spot, sweetie. But I know your heart was in the right place."

"You want me to put it somewhere else?"

"What are you two talking about?" Brad said.

Time to face the firing squad, I told myself. "It's something down in the basement that I inadvertently smuggled into the country. I didn't mean to." I cringed. "And now Tabatha says it's in the washing machine."

"It is," Tabatha said. "I'm telling the truth."

Like a herd of elephants, everyone got to their feet—even Brad, who apparently had forgotten about his back pain—and thundered down the staircase to the basement. Leading the way, I reached the front-loading washing machine and tugged open the door. Empty. "Are you sure you put it in here?" I asked Tabatha.

"Is this a joke?" Mario asked her.

"No. Oh, isn't that the dryer?" Tabatha asked, obviously thrilled with all the attention. "I've never done the laundry before. We have a cleaning lady."

I felt like giving her a lesson but knew I had more important things to do. I moved to the dryer. "This is a dryer."

Tabatha tittered. "Silly me, I didn't know."

Mario stepped over to it and tugged open its door. "*Eccolo*. Here it is." Mario extracted the parcel with care. He unwrapped the painting.

"Please be careful," I said.

"I will." He passed it to me. "Here, you take it."

"Thank God," I said when I saw the painting illuminated by the overhead light.

"It's an angel on Christmas Eve." Mama moved in for a closer look. "This painting appears to be very old."

I marveled at its beauty and the exquisite workmanship that could land me in jail. "I think it's by the Dutch painter Rembrandt, who lived in the seventeenth century."

"Maybe stolen and never found," Mama said wistfully.

"Well, obviously someone found it," Brad said.

"It may be a forgery for all I know," I said.

"It sure looks real to me." Mama peered at the painting's surface.

"I Googled works of art still missing from WWII last night," I said, "and found a painting that looks like it."

"My mother told me my grandfather owned a Rembrandt, but she never described it." Mama gave her head a small shake. "No, that would be too much to ask for."

"You should call Maureen," I said.

"Oh no, I couldn't."

"Or at least look at her website."

Mama said, "I've scoured her website and never seen a painting of an angel."

"Maybe Hitler gave it to Mussolini," Tabatha said.

I shrugged one shoulder. "Anything's possible."

"If this painting was stolen, we should call 911," Brad said.

"That's a little extreme." Tom came to my rescue. "This isn't an emergency. I'll bet they have their hands full tonight."

"You want them to come and arrest her?" Mario said. "I won't let you."

"Don't you tell me what I can and cannot do, you twit."

Carrying the painting with the greatest of care, I brought it upstairs and set it on the sideboard.

His hands clasped behind his back, Mario stood staring at it. "Magnificent. If only it were by an Italian master."

I couldn't help smiling.

"Give me a break," Brad said.

Tabatha cut in. "Oh yeah, what do you know about painters, Brad? The Italians have been masters since before the time of Christ."

"Yeah, right," Brad shot back. "Except for tiny sports cars what do Italians make?"

"Please," Mama said, "don't get into a fight and knock over the tree again."

"Sorry for raising my voice," Mario said.

"It was all his fault," Brad said. "He pushed me into the tree."

"Aren't you getting your story mixed up?" Mario asked him. He glanced through the front hall to the Christmas tree. "But, Gladys, we'll be careful. Although I did see some broken china in the living room when I arrived."

"Yes, we had an accident earlier," Mama said, tilting her head to Tabatha. "I assume that won't happen again either. Right, Tabatha?"

"Yeah, I guess not."

"Nothing can happen to the painting," I said. "Hey, I just had a thought. I can call my former professor at UW. He must be retired by now, but still alive."

"Darling, you can't expect anyone to come out in this storm tonight. Call him in the morning. Oh no, that's Christmas Day. Well, sometime this week."

"If you promise to call your sister after we eat."

Mama looked unconvinced. "We'll see." She glanced down at her slacks. "Oops, I need to get dressed for dinner."

"You look fine," I said, realizing I was wearing sweats.

"No, this is Christmas Eve, a special occasion." She headed for the staircase to the second floor.

"Guess I need to change clothes myself." I didn't own a Christmas sweater, but I'd purchase a midi-length burgundy-red dress several months ago and had never worn it. No room for it in my luggage. I figured unless I was invited somewhere special there was no need to bring it on the trip. In hindsight, the dress would have been perfect at the opera.

I patted my tummy, and I hoped the garment still fit after all the eating I'd done in Rome. I was thankful for my walking on the cobbled streets. Oh, I missed Rome.

CHAPTER 26

TWENTY MINUTES LATER, after a quick shower, I descended the stairs a transformed woman, wearing makeup and a flowing dress that revealed a bit of cleavage and accentuated my slim waist. I'd pulled my hair back into a French roll and donned the garnet earrings Mama gave me years ago, which once belonged to my Grandma Louisa, her mother.

Three pairs of male eyes watched my descent. When I reached the first floor, I saw looks of appreciation on their faces. Then Tom turned away and gazed at Mama—now wearing a gold lamé top and a cream-colored skirt. She wrapped an arm around his waist. Her smile said she was happy and proud of me.

"Wow, you look fabulous," Brad said to me. "You should wear that dress more often. I'll take you out to dinner. Your choice of restaurants."

"You look like a princess or a movie star," Tabatha said. "I wish I'd brought fancy clothes over with me." Her chin slumped down, and her features flattened.

"If you'd like, I'll lend you something," I told her.

"No, they'd be too big." She let out a lengthy sigh.

"You look pretty as you are," Mama said. "I could brush your hair if you like."

"You're beautiful," I told her.

"Never mind, I'd still be ugly no matter what I wore."

"How about a sweater or a scarf?" I said. "I have some scarves in the hall closet."

"I'd still look ugly. Where are my parents?"

"I'll try texting them again, but this snow has stopped all flights from arriving at Sea-Tac." My heart went out to her, but I couldn't perform a Christmas miracle.

"They're not here because they don't love me." Her chin quivering, Tabatha looked despondent.

"I'm sure they do," Mama said and glanced to me. She'd been two parents in one.

I nodded. No need to tell everyone about my father. I vividly recalled our first Christmas without him.

"Yes," Mario said. "Sometimes, parents . . . my own divorced when I was your age. It was very hard on me. One reason I don't care if I go home for Christmas."

Tabatha inched over to him. "I'm sorry," she said.

"Yes, I had no idea." I should have asked him why he showed up here. Probably not only to spend time with me. Yet when I looked into his eyes, I saw desire. Or was that my imagination?

"Do you have brothers and sisters?" Tabatha asked him.

"Yes, three of each. But we don't always get along so well. Usually, at family get-togethers, we end up quarreling."

"I wish I had a sister or a brother," Tabatha said.

"For tonight, I'll be your big brother," he said.

Her eyes teared up. "Thank you."

"And I'll be your sister."

I glanced at the painting and knew it would take Herculean strength not to stare at it all night.

When we seated ourselves at the table, Tom positioned himself at the head, which seemed all wrong. But I needed to grow up and accept that Papa was never coming home.

"I want to sit here," I said. Across from the painting so it would never be out of my sight. But, of course, it eventually would be. I'd have to give it up and find its true owner if my aunt and cousin would assist me. "First, I'll help Mama serve her pot roast."

"So will I," Tom said in a way that told me he knew his way around our kitchen. Which should make me happy. Mama had a new beau, and I should be delighted for her.

"And I want to sit next to Lucy," Brad said, lowering himself into that chair and walking it in.

"May I assist you in any way?" Mario asked Mama.

"Thanks, but I think we have things under control. It's fun having extra company. A party."

"I hope I'm not intruding," Mario said.

"Heavens no." She pulled out a chair for him and surveyed the festive table. "We're glad to have you here."

"I, for one, am not glad," Brad said.

"All are welcome at our table." Mama replaced the poinsettia with a lower arrangement made of pinecones and tiny gold and silver round ornaments.

"As I recall, you showed up without an invitation," Mario said to Brad.

"To ask Lucy to marry me. I'm not some Italian gigolo she met on the plane."

Mario said nothing in his defense. Maybe he had no interest in me after all. He sure had the dreamiest eyes—like two deep pools. I recalled meeting him on the plane and remembered my iPhone suddenly turning up in his carry-on. And then Mario happened to show up at St. Peter's, then saved the day when Tabatha came close to being arrested. He'd seemed like our hero, but was he? He'd reeled us in like two minnows in a stream.

I glanced to Brad—the man I'd been pining over all year. He'd brought me a ring. But he hadn't told me he loved me. Would those precious words make him right for me?

"Are you even here legally?" Brad pressed Mario.

"Yes, I have a green card." Mario folded his arms, leaned his elbows on the table.

"But the minute Amazon fires you, I bet you're out of here looking for a new job."

"They won't fire me. They have no reason."

"How about when they hear about you and a stolen painting?"

"I had no knowledge of the painting." Mario glanced to me. "Honestly, Lucia. I'm as baffled as you are."

My mind rattled like a pebble in a tin can—a trick Mama and I learned to keep Sassy from barking. She hated that sound as much as I hated the words Brad was spewing from his mouth.

"A husband doesn't have to testify against his wife, Lucy," Brad said. "You're safe from me. But not this guy." His mouth stretched into a grin. "Let's get married on New Year's Eve. Wouldn't that be fun? Neither of us would ever forget our anniversary."

The words I'd been waiting to hear, but I felt as flat and parched as the Sahara Desert.

"I don't understand what you see in Brad," Mario said to me. "I admit he looks good on the outside."

"You've got your nerve." Brad wrapped his beefy fingers around the stem of his glass.

"Now, boys, behave yourselves." Tom poured wine for Mama, Mario, Brad, and himself, and sparkling cider for me and Tabatha. My entire body craved a white pill. I chided myself and gazed at the festive Christmas tree. This was a night of new hope, I reminded myself.

I passed the green beans and mashed potatoes around the table. My eyes focused on the painting. "From what we read online, if this is the original Rembrandt, it was kept in a French château in the countryside before being discovered by the Nazis, then taken to Paris."

"That painting could be worth a mint." Brad slurped his drink.

"Unless it's a forgery." I turned to Mama. "Did your family own a château in the French countryside?"

"I've never seen it, but family lore says yes, at one time we did." She tilted her head. "Lore also says my grandparents were fortunate to have escaped occupied France when they did. This I believe. And I'm thankful they did." She turned to the painting. "I suppose I do need to call my sister. If she'll speak to me."

More than ever, I wanted to ask Mama about the painting in her bedroom. Tom must know about it, but no need for Mario and Brad to become privy. Of the two men, which did I trust?

I noticed Tabatha wasn't eating.

"Not hungry?" Mama asked her.

"I want my parents. Where are they? Isn't it Christmas Eve all over the world? How could they forget me?"

During dinner, I found that Mario and Brad had nothing in common. Yet I was attracted to both men for different reasons.

Our doorbell chimed, followed by knocking. Tom answered it and then announced that Mark, Brad's older brother, had arrived to fetch Brad.

"Come on, bro." Mark was tall, muscled, and blond, like Brad, as if he'd stepped out of an Eddie Bauer catalogue. "Mom's having a fit you're not home."

"How did you get here?" Tom asked.

"My Land Rover had no problem. I'm used to driving on snow when I go to Crystal Mountain. This snow means premium snowboarding."

"Want to come with us for dinner?" Brad asked me. "Our mother would love it."

"Go ahead if you like, Lucy," Mama said.

"What about me?" Tabatha shot to her feet. "You'd leave me here by myself?"

"I'd be here, Tabatha," Mario said.

"No, thanks," I said, "I want to stay at home." No way would I brave the storm. Yet Brad still tugged at my heart because he represented all I thought I'd never have.

"We're going snowboarding tomorrow if you want to join us," Brad said, but I bowed out.

"Thanks, but I want to stick around here."

"I left the ring on the mantelpiece in the living room." Brad stuffed his arm in his jacket. "Thank you so much for having me over, Mrs. Goff."

"You're most welcome." Thankfully, Mama stopped short of inviting him back again. "Merry Christmas."

"I'll come back tomorrow, if that's okay," Brad said.

"We'll be here." Mama sipped her wine.

"See if you can get Lucy to change her mind, okay?"

"My daughter has a mind of her own. I know better than to try to interfere."

Once he and Mark left, the street grew quiet. Not a vehicle drove past our house, leaving us with a beautiful and peaceful silence as the snow continued to fall.

Drifting in the background, "Silent Night! Holy Night!" floated throughout the house, thanks to Tom's mini sound system. Tabatha joined in, then Mario, Mama, Tom, and finally I sang. I was filled with tranquility. All was calm.

"I'm glad he's gone," Tabatha said when the piece came to an end.

I couldn't help chuckling. "Me too." I sipped my sparkling cider, feeling the bubbles tickle my throat. Yet I yearned for a glass of wine.

"And are you happy to have me here?" Mario asked.

"Yes." Tabatha's voice rang with exuberance. "Let's talk about *Roma*."

"That would be lovely," Mama said. "Tom and I plan to travel through Italy."

"In May," Tom said. "On our honeymoon."

"What?" My jaw dropped open in surprise.

"We intended to announce it tomorrow," Mama said. "But tonight, on Christmas Eve, is better." She placed her hand on the table to show me her engagement ring, a single oval diamond—valuable but understated, like my mother.

"Why weren't you wearing it earlier?" I asked.

"I wanted to show you at the right time. Which turns out to be now."

"It's lovely." The words clogged in my throat.

"Aren't you happy for us?" she asked.

My mind was a battleground of uncertainties. Where would I live?

"Yes, Mama, congratulations. I am happy for you," I said. "You caught me off guard. I didn't even know you had a serious boyfriend a few hours ago."

Tom's mouth lifted into a smile. "We decided to seize the moment. We're not getting any younger."

"Yes, love at first sight." Mama grinned back at him. "And we planned the honeymoon before we knew you were going to Rome."

Tom nodded. "But now Mario can help us with our itinerary, if he would. Neither of us has ever been there."

"I'd be delighted to be of assistance," Mario said. "And congratulations. We should have a toast."

"I just happened to have a bottle of champagne," Tom said. Getting to his feet, he slipped into the kitchen and returned with a bottle of Dom Perignon while Mama brought out fluted glasses.

"Allow me." Mario uncorked the champagne like a pro and filled the glasses. "I congratulate Gladys and Tom on their engagement."

I could smell the sweet, bubbly champagne from where I sat and recalled nights of drunken hilarity and laughter, followed by staggering hangovers. And white pills.

"Congratulations to both of you." I picked up a glass, then put it down. I raised my sparkling cider glass. "I'd better stick to this."

"This is cool." Tabatha raised her glass of sparkling cider.

We all clinked our glasses. "Cheers!"

"Are you truly happy for me?" Mama asked me.

"Honestly?" I said. "I need time to get used to the idea. Which I will."

CHAPTER 27

To say I had a restless, agitated night is an understatement. As I sank into my familiar mattress and pillow, my mind raced with conflicting thoughts. The image of the mysterious painting floated through my brain; I wanted to keep it. But I knew I should track down its owner's ancestors. If they could be found.

Brad's ostentatious engagement ring sat on the mantle. Mario slept on the couch, covered with a quilt Mama had sewn, in what we called the TV room, its door shut. I worried about Tabatha but doubted she'd leave the house with Mario close by.

Once, I heard heavy thudding noises. Santa trundling down the chimney? Nah, most likely snow sliding off our roof and hitting the ground. I peeked out the window and noticed the snow had eased but still continued.

I was grateful I hadn't succumbed to the wine or champagne. Or foraged through Mama's bathroom cabinet looking for pain pills. The thought of waking up with a hangover or day-after regrets filled me with dismay. I needed to text Sharon and tell her I was okay.

With so many people in the house, I couldn't descend in my bathrobe. I tiptoed to the bathroom, swished a quick shower, and combed my hair. Keeping quiet, I returned to my room and dressed in my seasonal plaid sweater Mama insisted suited me and a pair of stretchy black jeans. Back out in the hall, the guest room door next to mine was closed, but I cracked it enough to see Tabatha sprawled across the bed snoozing with earbuds in place. Mama's door was also closed. I wouldn't open it. Oh no, what a ghastly thought. Sometimes ignorance is bliss.

Which left Mario in the TV room. I wondered how he'd slept on that couch meant for an apartment. The thought of him evoked a warm fuzzy feeling through my chest. I might as well admit I was infatuated with him. But were the two of us suited to have a long-term relationship? The fact he was here seemed crazy. Not that Mama hadn't always welcomed my friends my whole life. Truth is Mario could jet back to Italy and resume his life without me. Maybe Brad was right: Mario was just some guy I met on the plane.

Outside, the cloudy sky hung with grays and purples. Garlands and red ribbon and luminous Christmas lights shone from around the neighborhood. A dusting of white powder continued. Since I was a child, I'd never seen Seattle cloaked in so much snow. I felt giddy, even though I knew the city would be paralyzed. But it was Christmas morning. My favorite day of the year.

Even without my father. I needed to get over him and enjoy myself, if possible. Yes, I would, no matter the circumstances. I had much to be thankful for. And I was hungry. And craving coffee with cream.

I pattered down the stairs. My feet, cozy in my slippers, felt light and breezy. I strolled into the living room and noticed the ring box on the mantel. I moved over to it, opened the box, and admired the opulent diamond. Wow. I recalled the song from an old Marilyn Monroe movie Mama loved. "Diamonds are a girl's best friend," Mama would croon along with Monroe. "These rocks don't lose their shape." I sighed.

I hate to admit I tried the ring on. But without love, it meant nothing to me. I removed it and placed it in the box and shut it. I mouthed the words. "Guess I'm done with you."

Mario's door stood shut, and I didn't hear the TV. I wondered what he'd think if I rapped on the door carrying a cup of java. I spun on my heel and headed to the kitchen. As the coffee brewed, I sidled into the dining room to admire the painting.

It was gone!

I bent over the sideboard to make sure the painting hadn't fallen behind it. No.

Had I been the fool by trusting Mario? Had he stolen the painting and then hit the trail in the dead of night? The thought brought a wave of nausea to the back of my throat.

I marched to the TV room and rapped on the door. No answer. I turned the door handle and elbowed the door open to find Mario asleep on the couch.

His eyes slowly opened. "*Buongiorno*," he said and yawned. "Morning already? *Buon Natale.* Merry Christmas, beautiful Lucia." He stretched out his arms. A lock of dark hair curled across his forehead. For a zany moment, I felt like sinking into his embrace and snuggling.

"Mario, wake up."

His face took on a look of alarm. "What's wrong?" Dressed in a T-shirt and sweats Tom must have loaned him, Mario sat resting his weight on his elbow. "*Che cosa fai?*"

"The painting. Did you move it?"

"You mean the angel painting? It's gone? Are you sure?"

"Yes, I'm sure. Where is it?"

"I have no idea. I didn't touch it." He raked his fingers through his hair. "Maybe your mother moved it to a safe place."

I clasped my hips. "My mother? What are you implying?"

"Would it be so bad if she or Tom hid it for safety? That would be the wisest thing."

Picturing Mama and Tom together made me cringe. But they would have been prudent if they'd hidden it. I should have slipped it under my bed. I could have kicked myself for being so blasé.

"I wouldn't have moved it without your permission," Mario said, bending his legs and sitting. In one fluid motion, he was on his feet and cruising into the dining room.

"How could I have been so stupid?" I asked the universe.

"No, you're not stupid; we'll figure this out." Mario looked sexy in the T-shirt and sweats. I was baffled that I even cared. "Where could it be?" I said.

"We'll find it." He glanced out the window. "Still snowing?"

"Yes," Tabatha said. I hadn't heard her coming down the stairs. "Isn't it too cool?"

"Merry Christmas, *Signorina* Tabatha." Mario followed her to the tree and turned on the lights. "I have an important question for you."

I decided he'd have better luck with Tabatha, so I pressed my lips together and remained silent.

"Tabatha," he said, "we seem to have lost the painting."

"The angel is gone?" She rotated to look into the dining room. "Maybe Mussolini came in the night and took her."

The corners of Mario's lips curved up. "That's the one person we know couldn't steal it. He died many years ago."

"No." She lowered her eyebrows "He's still alive. I saw him when we were in Rome looking out his balcony."

"Sweetie, it must have been a worker." I envisioned a grisly black-and-white photo of Mussolini and his mistress—both dead.

"Many of us Italians look the same," Mario said, keeping his voice upbeat.

"None of them are as handsome as you."

He grinned. "Thank you for the compliment, Tabatha. But you must be mistaken. Mussolini is no longer living."

"Think what you like. I spoke to him."

"Last night?" I asked.

"No, dummy, like while we were in Rome." She returned to the tree. "I want to open my presents."

"We have to wait for my mother to wake up."

Before I could stop her, Tabatha bounded up the stairs and knocked on Mama's door. I followed Tabatha halfway up the staircase.

"Time to rise and shine." Tabatha persisted in knocking until Mama cracked her door.

"Merry Christmas," Mama said. "It's only six o'clock. How did you sleep?"

"Fine, except for when Santa came. I heard him chuckling, but he didn't leave any presents."

"I think I heard him too," Mama said. "Or my naughty little Sassy was yapping and scratching on the door for nothing."

"Mama," I called up the staircase. "Are you decent?"

"Not quite dressed yet, dearest. Give us five minutes." Us?

"Should I call the police?" I asked Mario.

"And tell them what? That someone stole a stolen painting?"

"That doesn't sound very good, does it? I could end up in the slammer."

"Or at least on the five o'clock local news," he said. "Let me look around the house first. Okay?"

"Sure, if you don't mind. I'll check upstairs." I jogged to Mama's door. "Do you have the painting in there?" I asked through the doorway.

Mama poked her head out. "I haven't seen it since last night. Is this some kind of joke?"

"I wish." I heard rustling in the bedroom, and a moment later, Tom stepped out wearing a jogging suit. He seemed perfectly at ease, while I couldn't bring myself to look into his eyes.

Mama and I combed the first and second floors while Mario scoured the basement.

"This is fun," Tabatha said, following me. "I bet Mussolini or Claretta came back from the dead to nab it."

I lacked the stamina to argue with her.

Mario exited the kitchen. "It appears someone— maybe two men—entered your back door last night."

We all jammed into the kitchen. "The window isn't broken," I said. "Not a forced entry."

"Who else has a key to your house?" Tom asked.

"No one," Mama said. "But we keep one hidden in the garage on a nail."

"Anyone know about it?" Mario asked.

"A few people," Mama said. "Like our next-door neighbors."

"And Brad," I said. All heads turned my way. "I locked myself out one day last year."

"He'd come back here in the snowstorm?" Mama asked.

"I checked the mantel, and the ring is still there," I said.

"Wouldn't a thief have taken it?" Mario said.

"Who else would have known about the painting?" I asked.

"This whole scenario is making my head spin." Mama's hand moved to the base of her throat. She looked to Tom. "What should we do?"

"Mario and I should go to Brad's house and wish him Merry Christmas."

"Sure, *Buon Natale*," Mario said.

"I'd better come." I dreaded the encounter. "I know where he lives."

"I want to go with you," Tabatha said.

"No, sweetie, not this time."

CHAPTER 28

I'D BEEN TO Brad's parents' humongous brick mansion only a couple of times but knew its location, even buried under a mattress of white. Tom's vehicle's tires gripped the snow; we fishtailed only a few times. Bundled up in winter gear and wearing my tall boots, I sat in the back seat alone, rehearsing what I was going to say but coming up empty.

When we finally reached the circular drive, Tom said, "I bet this place is six thousand square feet." He cut the engine.

If I married Brad, I could live in a mansion like this someday, I told myself. But at what price?

"Look over there. Mark's Land Rover is only partially covered with snow." Mario turned to speak over his shoulder. "Do you want us to come with you?" he asked.

"Under the circumstances, I think we should," Tom said. "I don't mind a little cold."

"Nor do I," Mario said.

We all got out and plodded through the two feet of snow toward the front door. The temperature had dropped. Icy particles bit into my face, causing me to squint.

Mario and Tom waited at the bottom of the steps as I picked my way up toward the wrap-around porch, all the time holding onto the black metal railing. I rang the bell and listened to the elaborate chime echo throughout the vast space.

Clad in a lavender-colored silk bathrobe, Brad's mother, a willowy blonde, opened the door and bestowed upon me a tight smile. "How lovely to see you, Lucy." She peered down her chiseled nose at me and said, "Isn't this a bit early?"

"Sorry to wake you." The sun hadn't even risen yet. I could see through the door's opening elaborate decorations and a sensational Christmas tree that reached to the ceiling.

"I hear you may be a member of our family soon," she said. I imagined I wasn't what she hoped to have in her grandchildren's gene pool.

"Is Brad home?" I asked.

"Still in bed."

"This is very important."

She huffed. "Come in, all of you. Stomp the snow off your boots first."

"Mom?" Brad called. "Who's there?" His face lit up when he saw me.

Then he glanced down at my hand. "Take off your glove and show my mother your engagement ring."

"It's at home." I wished I'd brought it along with me to trade for the painting.

He gaped at me as if I'd lost my mind. Maybe I had.

"What's he doing here?" Brad pointed at Mario as if he were a panhandler.

Mario kept his cool and smiled. "Something is missing from Lucia's house."

"What does that have to do with me? My car's totaled."

"But not your brother's Land Rover," Mario shot back. "Is he up?"

"Not yet." Brad stepped forward to shield his mother. "Hey, man, it's Christmas morning. And we stayed up late. Had too much to drink."

"Please," I said. "Or I'll be forced to call the cops." Not that I would. How could I?

Tom moved forward. I was glad to have another man with us. He carried with him an air of authority. "I believe you may have something that belongs to Lucy and her mother."

"I don't know what you're talking about."

"Pipe down, I don't want to wake the neighbors," his mother said.

We all removed our hats, whisked snow off our shoulders and stomped our boots, then crossed the threshold into the splendid home.

"Is everything okay?" a gruff man's voice called down the grand staircase. I recognized Brad's father, Howard, dressed in a plaid robe, and remembered his petulant temper. According to Brad, he was a rattlesnake, coiled and ready to strike. Tough to grow up with. Maybe that's where Brad picked up the aggressive side of his personality.

"Are we serving breakfast to street people?" his father asked.

"You remember Lucy, don't you?" Brad said. "My fiancée."

I fluffed my damp hair. "Brad, we're not engaged. And we have a serious matter to contend with."

"Are you trying to ruin my family's Christmas?" Howard barked.

"Lighten up, Dad," Brad said.

"The Goffs are missing a valuable painting." Tom took on a military stance.

"What does that have to do with us?" Brad's mother said, all defensive.

"I think you'd better leave," his father said. "I should call the police."

"Wait, Dad." Brad moved over to him. "Please don't do anything hasty."

"What would be hasty about that?" his mother said. She turned to me. "If you're accusing one of our sons of theft, you've got a lot of nerve." She frowned down at me as if I stood half her height. Trapped in her haughty glare, I felt myself shrinking.

Mario strode over to Brad. "Where is the painting?"

"How should I know?" Brad balled his fist, bent his arm at the elbow. "Look, buddy, I've wanted to deck you since the moment I met you. All the time, you were trying to steal my girl."

Mario stood his ground. "I admit I'm attracted to Lucia, but that has nothing to do with the painting."

How I wished I could believe him. I wanted to.

Mark slogged down the stairs wearing sweats. He yawned as we exchanged a brief greeting.

"I'll be right back." Tom loped out the front door and over to Mark's vehicle. He checked the tires, then returned. "Same tire tread we saw at your place, Lucy."

"Are you an expert on tires?" his father said, his words filled with venom.

Tom leveled his gaze. "I am an expert on lying, as a matter of fact."

"I will not tolerate this mean-spirited drivel," Brad's mother said.

"Look," Tom said. "We can come back with a cop and a search warrant."

"I wouldn't do that if I were you," Brad said. He narrowed his eyes at me. "If I go to jail, so does Lucy."

"Maybe we'd just better go home." My voice came out above a whisper.

"No," Mario said. "We stay until we get the painting."

"It's yours?" Brad asked. "I think not."

"Brad said you work for the Williamses," his mother said. "We are loyal customers and know them well."

"Your job could be in jeopardy if we complain about you," his father added.

Strength permeated me, loosening my tongue. "Or you could be in jeopardy if I tell anyone your art was possibly obtained illegally."

"It's the truth," Mario said. "Do you want to see yourself in the news as owners of stolen property?"

"We didn't know," his father said. "In fact, we still don't know." But he drew back and looked troubled.

He turned to Brad and Mark. "Is it true? You broke into Lucy's home?"

Mark lowered his brows. "Better get it," he said to Brad.

"Be careful," Mario told Brad's departing form as he ascended the staircase. "It could be very valuable."

"Or not," I said. But I'd learned priceless information about Brad.

CHAPTER 29

TEN MINUTES LATER, Mario and I were in Tom's SUV. I sat in the back, the painting housed in a towel and a plastic bag in my lap. I envisioned Brad's family's impressive home, decked out for Christmas. My relationship with him and his parents was severed forever. Unless they reported me, in which case I might see them in court.

How and why did Brad and his brother pilfer the painting? Revenge to hurt me or greed? I pictured them sneaking in our back door after drinking a few too many. I could hear them chuckling. Some big spoof at my expense.

I'd have to return his ring somehow. He could give it to his next girlfriend. I doubted he'd be heartbroken for long over losing me.

My thoughts turned to Mario as I gazed at the back of his head. I wished we were in Rome amid the fabulous archaic buildings and ruins. While there I'd learned that beneath the modern buildings lay centuries of ancient structures, uncovered when new architecture was erected. How fascinating. I wanted to return more than ever. But only if Mario were there.

He glanced back at me. "Are you okay, Lucia? You're awfully quiet."

"Depends on your definition of okay."

"Tom, did I do the right thing in taking the painting?" I said.

"Lucy, your mother would have tanned my hide if I'd brought you home without it."

"Guess you're right. I'll give it to her for Christmas." Mama could handle anything.

Cruising and sliding through the snow, Tom's vehicle skidded to the right as if on an ice-skating rink, then bumped into a curb, thankfully missing several cars. It lurched to a halt. He tried several times to back up, but the tires spun.

"Want me to get out and push?" Mario asked.

"That would be great. I'd better push too."

With me at the wheel, the men shoved the vehicle without success. Two lights shone on us, emanating from a substantial police vehicle with chains on its tires. One of the officers got out. Flashlight in hand, he glanced into the back seat but said nothing. My throat tightened around a lump.

I rolled down my window and said, "Hi."

"We could give you a push," the officer said. "We've been helping folks all night."

"That would be great," Tom said. "We don't have far to go."

The officer hopped back into his vehicle. His bumper pressed against Tom's until we were moving. Mario dove into the back seat. The officer gave us a high-five, and I waved.

"Thank goodness," I said.

As Tom drove, we passed abandoned cars left in willy-nilly awkward positions. We saw elaborate Christmas lights on homes and trees. A few kids were having a snowball fight, laughing and joking. The interiors of many houses were still dark. I assumed children were inside, checking their stockings or searching under trees for presents. The city looked peaceful and calm. Quiet, save a couple of cars on the side streets.

Minutes later, Tom's SUV slid into our drive. Careful not to lose my balance, I opened the front door. Luscious aromas of toast, butter, and cooking eggs filled the interior.

Mama welcomed us with a "Merry Christmas." Her gaze traveled to the painting I carried. "Good, you got it. I was so worried."

"Here," I said to her, "take this." I gave her the painting. She made sure no snow touched its delicate surface as she removed it from the plastic bag and towel.

"Can you believe the man I almost married stole this?" I asked her.

"I'm sorry, dear. At least you're home safe and sound now." She turned her attention to Tom. "I was worried about all of you." He kissed the top of her head. Finally, a man loved her. I thought of all the years she'd lived without love. And me too.

Tabatha burst onto the scene. "Did you find Santa Claus?"

"No, but we retrieved the painting."

"Which we need to put out of sight," Mama said. "Somewhere safe." She cradled the painting as she scaled the stairs. I started to follow her, but she said, "I have a hiding place you don't know about."

"You do?"

"Yes, and you'll be able to say you don't have a clue if someone asks you where it is."

"Well, that's for sure." I was dying to know. "No hints?"

Her eyes sparkled. "No, then it wouldn't be a hiding place. Now go back downstairs and set the breakfast table."

I thought I knew every square inch of this house, but apparently not.

Tabatha searched under the tree. Surely, at age fifteen, she didn't believe in Santa Claus.

"No presents from Santa?" Tabatha asked.

"We'll open presents after breakfast," I said. "I still have a little wrapping to do." I hurried to get my chores done.

Tabatha turned gleeful again as she helped me place the plates and flatware on the table.

"This looks great," I told her, admiring the folded red-and-green napkins.

"I learned how to set the table from Martha Stewart."

"Too bad she can't join us," I said.

"She's all tied up," Tabatha said. "She told me herself."

Mama trotted down the stairs and hurried into the kitchen. I'd always enjoyed her special Christmas morning egg casserole. The cheesy aroma wafted throughout the house. And coffee! No wonder I was still so loopy.

At that moment, Mario handed me a mug of strong java with cream.

"Thanks, you just saved my life," I said. How could he look so good in the morning?

"I want to open presents." Tabatha's mood seemed to be deteriorating.

"First, we eat and give thanks." Mama led us to the dining room.

"I certainly am grateful," Mario said. "To be here. To have met Lucia."

"I'm thankful Brad's not here," Tabatha said.

Soon we were seated at the table enjoying breakfast. I could tell Tabatha was downhearted, but Mario did his best to entertain her by teaching her some Italian. She had a knack for it. I joined in, determined to master the language too.

My iPhone rang. "Now what?" Tom asked.

"The police?" I said, voicing my worst nightmare.

"No, it's Tabatha's mother."

CHAPTER 30

"**A**NSWER IT." TABATHA sprang to her feet. "Hey, you have an iPhone, Lucia. Put it on Face-Time so I can see her."

Sure enough, the Williamses emerged on my screen. Both of Tabatha's parents looked bedraggled.

"You made it home?" Tabatha asked. "I was afraid you weren't coming and that you didn't love me anymore."

"Oh, darling, I'm so sorry," Gretchen said.

"We got tied up." Her father's hand encircled his wrist. "You wouldn't believe how much we had to pay to get out of . . . out of—"

"Rome," Gretchen cut in. "We had to fly to Port-land, Oregon, and then hire a car." Stan seemed to be searching the room. "Lucy, is that you?"

Well, I wasn't going to make things easy for them.

"Merry Christmas," I said, with as much enthusiasm as I could muster.

"Please do come over and join us," Mama said, although I doubted they could see her.

Both looked awkward as they explained they were still stuck in transit in an Uber.

Tabatha took the phone from my hand. "Hurry and come here. That would be the best Christmas present ever."

"We will," Gretchen said. "As soon as we can." I was sure she had plenty of questions for me. But not half as many as I had for them.

"You're missing Christmas." Tabatha pointed the phone to the tree. "I decorated that tree. Isn't it fantabulous?"

"Yes, it is. I'm glad you're having fun." I figured Gretchen's gaze canvassed the room—as best she could.

"We hired a private jet," Stan said. "But Sea-Tac closed its runways. Even Boeing Field is closed, so we had to land in Portland."

"But at least you tried," Tabatha said. "Just for me."

"Yes, darling. Is that you, Lucy?" Tabatha pointed the phone my way. "I hope you'll be coming home with us when we get there."

"No, I don't think so." I took hold of my phone.

"We want her here with us," Mama said, for which I was grateful.

"Yes," Tom echoed. "Here with us."

Tabatha scooped up my phone. "Where are my presents?"

"Uh . . . we lost track of our luggage," Stan said.

"Yes," Gretchen said. "We left in a hurry. To be there with you, Tabatha."

"They should arrive in a few days." Stan paused. "Maybe tomorrow if we're lucky."

"You lost my presents?" Tabatha sounded as skeptical as I felt. "For real?"

"We'll have to wait and see," Stan said.

"What did you buy me?" Tabatha asked.

"All sorts of marvelous things," Gretchen said. "If they don't arrive, we can go shopping soon. When this miserable snow lets up."

"Maybe it'll turn into rain this afternoon and Sea-Tac Airport will open and our luggage will show up. Although that could take days." Stan yawned. "We'd better ring off and save our battery, honey. Both phones have run low."

Without a further farewell, the screen went black.

"Daddy?" Tabatha said. "Mommy?" She turned to me. "Did you hang up on them?"

"No, honest, I wouldn't do that. Maybe we just lost the connection."

"That happens sometimes," Mario said. "Please forgive me, Tabatha, I couldn't help but overhear your conversation." He scratched his unshaven chin. "With the temperature dropping, I doubt the airport is going to open any time soon."

Leaving half of her breakfast uneaten, Tabatha looked like a wilting dandelion.

"Let's go into the living room and open presents," Mama said. "I could make hot chocolate, Tabatha. With marshmallows."

"Okay." Tabatha remained slumped in her chair. "But I won't have any."

"What's this?" Tom headed into the living room. "A present for Tabatha."

"For real?" Tabatha shot to her feet. "Who's it from?"

"I can't quite read the signature."

She sprinted across the carpet and read the gift tag. "Mario. You got me a Christmas present?"

"*Sì*. I hope you like it." He followed her into the living room and settled on the couch.

She ripped open the parcel, then squealed with excitement. "I love it." She cuddled the stuffed plush puppy under her chin.

"I hope it will comfort you until your parents buy you a real dog."

"If they ever come home."

"Eventually they will." I hoped sooner than later. Not true. I could hear them accusing me of theft.

Sassy frolicked over to sniff the beige-and-white stuffed animal.

"Is it a boy or girl?" Mama asked Tabatha.

"It's a girl." Tabatha rubbed its fur against her cheek. "She's so soft." She cradled the stuffed dog.

"What will you name her?" I asked.

"Claretta."

"Really?" I said. "I thought you'd call her Fluffy or something like that."

"Who's she named after?" Mama asked.

"Someone you met in Rome?" Tom said.

"I wish." Tabatha expelled a dramatic sigh. "If only I could have."

"Sweetie," I said, "the real Claretta died years ago."

Tabatha plugged her ears and let out a scream.

"Ignore her," I told Mama when she stepped toward Tabatha to comfort her. "Do you know who Claretta was?"

"Not a clue."

"She was Mussolini's favorite squeeze," Mario said, his face somber.

"Tabatha seems to have a fixation on him," I said.

"That's a first." Tom parked himself on the armchair. "Why on earth?"

"Darned if I know." I scanned under the tree.

Tabatha quieted. "Claretta was so beautiful and clever that Mussolini loved her." Tabatha clutched her new stuffed dog. "I want to be just like her."

"Mussolini had many women," Mario said. "And he was a despicable anti-Semite."

"I know. I read her diary." Tabatha sent him a sly grin. "Well, almost."

"But how?'

"Claretta kept a diary," she said. "A few years ago, a guy wrote a book about her entries. I've got to learn Italian so I can read it for myself."

"Why would you waste your time reading that?" I asked. "Do your parents know?"

"Like I'd tell them anything." The corners of her mouth angled down. "They don't care what I do."

"Sure, they do." I wanted to change the subject. I spied a package labeled with my name, from my mother, under the tree. "Let's open more presents," I said.

Mama grinned. "Good idea." She reached under the tree to retrieve the present and handed it to me.

I was hoping to spot a gift from Mario but saw none. "Thank you," I said to her.

"Don't thank me yet," she said. "Come on and open it."

I removed the paper to find a teal-green cashmere sweater that echoed my eyes. "I love it, Mama. My favorite color. Thanks so much."

"You are most welcome, my darling daughter. I can't tell you how delighted I am that you're home for Christmas."

"I have something for you," I said and handed Mama a present.

"You shouldn't have," she told me as she unwrapped a stylish purse and a pair of matching leather gloves with hand-stitching. "But I'm glad you did. I love these, Lucy."

"Sewn as only the Italians can," I said.

Tabatha noticed the movement and conversation around her. Cradling her stuffed puppy, she plopped down on the couch next to Mario.

"Don't try to talk me out of calling her Claretta," she advised him.

"I didn't say a thing." He retrieved another present for her. "*Allora*, what's this? It has your name on it."

Tabatha turned into a giggly teenager again. "You got me two presents?" She ripped off the brown paper and string, opened a decorative metal box. "Yummy. My favorite pastries." She closed the lid. "I might save these for later."

Figuring she had no plans to share them, we adults all chortled. How thoughtful of Mario to remember her favorite morning treats, but he'd apparently forgotten about me. What a dummy I was to think he would remember.

I gave Tabatha her present, a bracelet I'd managed to purchase without her seeing the transaction. She seemed to like it. But instead of placing it on her wrist, she clasped it around her stuffed animal's neck. "There, don't you look pretty, Claretta?"

A thunderous, metallic thud followed an ear-splitting crack. Without thinking, I covered my head and bent at the waist as I envisioned our Atlas cedar losing another branch. Papa had loved that enormous tree, but it was a poor choice made by our home's previous owners. Our pruner told us years ago the specimen was meant to grow at high altitudes, not at sea level where its branches were weak.

"What was that?" Mario asked, also hunched over.

"One of our tree's branches is my best guess," Mama said.

Mario sat upright and breathed a sigh of relief.

"The accumulated snow must have been too heavy for it," Tom said with a grimace.

"I hope it didn't land on your car," Mama said. "I'm afraid to look."

"Exactly what I was thinking." He got to his feet.

We all proceeded to the front window to survey the damage. A hefty branch lay across his SUV's hood. Tom swore under his breath. "I'd better call an arborist," he said. "If one's available today."

"I'm so sorry," Mama said. "I've been meaning to have that tree thinned out, but it requires a permit."

"In this city, you can't prune a tree on your own property?" Mario asked.

"Nope," I said.

"That's ridiculous."

"That's Seattle for you," I said.

"I don't suppose you know an arborist," Tom said to Mama.

"We have a guy who prunes bushes out in the yard, but he's not exactly an arborist," Mama said. "I'll call him and see if he owns a chain saw. I feel terrible about this. Your poor Acura."

"It's not going anywhere today." Tom punched his arms into his jacket. "I'd better check the damage, and I might as well take a broom and knock the snow off the rhododendrons and camellias, so their branches don't break too."

"You're sweet," Mama told him. "How did I get so lucky?"

"How about the bushes in your own yard?" I hoped that didn't come out snarly. I really had acted rudely toward him earlier. When did I turn snarky?

"Neighbors are looking after them." He cupped Mama's hand under his. "There's no way I'm leaving now."

Mama gazed up into his eyes. "I'm so sorry," she said. "I hope my insurance company covers acts of God."

"Do you think God is punishing us for having the stolen painting?" Tabatha asked.

"No," Mama said. "That's just a saying used by insurance companies."

"And we didn't steal it," I said.

Minutes later, clad in warm attire, Tom and Mario sauntered out into the yard wearing rubber boots we'd accumulated over the years and carrying brooms.

"I want to go outside too," Tabatha insisted.

"Okay, you can wear my down parka and a knit hat," Mama said. Tabatha wriggled her arms into the sleeves and propelled herself out the door.

Good, maybe she'd work off her extra energy and angst. "Do you think her parents will show up?" I asked Mama as she stood at the window.

"Eventually, don't you?"

"Ugh, I wonder what they'll do." I imagined the two policemen who'd helped us this morning coming back to arrest me. I was glad I didn't know the painting's whereabouts.

"I should call Anna," Mama said. She looked nervous, even shaken.

"Mama, why don't you two get along?"

"My sister hates me," Mama said.

"But why?"

A long pause ensued. "The truth? I think she was in love with your father. Well, I know she was."

CHAPTER 31

"EVEN AFTER YOU got married?"
"Let's just say we were rivals, and he chose me.
I'm still not sure why since she was always prettier and
smarter than I was. She thought our parents favored
me over her too."

"Did they?"

"Maybe. She was five years younger than I was, always
trying to keep up and win their approval."

"Why blame their actions on you?"

"When she met your father, she fell head over heels
in love. Practically threw herself at him."

"And?"

"Are you sure you want the truth? Sometimes it's
better to let sleeping dogs lie."

"Yes, of course I want to know."

Her features turned serious. "Almost thirty years
ago . . . I found them together—"

"While you and Papa were married?"

"Yes. I got home and recognized her car out front." She pursed her lips for a moment as if trying to decide if she wanted to continue. "I quietly unlocked the door and tiptoed inside. They were in the bedroom."

I did the math and juggled the consequences. "Maureen's about my age. We could be half sisters." Or was I nuts?

"I've always wondered. You and your cousin look so much alike. Almost like twins."

I hadn't seen Maureen in many years. I wouldn't recognize her if I passed her in the grocery store. I knew I was jumping ahead of myself, but I wondered if she and I should get a DNA test. If she would. I'd wait on suggesting anything like that to her. One hurdle at a time. My plate was already heaped with too many uncertainties.

"And you still want to call her?" I asked. Mama paused.

"Time to end our family feud. Christmas is a day for reconciliation," she said. "And we need Maureen to see the painting. If it's on the internet, she probably knows who it belongs to."

Before I could stop her, Mama pulled out her phone and tapped in a number. "Merry Christmas, Anna," she said, her voice jubilant. Then, "Fine, we're both fine. In fact, Lucy is right here."

Anna spoke nonstop for several minutes. I was dying to know what she was jabbering on about, but in the end, Mama said, "I want to see you too. And we have questions for your Maureen about a painting that Lucy unwittingly brought back with her from Rome."

"No, no, that's not the purpose of my call, but it prompted me. I miss you, Anna." A tear trickled down Mama's cheek. "It's been too long." Another pause. "Okay, as soon as the snow melts, we'll have a second Christmas. Here or at your house, whatever you prefer."

Mama jimmied the phone back into her pocket. "There."

She sounded as if she'd solved the turmoil in the Middle East, when in fact she'd possibly started a skirmish. "Water under the bridge." She flipped her hand. "Time to let go of the past. I should have forgiven Anna years ago."

"I'm glad you and your sister are burying the hatchet." I tried to keep my face placid, but I felt dumfounded, my world oscillating one notch more off-kilter, making me dizzy.

WITH MARIO, TOM, and Tabatha outside, Mama and I strolled into the living room and glanced under the tree.

Strips of wrapping paper, bits of string, and several open boxes lay helter-skelter. Sure enough, no present to me from Mario. I admonished myself for being such a baby. I had plenty of stuff.

"Dear, I see something between the branches," Mama said. "An envelope with your name on it."

"Really?" I wandered over to have a look. "Is it from you?"

"No, not from me. Must be Mario."

"Oh dear, I don't have anything for him."

"That's understandable. How did you know ahead of time that you'd see him on Christmas?"

"Good question." As she straightened up, I said, "There are several questions I have about him."

She tilted her head. "Such as?"

"This may seem insignificant, but after the flight over, he found my phone in his carry-on."

"And you wonder if you'd really lost it?"

"Yes, then he called me at our hotel in Rome." I searched my memory bank. "And then we happened to run into him at St. Peter's."

"Did you ask him about these things?"

"Yes, and his explanations seem rational enough—at the time. Still, I have to wonder if he's being completely straight with me." I glanced out the window and saw Mario and Tabatha enmeshed in a snowball fight. Tabatha was laughing and enjoying herself.

Mama followed my gaze. "I always think of you as a good judge of character."

"I wish. Look at Brad." I shivered as I contemplated traipsing off with him to the other side of the world. I wouldn't tell Mama what a bully he was. Too humiliating. "What should I do with his engagement ring?"

"If you like, I'll find a way to get it back to him," Mama said.

"That would be great. Maybe through his parents."

"I could arrange that." She stroked my shoulder. "I'm sorry, dear daughter."

"I wonder what's in the envelope from Mario." An idea bloomed in the back of my brain. "Mind if I use some of your *Seattle* magazines to make a collage for him?" I asked.

"Not at all," she said. "I was going to give them a toss. And I saw a nice piece of cardboard in the basement."

"I need glue."

"We have Elmer's in the kitchen. It dries quickly."

"Perfect. Please keep Mario busy when he comes in." I grabbed an armful of magazines, the glue, and the nine-by-twelve-inch board and headed to my room. I hadn't made a collage in years but no matter. I flipped through the magazines, found photos of Puget Sound and Seattle's highlights, and affixed them to the board. Using dots of glue, I hoped the collage would dry in time. It's the thought that counts, I told myself. When done, I left my creation in my bedroom to dry.

As I descended the stairs, I detected the aroma of cooking oatmeal. I found everyone sitting at the dining room table.

"Tabatha decided she was hungry for oatmeal," Mama said. "Care to join us?"

Mario's face was flushed with exuberance. "You missed a great snowball fight, Lucia."

"I won, I won." Tabatha balled her fingers and fist-pumped.

"Hands down," Mario said. "You are the winner."

I was delighted to see Tabatha happy, but my predicaments lingered. Her parents showing up. The painting. Mama's sister—would she come over and start a screaming match? Had Papa gotten her pregnant those many years ago? Was my cousin actually my half sister? Would a half sister be a blessing or a curse?

More than I could cope with. My head spun.

CHAPTER 32

KNUCKLES DRUMMING ON the front door made our necks snap. Sassy streaked to the front hall and yipped. She was small in stature but a fine watchdog—most of the time.

"The pruner already?" Tom asked.

"Unlikely," Mama said. "I called him, and he said he can't get here for a couple of days."

"There's nowhere I'd rather be stuck," Tom said.

Mama stood and walked to the door, looked out the peephole. "Oh my."

Tabatha grabbed her stuffed animal, flitted to her feet, and followed in Mama's wake.

Mama pulled the door open. "Anna, what a surprise. I can't believe you're here so quickly. Come in, please."

My Aunt Anna stomped the snow off her boots and stepped over the threshold, then stood stiffly as Mama hugged her. "You want to wear a pair of my slippers?" Mama asked her. "I have several in the closet." Mama opened the nearest door and revealed a dozen slippers from years past.

"I suppose I could, if you insist," Anna said, stepping into a pair of Uggs.

"And Maureen, please come in, dear," Mama said with exuberance that seemed forced. Or maybe she was just startled. I know I was.

My cousin Maureen stomped the snow off her boots, found a pair of slippers that were actually mine, and minced her way into the front hall. She looked equally as uncomfortable as her mother. I supposed Maureen and I had many similar traits, such as greenish blue eyes and hair color—nutmeg brown. I wondered if she was thinking the same thing. Had Anna filled her in? Unlikely.

Mama said, "This is a lovely surprise, Anna. How did you make it over here so quickly?"

"Karl put chains on his pickup. He had something to do at home."

Sassy jumped on Aunt Anna's legs. "No, bad dog, get off of me," Anna said, and Mama directed our terrier to the kitchen.

Aunt Anna kissed the air near my ear Hollywood style. "It's been too long, Lucy."

"Yes, it has. Good to see you, Aunt Anna." I was steeped in confusion as I introduced them to Tabatha, Mario, and Tom. Mario and Tom helped the two women remove their puffy jackets. Both Anna and Maureen wore what appeared to be new turtleneck sweaters—Anna in gold and Maureen in turquoise blue. Presents from my Uncle Karl, Anna's husband?

For a few minutes, the front hall was awash with conversation, then it fell silent again.

"And don't forget to introduce Claretta." Tabatha held up her stuffed pooch. Neither Anna nor Maureen said hello to it. My best guess was the name was not missed on either woman.

Anna rotated away from Tabatha. "Whose poor SUV is that out there?"

"I claim that privilege," Tom said.

"Lucky you." Aunt Anna directed her attention to me. "How have you been, Lucy?"

"Fine."

"It's been a while. You've aged."

"Thank you." What else could I say?

"Your mother tells me you have questions about a painting," Anna said.

I nodded. "Yes, I do."

"You're kidding. A painting?" Maureen came to life. "Why didn't you mention it to me earlier, Mom?"

"Because we don't even know if it exists."

"It exists all right," Tabatha said.

"Then I want to see it," Maureen said, her voice swooping. "Where is it?"

"It was in the lid of Lucy's suitcase when we got home." Tabatha seemed to enjoy the spotlight.

"Now just a minute," Mama said. "She had no idea it was there."

"In her suitcase and she didn't know it?" My aunt tossed Mama a look of disbelief. "Does Lucy have possession of a painting or not?"

"Stolen by the Nazis," Tabatha said.

"Is this true?" Maureen asked me.

I was glad the painting was out of eyesight. "I have no verification it's an original," I said.

"An original what?" Maureen circled me like a shark. "Who's the artist?"

"Hey, lighten up," Tom said. "She said she didn't know if it's for real."

"Who are you anyway?" Anna glared up at Tom with a look of disdain.

Mama held out her hand to display her engagement ring. "He's my fiancé."

"And also an expert in art?"

"I'm an invited guest," he shot back. "And soon to be Gladys's husband."

"I hope you know what kind of family you're marrying into," Anna said.

"Whoa," Mario said. "Let's cool down, everyone."

I glanced at our Christmas tree as the words "all is calm . . ." vibrated into my ears from the sound system. Time for new music.

Mario moved in behind me. "I have perfect confidence in Lucy and her mother."

"Wait long enough, and you'll come to regret it," Anna said.

I glanced up to him. "A family feud I recently learned about," I told him.

"Christmas is the perfect day to lay old disputes aside," Mama said.

"Too late," Anna said.

"What are you talking about?" Maureen asked Anna, who clamped her lips shut. Maureen rotated her neck and stared into my face. For a moment, I felt as if I were looking in a mirror; our facial features indeed reflected each other.

"I remember when we used to be friends," she said. "Back before your father died. You're one reason I was so interested in art history."

She wanted to be like me? "I still have a ton of art history books you're welcome to look through," I said. "Or take home with you."

"We came over to look at a painting," Anna broke in. She riddled her words at Mama. "But then you've always tried to louse up my life, sister dearest. Is this some kind of sick joke?"

"You've got a nerve blaming your problems on me," Mama's voice grew fierce.

"Sis, you called me, not the other way around." Aunt Anna crossed her arms. "So show me the painting already. Or was that just a ploy to get me over here?"

Mama hesitated, then looked to Tom. "What should I do?" she asked.

"Might as well go ahead and show her the painting." Tom's voice lacked conviction. "You have nothing to hide."

"Wait until my parents get here," Tabatha said.

CHAPTER 33

MAMA INSISTED EVERYONE remain on the
first floor while she scaled the stairs to fetch the
painting. All sorts of crazy scenarios looped through
my brain as I waited. I noticed Mario and Maureen
eyeing each other, sending a slush of jealousy and anger
through me. No doubt about it, their gazes were locked.
He found her desirable; that was evident. I should
have spruced myself up today. Hard to compete with
Maureen in her skinny jeans accentuating a shapely
figure, her flirtatious voice.

Finally, the patter of Mama's feet alerted us of her
return. I glanced up the staircase to see her carrying
the painting, now in a pillowcase.

Maureen rushed to Mama's side, followed by Anna.

"Wait, don't trip me," Mama said, holding her
ground. "Be careful, will you?"

I moved ahead of her to the coffee table in the living room. "Tabatha, please help me clear off this table," I said.

"Sure." Tabatha reminded me of Tinker Bell in the Walt Disney movie *Peter Pan*. Light on her feet and full of mischievousness, she swiped used wrapping paper into a bag.

Mama walked with care, laid the painting on the table, and pulled back the pillowcase.

Maureen appeared as if she might swoon. "It's a Rembrandt. But I'm not sure it's the angel listed in your grandfather's art catalog."

"It looks like it to me." Anna peered over her shoulder. "It is."

"No, Mom, there are slight differences." She peered closer. "I think. There are no photographs of his collection, so I can't be sure."

"No signature," Mario said.

"Many others aren't signed either."

"But I can recognize a Rembrandt when I see one," I said without thinking. "He was a prolific master."

"You already knew?" Maureen asked.

"Well, of course she did," Aunt Anna said. "That's why she stole it."

Mama narrowed her eyes. "She stole nothing."

"We should show this to the curator of the Seattle Art Museum," Anna said. "Bet he'd have an opinion."

"This painting isn't going anywhere," Tom said. "Not until my future wife and Lucy say so."

"Or my parents," Tabatha said.

"What do they have to do with this?" Anna asked.

"I'm not exactly sure." I still had no proof.

"They own an art gallery," Tabatha said.

"But they're out of town." Mario gave Tabatha the evil eye.

"When will they get home?" Anna asked.

"Lucia, try calling them again." Tabatha tugged on my arm. "Pretty please."

I shook my head. "They said their phones' batteries had run low."

"Sounds fishy to me," Anna said.

"They might just show up," Mario said.

"Well, they can't take this painting." Maureen's hands clamped her hips. "I won't let them."

"Who do you think you are?" I asked.

"If that painting is the one I think it is, it belongs to me as much as to you." She turned to Anna. "Right, Mom?"

"Yes . . ." Anna shrugged one shoulder. "But we need proof this belonged to him before we can claim it."

"I wonder where it's been all this time," Mama said.

Maureen examined it more closely, her face dreamy. "It was finding its way back to its rightful owners."

"I should change my story for school," Tabatha cut in. "I have a cool idea. In my new paper, Hitler will give Claretta this painting instead of *The Swing*. I can go back and switch them easy."

"As you like," I said. I didn't want to extend this conversation in front of Anna and Maureen.

I noticed Mario taking photos with his iPhone of the painting as it again sat on the sideboard, which made me feel uneasy. Why would he? I decided to keep quiet.

"Gladys, honey, why don't you make tea for our guests?" Tom ushered Mama toward the kitchen. He stepped back and cleared the table with Mario's help.

"Nothing for me," Anna said. "I did not come over here for a tea party."

Tom pulled out a chair for Anna. "Please, have a seat." He carried the soiled baking dish into the kitchen and set it in the sink.

"Yes, please stay," Mama said. Minutes later, the kettle shrilled, and Mama excused herself. She brought out a tray and her favorite teapot. "I hope you still like Earl Grey," she said to Anna. Mama extracted half a dozen teacups from the glass-fronted cupboard in the corner of the dining room and brought them to the table.

"Hey, Sis," Aunt Anna said, "are those our mama's teacups?"

"Yes, as lovely as ever." Mama arranged them on the table.

"So you're the one who took them? I wanted these teacups."

"Really? You never said a word."

"I did so. But suddenly, poof, they were gone."

"I wish I'd known that," Mama said. "Seriously, I had no idea. They were on the estate agent's table. She said no one in the family wanted them."

"I don't believe that for a second," Aunt Anna said.

"Mom, who cares about these cups?" Maureen said. "It's not as if you and Dad ever drink tea." She tipped her head to the painting. "We have bigger fish to fry."

"I suppose you're right. We have enough knickknacks cluttering the house." Aunt Anna's lips flattened.

"The tea should be steeped by now." Mama served her sister first.

"I suppose, if I must," Anna said. "With milk and sugar." Anna stirred her tea and swigged it down. "We didn't come over to get chummy."

"Aren't you glad you're here now?" Tom said.

"Yeah, for sure," Maureen said. "We wouldn't know about the painting."

CHAPTER 34

AFTER SOME NEGOTIATION with my aunt and cousin, Mama, Mario, Tom, and I huddled in the kitchen. Tabatha hung out in the dining room, enjoying hot chocolate, heavy on the marshmallows, and entertaining Anna and Maureen.

"I called my cousin to wish him a Merry Christmas," Mario told us. "According to him, the Williamses hired a lawyer who costs a bundle and has friends in the highest places."

"What was the charge?" Tom said.

Mario stirred sugar into his tea. "Dealing in stolen art."

"What Tabatha told me," I said. "I should have believed her."

"Poor girl, I hope she doesn't get in trouble." Mama sipped her tea.

"Nah," I said, "she'd squirm her way out."

We all chuckled.

Just then, as if she knew we were talking about her, I received a text from Gretchen. *We should be over in an hour.*

"Now what?" I said, when I showed them the text. "They'll want the painting."

"Can't we just say 'no way'?" Tom said.

"They might insist," I said. "They can be forceful." I pictured the quarrelsome scenarios as they tromped into the house. All were bad.

"I have a thought," Mama said in a hushed voice. "We give the painting to Maureen to take home."

Her idea flabbergasted me. "Why on earth?" I asked.

"The painting isn't yours, Lucy." Mama wagged a finger. "Don't you figure the Williamses will come looking for it and raise a stink?"

"Yes, but it isn't Maureen's either." I sucked in a mouthful of air. "And it never will be if I have anything to do with it."

"What, you love that little angel painting more than you love your freedom?" Mama asked.

"That's not fair."

"Often life isn't fair."

"I could take it; you can trust me," Mario said. "But if I get caught with it, it's goodbye green card."

"You could lose your job," Mama said.

"Or worse, land in prison," Tom said. "I could take it, once I get my SUV unburied, but I'd rather not leave." He looked into Mama's face. "Only if you asked me, dearest Gladys."

"No, I wouldn't." She took his hand and kissed his fingers.

The thought of Maureen procuring the painting and keeping it for herself after she'd snubbed me for years irked me. How could my life get turned upside down in one morning? I needed to get ahold of myself before I said something I later regretted.

"The Williamses have a vault full of old paintings in their basement," I said. "But then they do own a swanky art gallery."

"You're kidding." Tom glanced over his shoulder; I assumed to make sure no one was eavesdropping.

"I wish I were." I moved closer to Mama, spoke in her ear. "Tabatha showed me."

"We'd better not let her know what we're thinking," Mama said. "She's young and seems to have some mental problems."

"I'm guessing bipolar disorder," Tom said. "A friend has a daughter who was diagnosed with it."

"When did you get so smart?" Mama asked him.

"Smart enough to snag a beauty like you." Tom grinned.

"Lucy?" Mama said, startling me out of my musings. "Does my idea sound so crazy now?"

"I'll take Tabatha outside," Mario said. "Another snowball fight. We'll have fun." He glanced my way. "The less I know about all this the better."

"Meaning you think Mama has the right idea?" I asked.

"Yes, after meeting the Williamses, I do."

"And you say they have a stash of paintings in their basement?" Mama asked. "Amazing."

"But we don't know if they're illegal," I said. "They could be legit." Yet my gut told me otherwise.

THIRTY MINUTES LATER, a burst of giggling filled the house as Tabatha and Mario bundled up to go outside. The block of laughter moved to the back door and into the yard. Mama, Tom, and I stepped into the kitchen to speak to Anna and Maureen, who were amazed at our offer.

"We're family, right?" Mama asked Anna. "So this is a lend."

"You mean you'd lend us the painting? I can't believe it."

"Can we trust you not to go to the press, Maureen?" I asked. "I don't want to see my mother's and my mugs on the six o'clock news."

"Yes, you can trust me." Maureen chewed her fingernail for a moment. "But I'd want to get it verified by an expert that it's not a fake."

"Okay," I said. "I'm curious too."

"Say, how do I know we can trust you?" She glanced to Anna. "Can we believe your sister and her daughter?" She looked me up and down. "Is this a trick to get rid of a stolen painting and put the blame on us?"

"No, not at all," I said.

"I want to put our family's conflict behind us." Mama poured more tea.

"So do I," Maureen said. "Mom still won't tell me what it's all about."

"Which might be for the best," I said.

"Meaning you know the source?"

I felt heat moving up my neck as I realized this was a pivotal moment in both of our lives. I didn't know if what Mama surmised was true—but I wanted to find out desperately. I pictured Anna's tall husband: sandy-colored hair and a hooked nose. Maureen's brother was his spitting image, but not Maureen. Proving nothing. Only a DNA test would verify if she was my half sister. And now was not the time to mention it.

"Let's save that complication for another day," Anna said. "It has nothing to do with this painting."

"Please take it home," I said, "and guard it with your life."

Mama was already slipping it into the pillowcase and then into a plastic bag from the dry cleaners.

"Hurry," I said.

"All right." Maureen's eyes were huge—like mine no doubt. She hugged me. "Thanks. You can trust me," she said.

I believed her, but what about Aunt Anna? And Uncle Karl, whom I hardly knew. Yet what other options did I have? Was I making the biggest mistake of my life?

I looked to Mama, who nodded, telling me we were doing the right thing.

"Get on your jackets and boots," she told Maureen and Anna. She cracked the door. Mama practically shoved Maureen and Anna outside. She put her fingers to her lips. "Shush." Anna gave her a quick hug before stepping out onto the porch.

The kitchen door burst open. Tabatha chattered and giggled. I heard clunks that I figured were Mario and

Tabatha kicking off their boots. More laughter and conversation as they dislodged their jackets.

Tabatha waltzed into the front hall, followed by Mario and Sassy. "You missed all the fun, Lucia." She scanned the room. "Where is your sister?" Tabatha asked.

"You mean my sister, Anna?" Mama said. "She and Maureen had to scoot."

"Oops, sorry," Tabatha said. "Well, Maureen looks enough like Lucia to be her sister."

"Never mind that," I said, listening to Anna's departing automobile. There went my painting. I doubted I'd ever see it again. "Tabatha, I got a text from your mother."

CHAPTER 35

WHEN TABATHA'S PHONE rang, she bounced
up and down like a cheerleader. She looked exu-
berant enough to do cartwheels. "It's Mommy!" She
answered her cell phone, pressed it to her ear.

"They'll be here in half an hour," she told us minutes
later. "I can hardly wait."

Mama and I turned into stone statues. Mario moved
in behind me and placed a hand on my shoulder. "It's
going to be all right," he said in my ear.

I swiveled my head to gaze into his dark amber eyes.
The term *dumb bunny* taunted me. How had I gotten into
this mess? And dragged my mother into it too. I might
have made her an accessory to a crime. I'd never forgive
myself if our ships sunk together.

"Then we can go home," Tabatha said.

"This is my home," I said.

"But, like, you'll come with us," Tabatha said. "Won't
you?"

"Not this time."

Tabatha stood waiting at the front window. Thirty minutes later, a black Suburban sporting chained tires pulled up front.

"They're here." With Mama and Tom on her heels, Tabatha charged to the front door and wrestled it open.

"Mommy." She threw her arms around Gretchen's waist. "I knew you'd come."

"Of course, we came darling." Gretchen brought with her a blast of frosty air.

"How lovely to meet you," Mama said to Gretchen as she extended an arm to shake her hand. "Careful of the ice on the steps," she called to Stan. He trudged his way over the threshold.

Mama should have been an actress, I thought. Well, she had been most of her adult life.

"Nice to meet you." Gretchen wore dark circles under her eyes—her mascara smudged. She looked as though she hadn't slept in days. Her hair, usually sleek, was a mess. Her clothes were wrinkled. She spotted Mario. "What are you doing here?"

"He's our guest," Mama said.

"Stuck in the snow," Mario said.

"As if I'd believe you."

He shrugged. "Believe what you like."

With Tabatha clinging on her arm, Gretchen turned to me. "Hurry, Lucy, we've just come by to pick you and Tabatha up."

"I won't be going with you," I said.

"Of course, you will. You're under contract."

"I never signed anything or made a commitment."

"You did, you little liar," Gretchen said. "We have a copy at our house."

Mama searched my face, and I shook my head.

Mario and Tom moved to my sides like Roman centurions. I cowered at what I fathomed might spew from Gretchen's mouth.

"Where's your suitcase?" Stan asked me.

"Yes, get it out and get packed." Gretchen scanned the room.

"My suitcase is in the basement," I said. "But it's empty."

"Then you won't mind if we take a look in it."

"Be my guest." I felt a smile tugging at the corners of my mouth.

Stan followed Tom to the basement and returned lugging the suitcase up the stairs. Sassy pranced at their heels.

Stan dumped it at Gretchen's feet. Sassy scrambled for cover.

"Empty," he said.

"It can't be." She fell upon it, opened the lid, and unzipped it. Then she popped up and swung around to face me. "Where is it?"

"Where is what?" I asked, determined not to look away. I saw Tabatha in the periphery of my vision and hoped she could manage to keep her mouth shut.

"Tabatha?" Gretchen said. "Is there something you want to tell me?"

Tabatha grinned. "You found my Christmas presents?"

"Sorry, darling. Not yet."

"What were you expecting to find?" Mama said.

"I think you know full well. At least Lucy does."

I wore my best blasé teacher mask.

Stan's phone rang. "Yes?" He turned to Gretchen. "It's our driver."

"Tell him to take a nap or go get something to eat, "Gretchen said. "We won't be needing him for a while. We'll stay here." She spoke to Mama. "If that's okay with you."

"Whatever you like," Mama said. "You're welcome to stay."

"Oh, goodie." Tabatha danced her rendition of a jig. "This will be the best Christmas yet." She sauntered up next to Mario, who looked relaxed as ever. I thought he'd shoot me a grin, but apparently, I'd grown invisible.

"Want to see my new dog?" Tabatha asked her mother. She skipped into the living room and returned clutching the stuffed animal. "Brought straight from Italy. A Christmas present from Mario."

Gretchen's lips turned white.

Stan's glare riddled Mario. "How dare you buy our daughter a gift without our consent?"

"I apologize," Mario said. "I didn't realize it would be a problem."

Gretchen hand swung out to take it from Tabatha, but she grasped the stuffed pooch and swerved away.

"I love her." Tabatha hugged her stuffed pup. "Her name is Claretta."

"Did I hear you right?" Gretchen asked. "Who taught you that name?"

"I named her after . . . Well, you know who she was. I've heard you speaking about her."

"Hush," Gretchen hissed. "Not another word, you hear me?"

"But—" Tabatha stomped her foot, landing on Gretchen's toe.

"Ouch." Gretchen looked mad enough to smack her daughter but controlled herself, plastering a smile on her face. "Now, darling, are you sure there isn't something you wish to tell us?"

"Well, okay. I wrote a story for school about her. And Mussolini."

Gretchen swung around to glower at me. "I've been paying you to look after Tabatha. Are you so stupid you'd let her write about that monster?"

"Just a minute," Mario said. "Don't speak to Lucia like that."

"Keep your Italian nose out of our business," Gretchen snapped.

"She wrote it the night we returned," I said. "I had no idea until then."

"Let me read it to you, Mommy," Tabatha said. "Bet you'll love it."

"I wouldn't be too sure about that," Stan said.

"But it's fiction," Tabatha said. "Like, you know what I'm talking about?"

"Yes, dear, I realize what fiction is," Stan said. "But some fiction is best left alone."

"Is there anything else you wish to share with us?" Gretchen asked her.

"Nope." Tabatha clutched her stuffed dog and buried her nose in its plush fur.

"In that case, I wish to search the house." She glared into Mama's face. "You're hiding something, aren't you?"

"What would that be?" Mario asked, moving between us. "There is nothing here you're looking for."

"How would you know?"

"Why don't you tell us what exactly you want?"

"I, uh . . ." Gretchen reexamined the suitcase. "I think Lucy knows."

Tabatha giggled. "Did you lose something, Mommy?"

"Honey, will you please tell me what was in the suitcase?"

"You mean what you wanted Lucia to smuggle into the country?" Tabatha shot back.

My mind spun with uncertainties. I tried to figure out what the Williamses would have seen through their security system. No, Tabatha said she'd turned off the interior cameras. The idea of being recorded before that vexed me, and yet I didn't dare complain.

"Whatever you're looking for is not in this house," I said.

"We'll see about that." Stan lumbered up the stairs.

I looked to Mama and was surprised to see her nonchalant composure as a stranger searched our home.

"Whatever it is you want, you won't find it here," Tom said.

After ten minutes, Stan returned to the first floor. "There's an interesting painting in the bedroom. We take artwork on consignment at our gallery."

Mama stared back at him. "It's not for sale."

"But if you ever do want to . . ."

"I'll keep that in mind."

"Now, are you satisfied," I asked. "If you want to search the basement, too, go ahead. It's not as interesting as yours, I can assure you." My hand flew up to cover my mouth.

"What do you mean?" Gretchen's words pierced into me. "Did Tabatha take you down to our basement other than to do laundry?"

Tabatha dug her big toe into the carpet. "We were going to decorate the tree, but Lucy asked me what was in the closet."

"Hey, don't you have your stories turned around, young lady?" I asked, but Tabatha remained silent.

Gretchen's face turned white. "Lucy, did you or did you not enter . . ."

"Uh . . ." I didn't want to get Tabatha in trouble, but I didn't want to serve as a human dartboard target.

"We haven't broken the law by storing paintings in our basement." Gretchen turned to me. "How dare you go poking around like that in our absence?"

"I didn't steal anything." I said.

"You must have realized no one was allowed to enter when Tabatha let you in." She spun to Tabatha. "Why did you lead Lucy into our vault?"

"This is sounding more and more interesting," Mario said. "Maybe we should move this party to your house."

"No way, I don't want to leave," Tabatha said. "Unless my presents are over there."

"I suppose our bags could have arrived," Gretchen said without conviction.

My phone pinged, telling me I'd receive a text message. I pulled out my phone and was amazed Maureen had left me a message.

Mother told me the truth.

Huh? I'd have to call or text back later. I stuffed the phone in my pocket.

"How about something to eat?" Mama said, snagging Stan's attention.

"Sure," Stan and Gretchen said in unison.

I've got to say, Mama beguiled the Williamses. Not that they were pushovers. My hunch was all four adults at the dining room table were keeping their guard up. On the staircase, Tabatha played with her stuffed puppy with Sassy at her feet.

"Pssst." Mario beckoned me from the dining room. I glided over to sink down next to him on the couch. "I have something for you, Lucia." He pulled the envelope out from between the branches of the Christmas tree and handed it to me. "Please open it," he said.

With my index finger, I slid open the envelope. My breath froze in my throat. "A round-trip ticket to Italy?"

CHAPTER 36

"I HAVE THE REST of the week off, until after New Year's Eve." He took my hand. "Will you come back to Rome with me to celebrate the arrival of the new year?"

"Seriously? An invitation to Rome?"

"Yes. You look surprised."

"I am. To put it mildly." Had I ever been more blown away?

"I looked up the weather this morning," he said. "It's fifty degrees in Rome. Blue skies." He brought my fingertips to his lips. "You like Roma, no?"

"And how about me?"

"Yes, I like you very much." His face moved closer to mine. Our lips brushed, then softened into a brief kiss. "But my feelings for you are much deeper than like," he said. "Will you come with me? Please say yes."

A wave of fondness rolled over me, but I felt unsure. "I made you a silly Christmas present."

"I'm sure if you made it, it isn't silly."

I hurried to fetch my collage: pictures of the Space Needle, Lake Washington, the Cascade Mountains. "These are the places I want to explore with you here in the Pacific Northwest," I said. I glanced out the window. "But not this week. Let's wait for spring."

Mario slipped his arms around me and bestowed a tender kiss. My arms encircled his shoulders.

"What's going on?" Tabatha said.

Mario pulled away. "A Christmas kiss."

"With no mistletoe?" Tabatha asked.

"I think we have some," I said. "Please go ask Mama where it is."

"Okay." She bustled off, leaving me and Mario on the couch.

A MOMENT LATER, Tabatha bounced back into the living room, carrying a sprig of mistletoe, but her lower lip jutted out. "My parents say we have to leave now."

I was conflicted because I hated to say goodbye to Tabatha, but not Gretchen and Stan. I would gladly bid them farewell forever.

The Williamses poked their heads into the living room. "We're out of here," Stan said. "Come on, Tab. Gather your stuff."

Mama and Tom wandered in behind them. "Thanks for looking after our daughter," Gretchen said. "And for the coffee and snacks."

"Why can't we stay longer?" Tabatha's voice sounded whiny.

"Our driver says he's leaving, with or without us," Stan said.

"Poor guy," Mama said. "We should have invited him in."

"If you knew how much we're paying him, you wouldn't show him any pity." Gretchen let out a yawn. "Anyway, he says he has a family waiting for him at home in Oregon."

As Tabatha and the Williamses layered up to face the storm, Stan paused. "Say, Gladys, I'm serious about selling your painting on commission if you change your mind."

She responded without hesitation. "No, thanks. I'm sure."

Minutes later, Tabatha and her parents picked their way down the front steps, then climbed into the Suburban. I waved from the front door, then shut it as a gust of icy wind hit my face, making me blink.

"Say, does anyone want hot cider?" Mama asked. "Warm and sweet. Perfect on a day like this."

"Sounds divine." I recalled the sticks of cinnamon she always inserted in each cup. Mario and Tom echoed my sentiments.

I followed Mama into the kitchen and watched her as she warmed the cider in a pot atop the stove. She turned to me. "You and Mario seem to have grown close," she said.

I tried not to let my conflicted emotions show on my face, but to no avail. The corners of my mouth tugged up into a grin. "Mario wants me to fly to Rome with him for New Year's Eve."

"And you don't know if it's a good idea?"

"I'm not sure what to think."

"Too many times in my life I've let opportunities pass me by." She gave me a quick hug. "Mario seems like a good man. I like him, if that matters."

"It does, you know that."

After she'd prepared the hot cider, she poured some into four mugs and passed me two. We meandered into the living room to find Mario and Tom chatting and laughing. I sat next to Mario, who accepted a cup.

"*Delizioso*, Gladys." He stole a glance at me. "Thank you, Lucia."

"I have a question for you." I looked him square in the face. "Why did you come back to Seattle if you plan to return to Rome?"

"My supervisor summoned me." He sipped his cider and offered a wry smile. "Simply for a Christmas party, so everyone in management could mingle and to strengthen morale during a hectic but profitable holiday season."

"You could have said no," Tom said.

"I did, but then I caught wind that Lucia was returning to Seattle." He gave me his full attention. He took my hand. "I swear I knew absolutely nothing of the painting in the lid of your suitcase. I only wanted to be where you were."

"You'd face jet lag again so soon?" I asked.

"Only if you'll come with me."

CHAPTER 37

"*BENVENUTI A ROMA*—WELCOME to Rome," the flight attendant spoke in Italian then English. "Please, seats and tray tables in the upright position. Remain in your seat with your belt firmly attached."

As the giant aircraft prepared to land, I looked over to see Mario gazing at me. "How did you sleep?" he asked.

"Like a baby." Apparently, my fear of flying had subsided. No nightmares about my father's death. Not that I didn't miss him. The hole in my heart left by his death may never be filled. When I returned home, I'd talk about him more with Mama. Knowing more wouldn't have helped me over the last decade, yet I had a right to know. Did he deliberately leave us? Would Aunt Anna know the truth?

Still in half-slumber, I realized I'd neglected to ask Mario where I'd stay when in Rome. Certainly not at the Hassler. That fantastic hotel would drain my savings account in a day. Yet I wanted to at least walk by it. I hoped it was still resplendent with Christmas decor.

"You could stay at my place," he said, stretching. "You two may share my bed. I'll sleep on the couch."

When I didn't answer, he said, "Unless you two would rather stay at a small hotel I know about."

Two?

Adrenaline shot through my veins as I reached full consciousness and remembered Maureen was sitting across the aisle from Mario. She'd begged to come once she'd heard that Mario and I were returning to Rome for New Year's Eve. Mama and even Aunt Anna said they thought it was a wonderful idea. A way to rebuild our relationship, Mama said. Or to act as my chaperone, I'd wondered.

I glanced out the window and watched Italy's glorious landscape come into view—a palette of sepia browns and burnt umber. My heart swelled with gladness, until I looked over and saw the back of Mario's head as he leaned away from me toward Maureen across the aisle. She seemed to be capturing his full attention as she slept, her eyes shut.

Earlier, when boarding, she'd raved that it had been her dream to visit Rome. A lifetime goal to see the ancient city. Or had meeting Mario been her catalyst?

The plane took a dip, then lifted again. My shoulders flattened against the back of the seat as the aircraft accelerated. A man's voice spoke over the PA system in rapid-fire Italian, then in English. "This is your pilot. The front landing gear, it's not coming down. We'll circle around again." A gasp resounded throughout the seating area.

"A belly landing," Mario said.

"How do you know?" I asked him.

"I was in the Italian air force for six years. Not to worry," he said. "We should be fine, but we might have to evacuate down the slide."

"*Per favore*. Please leave your belongings on board," the pilot said over the speaker system. "Attendants, return to your seats." Then he spoke again in Italian as the flight attendants hurried past us.

"Where is your passport?" Mario asked me.

I indicated my purse.

"Put it in your pocket."

"Okay." Reaching to my purse took all my effort, but I was able to retrieve it and find my wallet and passport, then stuff them in my jacket pocket.

"*Va bene*, leave your purse here."

Was I about to die as my father had? Bitter irony, I thought. I wished I were sitting by Maureen. I hadn't had time to speak to her, to reveal what Mama had told me, that Maureen might be my half sister. The longer I was with her the more I believed it.

As the aircraft circled around to land again, I saw six fire engines and several ambulances traveling in our direction, moving along next to us as we lowered.

Mario took my hand. "We'll be okay," he said, but I didn't believe him. This was my nightmare unravelling itself. But unlike Papa, I wasn't ready to die.

I watched the tarmac leaping up to us, then felt the 767 bounce on its rear tires. Everything was fine, I told myself. But then I heard a scraping, grinding sound as the front of the plane met and crunched into the tarmac. I jolted against my seat belt. My head snapped forward once we came to a halt. I sniffed the air for smoke but smelled none, yet I assumed fire was a ghastly likelihood. I needed to escape.

Everyone onboard fell silent for a moment and then spoke at once.

"Please remain in your seats," a flight attendant said, but many were already on their feet, heading toward the exit aisles, impeding the attendants. Moments later, the emergency doors on one side opened, slides shot out, and people scrambled to skid down them.

"Come on," Mario took my hand.

"I can't leave Maureen," who sat like a zombie, still conked out. "Maureen," I shouted, "are you okay? Wake up."

No answer.

An attendant, cool and calm, asked Mario and me to exit the aircraft. "Leave your belongings. You know this woman?"

"Yes," I said. "Wake up, Maureen."

"I couldn't rouse her earlier," Mario said.

"Why didn't you tell me?" I said.

"Medics will come in and attend to her," the attendant said. "Hurry, you two must evacuate right away."

"I can't leave her." My legs wouldn't work.

"Come on," Mario took my hand. "We're making their job harder for them."

The passenger on the other side of Maureen had already escaped. He must have jumped over her. I noticed most of the men carried their briefcases in spite of the pilot's request.

Moments later, I shot down the slide behind a woman who let out a scream when she reached the tarmac. Mario followed me. Attendants helped passengers too jolted to walk get to their feet.

"What if the plane catches on fire?" I asked him once we were standing a safe distance from the aircraft. "What's wrong with Maureen?"

Mario shrugged. "Too many sleeping pills? Too much to drink?"

First responders carried Maureen down a set of stairs, and medics scrambled to examine her vitals. I wanted to run over to her, but Mario wouldn't allow me. "Let them do their job," he said.

Finally, I broke away and dashed over as they lifted her into an ambulance. "Stop, I know her." I was shaking so much I almost couldn't speak. "She's my sister. Where are you taking her?"

"Emergency room—acute trauma—at the Salvator Mundi International Hospital." He jumped in, closed the rear door. A deafening siren erupted as the ambulance sped away.

"Wait, I want to ride with her."

Another uniformed man said, "Come, you must go through customs." He took my elbow, steered me toward the terminal.

"Can't we skip this?" I asked Mario.

"I'm afraid not. I need to get our carry-ons and your purse."

I turned to assess the plane, its nose resting on the tarmac, a black ribbon of smoke rising. A fire truck sprayed the front of the jet with white foam. Dozens of workers waited to remove the luggage; reporters swarmed.

"We were lucky," Mario said.

"But how about Maureen?"

"I know where the hospital is, once we get through customs."

"But I don't even want my carry-on or my purse." My lips were chattering.

"Cold?" he asked.

"Yes."

"You're in shock." Mario wrapped his jacket around my shoulders. "Come on, we'll get in line. Unless you feel faint."

"If I fainted, they might take me to the hospital with Maureen."

"Or another hospital."

A medic must have noticed my distress and wobbly gate. "Are you all right?" he asked me.

"Just my neck hurts." I felt disoriented, the tarmac swaying.

"You must fill out this customs form." A uniformed man handed me a slip of paper with an army of questions.

My vision swam. "No time. I've got to find my sister."

"Why did you call her that?" Mario asked.

"I figured I'd get better service that way." I caught his glance. "She actually may be my half sister. I don't know."

"Do you still have your phone?" Mario asked. When I showed it to him, he said, "You'd better call your mother and Anna."

CHAPTER 38

MARIO AND I waited with the other passengers to get through customs, then I called Mama.

"Thank God you're okay, darling," Mama said over the phone. "I've been worried sick ever since I saw the plane skidding down the runway on TV just now."

"You saw it?" My hand shook.

"Yes, Tom was watching TV and called me in." Mama sounded breathless. "Has Maureen called her parents yet?"

"She can't." How transparent should I be?

"But she's okay, isn't she?"

"I don't know. They took her to the hospital." My carry-on would have to wait. "Mama, I just called the hospital while in line and was told she has not reached consciousness."

"Tell me you're joking." Mama sounded on the verge of tears. "I feel like this is all my fault. If only I'd never invited Anna and Maureen over."

"Mama, no time to talk. Are you going to call Aunt Anna, or should I?" I felt guilty for the impatience in my voice, but one of us needed to contact Anna before the authorities did.

"Yes, yes, I'll place the call right now. Wait—I'll fly over too."

"But what about Sassy?"

"Tom can look after her. She adores him."

MARIO CALLED AN Uber. "Are you sure you feel good enough to go see Maureen?" he asked me.

"No, but I have to."

Mario directed the driver to the hospital. As our sedan cruised through the busy streets, Rome still looked marvelous, bedecked with Christmas trees and lights. But the city's grandeur had lessened. I wouldn't admit my head throbbed and my shoulder ached. I kept reliving our terrifying landing. I'd never felt more helpless.

"If I had sat where Maureen was, would she be okay?" I asked Mario.

"Let's wait and see what her problem is," he said. "She had a lot to drink, and I saw her pop more than one pill during the flight."

"What kind?"

"No idea."

The Uber dropped us off at the bustling emergency entrance. Mario led the way. He did all the speaking as he gave Maureen's name and asked for information in Italian.

"What would I do without you?" I said.

"I have little doubt you'd find your way." He had more faith in me than I did.

"Can I see Maureen?" I asked.

"Yes, but only because I said you were her sister."

We found her in a room designated for trauma patients. People on surgical tables lay almost next to each other with nurses and doctors attending them, drip-bags everywhere. The air was charged with uncertainty.

Mario translated for me what a man wearing a physician's badge said. "They x-rayed her brain already. There seems to be no injury—no bleeding in her head, no aneurism. But she is unresponsive."

"She could have hit her head when we landed," he said. "That was a serious jolt."

Maureen appeared near dead, pale, her eyes closed. Tubes ran to her arm like snakes. Good, she was getting fluids. And she was breathing. Her chest raised and lowered through her gown.

The doctor spoke to me. "*Sua sorella?*"

Mario said, "He wants to confirm you're her sister."

"Sì," I said and nodded. "*Mia sorella.*" I hoped she was. I wasn't totally convinced. Mama's bitterness to her sister might have done a backflip. Wishful thinking wouldn't pass a DNA test. If Maureen lived. I would be devastated if she died. I prayed she would survive, whether she was my sister or cousin.

As my musings zigzagged through my mind, I rebuked myself for not asking Maureen where she and Aunt Anna had stashed the painting. I hoped Uncle

Karl was guarding it, but he might drop everything when he learned Maureen was in the hospital.

"Lucia, they need to move her." Mario harpooned me to the present.

"You mean they've given up?"

"No, but they need the space for another patient."

I spun around to speak to the doctor, who was conversing with a nurse. "You haven't given up on Maureen, have you?" I asked.

"No, no, *signora*. Your sister, she's getting moved to Intensive Care where we'll look after her."

"But why won't she wake up?" I reached out and touched her arm, felt her smooth skin for the first time since we were children.

"We don't know yet," he said. "We need to run more tests."

"When do you think she'll wake up?"

"I'm sorry, but again we have no idea. She has a rapid heartbeat and shallow breathing." He stared into my eyes. "Do you think she's using drugs?"

His question speared into my heart. "You mean opioids?"

"Yes, or any other drug. Alcohol consumption."

"I saw her taking pills and drinking wine," Mario said.

"They could have been sleeping pills or antianxiety medication," I spoke loudly enough for everyone in the room to hear me. "I've battled opioid addiction for years." Heads turned, but my secret was helping no one.

"Then you understand," the doctor said. "Plus, we must keep in mind that both of you were in an accident. I heard about your plane's landing. Enough to give any of the passengers a terrible jolt. Possible brain and neck injury." He stared into my eyes as if inspecting my pupils. "Do you feel all right?"

"I've been too worried about Maureen to think about myself."

"My advice is that you take it easy for the next few days and visit a doctor if you get a headache or feel neck pain." His features softened. "And no alcohol or pain pills other than ibuprofen or Tylenol."

"Okay."

"I'll keep an eye on her," Mario said.

Just then, a nurse brought the doctor's lab results. "As I suspected," the doctor said. "Overdose on opioids mixed with sleeping aids and alcohol. But her vitals are becoming stable."

As Mario and I found our way to the cafeteria to buy coffee, I vowed that when Maureen woke up—I prayed she would—I'd help her. We had much in common.

I heard a text come in from Mama, asking about Maureen's condition. I filled her in as best I could.

Anna, Karl, and I are on our way, she texted. *I'll let you know when we land.*

What about the painting? I knew this should be the last thing on my mind, so I added, *Maureen will want to know.* When and if she woke up.

It's safe.

CHAPTER 39

MAUREEN SAT IN a hospital bed sipping water when Mario and I located Intensive Care. A tube still was affixed to her arm, and a nurse hovered close by. The room was large with partitions between the dozen patients.

My heart fill with gratitude when Maureen noticed me and smiled. A weak smile, but nevertheless, the corners of her mouth raised a skosh. "Lucy."

For a moment, my mouth refused to function. "Maureen." I realized I hadn't been breathing. No real deep breaths anyway.

"Welcome to Rome," Mario said.

"Not what I expected." She surveyed the windowless room, the white curtains hanging on either side of her bed. "When can I leave?"

"As soon as we get the doctor to discharge you," he said. "This hospital is like a whole city with rules beyond our choosing."

"I'm just glad you're alive." My throat constricted. "I was so worried. Thank God you woke up."

"How long was I sleeping?"

"Several hours. Long enough for me to worry that we'd lost you."

"What, and miss my chance to see Rome? I didn't sleep through New Year's Eve, did I?"

"No," Mario said. "It's several days away."

"Maureen, it seems you and I have a lot in common," I said. "I'll help you as much as I can."

She gave me a blank look.

"I was hooked on opioids. When we get back to Seattle, I'll attend NA—Narcotics Anonymous—meetings with you."

"I don't want to go to any meetings. I'm too tired." Her eyelid slid closed.

"Be patient," Mario said to me.

I sat by her bed for hours; eventually, I crawled up next to her and fell asleep. I heard nurses speaking, wishing patients *Buon Natale*—Merry Christmas—and the rattle of wheeled tables, but sleep consumed me through the night. Mario must have sacked out on a couch in a waiting room.

I awoke with a stiff neck and shoulder to see Maureen struggling to sit. "I need coffee," she said. "If I don't have caffeine, I'll get a headache." The nurse helped her to a sitting position. "And I need pain medication for my shoulder," Maureen said to the nurse.

"I'll get you coffee," I said, "but we'll have to wait for the doctor for anything else." I was glad I could rely on a physician to regulate the medications. I assumed the new staff would read her chart and see she might have an opioid addiction. If not, I'd tell them.

"*Buongiorno*," Mario said, carrying lidded coffee cups.

The nurse spoke to him in Italian, what seemed like a rebuke for bringing the coffee. But he smiled and said something to appease her. She sent him a grin. No doubt about it. Mario was a charmer.

"How is our patient doing?" He placed the cups on a side table.

"As you can see, she's much better," I reached for a cup and handed it to Maureen, who thanked me and Mario. "You two are lifesavers." Her smile turned into a wince. "But I'm in so much pain. I wonder if I broke something."

"You poor thing, but they x-rayed you," I said. I was on to her antics. There was a time I'd do anything to get opioids, even buy them off the street not knowing with certainty what they were.

"Are you sure?" she asked. "I don't remember."

"Yes, the doctor or nurse can show you the results." Did I even want to tackle this conversation?

I heard the familiar ping from my iPhone informing me I'd received a text from Mama.

We just landed and will head over to the hospital.

Who's we? I wrote.

Aunt Anna, Uncle Karl, and me. Tom stayed home since you're okay.

I hesitated, then wrote to Mama: *Maureen almost OD'd on the plane. Thought you should know. Your call on what to do with this information.*

I imagined my mother's shock and wondered if she'd tell her sister.

"Your parents just landed," I told Maureen. "They're on their way over here."

"Oh, no, I don't want to see them." She tried to leap out of bed, but the nurse restrained her.

"I don't know how you'll avoid it," I said. "Although at your age, maybe you can keep your problem under wraps." I motioned to the nurse and to Mario to give us space to speak in private. "But don't you want your freedom back? How did you get hooked?" I asked.

"Who says I am?"

"I do. Because I have the same struggle—I mean, addiction." I lifted a long strand of hair off of her cheek and out of her eyes. "That plane crash could have saved your life, if you think about it. If you'd been home alone, you could have died. I can think of a dozen scenarios, because I was once in your shoes." I took her hand. How would I gain her confidence? "Maureen, I gave you the painting because I trusted you."

"I was blown away when you did." She examined her plastic hospital bracelet. "Mom told me we might be half sisters. What do you think?"

"I don't know." I waited for her to raise her chin, look up at me. "We could have a DNA test when we get back to the States. But that means staying alive. Know what I mean?"

"I'll do my best. But my father. He'd be heartbroken. Might even divorce my mother."

"We might really be cousins after all." I felt as though I was sinking in quicksand. "Maybe digging into the past will unearth unneeded pain and heartache." I couldn't bring myself to tell her how Papa died. If Mama was correct. She and I had no concrete proof.

I recognized Mama's voice in the hallway. "Lucy, darling." She swooped over to me. "And Maureen, you're awake. Good."

CHAPTER 40

AUNT ANNA PUSHED past Mama. "Maureen, dearest. We saw it on the TV. They actually showed your picture—you on a stretcher. I was scared to death."

Uncle Karl followed her. "You had us worried, kiddo. How do you feel?"

"Not good at all, Daddy. They must hate Americans. I'm in pain, but no one will help me. I need pain medication." Karl glanced at Anna. "We'll talk to the doctor as soon as he comes in."

Maureen was far from admitting she was powerless over drugs. I decided to say nothing as I relived days of withdrawal. First things first. Get her out of the hospital. Although maybe she was safer here.

Her physician today turned out to be a personable woman, who said Maureen could leave. "Take it easy for several days by resting and riding in an automobile rather than walking."

"How about pain medication?" Maureen asked.

"I'll give you four days' worth, to be taken when necessary." The physician was about my age by a few years but seemed to know her stuff. "If you are still experiencing pain, please find a doctor to help you locate its source."

"We're her parents," Aunt Anna said. "Does that mean she can leave here? We'll take good care of her."

"Wonderful that you're here," the doctor said. "I take it you weren't on the plane."

"No, we flew over right after. We'll make sure our daughter is well cared for."

The physician gave Karl the prescription slip to take to the pharmacy, and he headed out the door promising Maureen he'd be right back. "Hurry, Daddy," she said.

The doctor excused herself and moved on to her next patient.

"Yay," Maureen said. "I can leave."

"We need to find us all a hotel," I said.

"There's a very nice and reasonable *pensione* near my apartment," Mario said. "It's like a hotel, but they serve breakfast and dinner. More casual than a hotel. Rustic. Like a B and B. The woman who owns it is very, very nice."

"Or we could stay where Maria was if it's vacant." Then I remembered it was located across the way from Mussolini's balcony. "No, never mind. Your suggestion sounds better. Can you call and see if she has rooms for us?"

Mario placed the call and found that several guests had cancelled. "They have room for you," he said. "It's casual but charming."

"Great." I warned myself not to expect the grand Hassler.

"When we leave, I want to drive through the whole city," Maureen said. "To see all the Christmas decorations before they come down."

"Are you sure you feel up to it?" Anna asked.

"I will as soon as Daddy gets back with my pain medication."

"Okay, dearest, after a driving tour, we'll get checked into the *pensione*, and you can rest as the doctor told you."

"How are you feeling?" Mama asked me.

"So-so. Nothing a good night's sleep won't help."

"I sure hope your neck didn't get wrenched, Lucy," Mama said. "What an atrocious landing."

"I could share my pain pills," Maureen said. "Well, give you one anyway."

"Uh, that's okay."

Mario summoned a minivan large enough for six passengers, out of place amidst the many small vehicles. We all crammed in while the driver wedged our carry-ons into the back. Mario explained our destination to the driver, who said, "*Certo*."

For twenty minutes, we wove our way through Rome. I watched out the window as the magnificent Victor Emmanuel II Monument flew by. I turned my head so I couldn't see Mussolini's balcony, which made me think about Tabatha. I expected she was home with her parents, scheming ways to recover the Rembrandt painting. Unless they already had. What a couple of dishonest shysters they were. Not that I was perfectly honest all the time. The words *lying by omission* came to mind.

Maureen wanted to stop at the Pantheon, the Colosseum, St. Peter's Basilica, and so did I. But darkness was blackening the sky, and I was stifling my yawns.

"For anyone in the vehicle who doesn't know, I used to struggle with narcotics addiction." I looked to Mama and said, "No more secrets."

She patted the back of my hand. "Of course, you're right."

"In other words, you think I have an addiction too?" Maureen said. "Well, you're wrong. How dare you bring it up when I'm having so much fun?"

Aunt Anna said, "Don't pay any attention to Lucy or her mother."

Mama clasped her hands together, massaged her fingers.

"My sister has always been jealous of me," Anna said.

I felt Mama rising in her seat, but she remained mute.

"Don't start a catfight, Anna," Karl said. "Let's just get settled so our girl will get better."

"I am all better," Maureen said.

I had to press my lips together to keep myself from reminding her she'd been unconscious a short time ago. Yet the doctor had released her from the hospital.

WE FOUND OUR *pensione* and its middle-aged and rotund owner charming. And the warmish weather was a welcome contrast from Seattle's snow.

As we exited the vehicle, Karl sang the first line of "White Christmas" in his bass voice, and we all booed, then laughed. Mama and I shared a room with doubled beds, and Maureen shared a suite with her parents. The *pensione* was on the old side, but tidy and clean. Potted plants sat in the windowsills, and patterned fabric covered the beds.

Upon receiving a phone call, Karl declared he needed to return to Seattle the next day.

"Our house was broken into." He downplayed the break-in, but I could tell he was agitated. "Nothing was taken. We have one of those doorbells that alerts our security system company who summoned the police right away. The thief was long gone. You know how that goes."

I assumed he was referring to someone trying to steal the painting, but he never mentioned it. I had to ask, "After the painting?"

"If they were, they're looking in the wrong place," Karl said.

"Never mind, let's all go out and explore the city," Maureen said.

Thankfully, Aunt Anna stepped in. "We're going to follow the doctor's advice, Maureen. You heard what she said about resting for a few days. And this place serves dinner."

I sniffed the air. "Something smells good. Let's give it a try."

"Real homemade Italian food," Karl said.

"But I feel perfectly fine." Maureen glanced in a framed mirror affixed to the wall. "Yikes, I look awful. I need a shower. Pardon me for a few."

While she showered in their room, Anna stressed the importance of Maureen's resting at least for the remainder of the day.

"Are you kidding?" Mama said. "She could have a concussion."

"They x-rayed her head and found nothing," Anna said.

"If she were my daughter," Mama said. "I would—"

"Well, she's not, is she?" Anna shot back.

"Hold on, ladies, she is my daughter," Karl said. "I've a mind to take her home with me if you two are going to argue."

Mama and Anna fell silent. They exchanged a brief glance, then set their sights on Karl.

"But the trip might be too hard on her," Karl said. "So the doctor thought—"

"Yes, too hard," Anna echoed. "She should rest."

"I will be happy to drive her anywhere tomorrow," Mario said.

Huh, what about me? I now knew the meaning of *crestfallen*. Mario must have seen my shoulders slumping because he added, "And Lucia. She knows my Alfa is trustworthy. And that I'm a careful driver."

"A private driver would be lovely," Mama said, "If we can all fit in."

"I'm heading for the airport early in the morning," Karl said. "So that's one less person, bringing you down to five. Still, I don't see how all of you will fit, unless Mario owns a passenger van."

Anna went to check on Maureen, then came right back. "She's sound asleep on her bed. Too tired to even take her shower."

Karl checked his wristwatch. "We need to wake her up every two hours all night," he said. "That's what the doctor said."

Anna moaned. "I know, you're right. All night long we've got to wake her up to make sure she's okay."

"I wonder how long she'll sleep," I mused aloud.

"Between fatigue and jet lag, she might sleep through the night," Mama said, yawning.

Her yawning was contagious. "Maybe I'll take a nap too," I said. "I'm not even hungry." I dove onto my bed and tumbled into slumber even though I knew better. I would worry about time zones tomorrow.

CHAPTER 41

I AWOKE TO SUNLIGHT creeping through striped curtains. Mama was sacked out in a bed only feet away. I checked my phone for the time, to see we had both slept ten hours. The previous day's ordeal swam through my mind, but it had apparently not bothered my sleep. More evidence I'd overcome my fear of flying.

The intoxicating aroma of freshly brewed coffee and baked pastries drifted under the door, beckoning me to get up.

"Mama," I whispered so not to startle her. "It's the next day."

"Already?" She stretched her arms.

"Yup. Ten hours later."

"Ten hours? I can't believe I slept that long. I woke up only once during the night."

"Let's go downstairs for breakfast before it's too late. And see how Maureen is doing."

Minutes later, Mama and I toddled down to the dining room, with its tiled floors and potted succulents in the windowsills. Aunt Anna sat sipping coffee and reading a Christmas book. A platter of pastries and rolls sat on her table.

"May we join you?" Mama said.

"Of course, have a seat."

"*Buongiornio,*" the waitress said. "Coffee American-style?"

"No, *un cappuccino doppio, per favore.*" I turned to Mama. "I need an extra shot of espresso. The American-style coffee is too weak."

"I'll have one too," Mama said. "Please."

"You two had a good sleep," Aunt Anna said. "I'm exhausted from getting up all night to check on Maureen and then helping Karl leave. Poor guy."

"It's a pity he can't stay." I was delighted to see our drinks arrive.

"As sole proprietor of his business and all his employees on vacation, he's itching to get back home," Anna said.

"People are getting bodywork done on their cars this week?" I asked.

"He says he never knows. I'll bet he's buried with customers with all the collisions caused by that snow."

"How is Maureen doing?" Mama asked her. "Breakfast in bed today?"

"No, she got up with Karl. In fact, she's with him and Mario, who's kindly driving Karl to the airport. The men arranged everything last night."

"What?" I sounded like a croaking frog.

"I saw no reason to stop her," Aunt Anna said. "She insisted she felt great and wanted to see the sights."

I selected a roll and tore it open. "I'd hardly call driving to the airport seeing the sights."

"You have a problem with that?" Anna said. "You and Mario an item? It hasn't seemed that way."

"We haven't made a commitment or anything like that." I smeared the roll with unsalted butter and apricot jam.

Mama searched my face; I had to look away.

"I don't know." Not true, I cared for him deeply. I bit into the roll and relished the butter and jam.

"By now you'd know," Aunt Anna said.

"Say, I have an idea," Mama said. "Why don't we three girls go out exploring the city on foot?"

"Without telling Maureen?" my aunt asked. "I'll text her."

Minutes later, Anna declared that Maureen and Mario had dropped Karl off at the airport and wouldn't be back for a couple hours. "She said they planned to drive through the city and admire the Christmas decorations while they were still up."

Without me? I felt like going back to bed but knew I needed to clamber into this time zone. So my cousin— or was she my half sister?—was trying to steal Mario away? Not that he was mine to steal. Still, I felt resentment seething and sadness growing.

"Want to meet up with them?" Mama said. She turned to Anna. "You need to make sure Maureen is okay, don't you?"

"We woke her up all night every two hours, as the doctor directed." Anna sipped her coffee. "She's sick of me by now."

"But is she all right?" Mama said.

"What about her pain?" I asked.

"She said she feels fine. We ate breakfast together hours ago. The owner scrambled eggs especially for her American guests."

"In that case, I say we explore the city," Mama said. "Lucy can be our guide."

"Okay." I sipped my cappuccino, enjoyed the flavor. "I need the exercise."

I was tempted to text Mario but didn't want to seem as though I was running after him the way Maureen was. In hindsight, I wished I'd told her I had a crush on him. Maybe she would have kept her distance. First, she took my painting and now the man I dreamed of. But neither the painting nor the man was mine. Or maybe I was just acting immature and competitive. Tossed back in time.

Mama's shoe nudged my foot under the table. She tipped her head toward me. "You should text Mario," she whispered. "Go on and stand up for yourself. He obviously likes you."

"What are you two talking about?" Aunt Anna asked.

I tidied my mouth with a napkin to save myself from speaking.

"I was telling Lucy she should ask Mario to swing by and pick her up," Mama said. "If anything happens to Maureen, you'd want her there, wouldn't you?"

"Are you insinuating I'm not a good mother?" my aunt asked, all huffy.

At that moment, a twenty-something couple strolled into the room. I could tell they'd been laughing, their cheeks rosy, their eyes bright.

"On their honeymoon," Mama said. "I'll bet you." She sent them a smile, and they grinned back.

"I, for one, am not going to spend the day sitting around," Aunt Anna said.

Mama agreed. "I'm dying to see the city. I haven't been here for decades."

I lingered over my meal. I still felt loopy from jet lag and too much sleep. I should have set my alarm. I received a call on my cell phone. Finally. I fished my phone from my purse. "The Williamses" I said. "Should I even answer?"

"I would," Mama said. "But be wary."

"Lucy?" Gretchen said. I did the math and figured it was evening in Seattle. "Tabatha is missing. Is she with you?"

"No, why would she be?"

"Because you and Mario are all she's talked about. And Mussolini, of all bizarre people."

"She's not with me, I assure you. I'm sitting here with my mother and aunt."

"Where are you?"

I cupped my hand over the phone. "Gretchen Williams wants to know where I am. Should I tell her?"

Mama wagged her head and mouthed the word *no*.

"What is this all about?" I asked.

"Tabatha was here one minute and gone the next." Gretchen's voice was filled with frustration. "I should call the police."

"Maybe that's not such a bad idea."

"She's only fifteen, but I doubt they'll help us."

"Have you called all her friends?"

"You know she doesn't have any." She spoke to someone nearby, probably Stan.

I waited in silence with Mama and Anna watching me.

"I don't know what you want," I finally said. I figured this call was all about the painting. If she was phoning me, the Williamses hadn't gotten it back. "Tabatha hasn't contacted me," I said, "and I have no idea where she is."

"We read the story she wrote about Mussolini and his mistress," Gretchen said. "She printed it out on our copier. Did you help her?"

"Absolutely not," I said. "I never would."

"Call me if you hear from her," Gretchen said. "Promise?"

Did I want to promise this woman anything? "I've got to run," I said. "My mother is waiting." Which was true. Mama had moved her chair over and leaned toward me to listen in.

"She's got her nerve," Mama said when I hung up. "Let's get dressed and explore the city."

CHAPTER 42

As MAMA, AUNT Anna, and I left the *pensione* thirty minutes later, Mario zoomed up and stopped. He and Maureen exited his Alfa Romeo. She was giggling, a high-pitched girlish laugh.

"Good, Lucia, you're up," Mario said. "Maureen said you were sleeping and that you didn't want to be disturbed."

Maureen looked sheepish, setting her gaze on my feet. "I just assumed," she said. "Mom said to let you and your mother rest."

"How generous," I said, feeling angry but not showing it. I hoped. I was gritting my molars. "What have you two been up to?"

"We dropped my father off at the airport, then drove around the city." Maureen took Mario's elbow. "He's the best tour guide in the world." She gazed up at him. "His knowledge of history is incredible."

"Any Italian would know the same." He shifted his weight in a way that made me think he was nervous. "We are all very proud of our history."

"Did Tabatha's parents call you?" I asked.

"Yes, we shared a brief conversation. They asked if I'd heard from Tabatha after they brought her home, and I said I had not. I figured they thought I was still in Seattle, and I saw no reason to set things right."

I wondered if I could trust him. Sometimes my gut-level reactions were correct. Although not with Brad or my father. Never mind, I didn't trust my judgment, or why would I have agreed to give Maureen a painting that might be priceless?

"Why don't you young folks go off and leave us to fend for ourselves," Aunt Anna said. "I'd prefer to go on foot. I need to walk off the calories I just ate."

Mama patted her tummy. "Good idea. I plan to eat the whole time I'm here."

Leaving me with Maureen and Mario seemed like a dirty deal. Maybe those two were perfect for each other. I should venture off with my mother and aunt. We could always grab a cab or Uber if needed.

"Where do you think Tabatha is?" Mario asked me.

"Not a clue." I spoke in earnest. "Maybe at a friend's house. Not that I know of any friends."

"I've heard you have a drug problem in Seattle," Mario said.

"We do," Maureen said. "Tabatha's probably high somewhere or living under the freeway."

"You have no right to say that." I felt like adding my two bits about Maureen's drug usage but knew it would serve only to distance her. My mind drifted back to the time I was confronted with my opioid dependency. A friend invited me to an NA meeting. She'd said she wanted my support in her uphill battle against alcohol and drugs, while all along she'd wanted to help me. She moved to Texas soon after, but I'd continued to attend the group. I had more in common with those strangers than I did with my girlfriends who went to happy hour after work every day.

Out on the street sunshine swathed my shoulders. Ahead a decorated Christmas tree beckoned me. I didn't miss the snowy slush I'd left behind.

"Ready to move to Rome?" Mario asked me. I hadn't noticed his following me.

"I thought you were going to continue guiding Maureen around," I said.

"She is welcome to come along, no?"

"Sure," I said. "I want her to have fun while we're here. What did you two see earlier?"

"We drove by the Colosseum, the Pantheon, St. Peter's. Why don't I take you to a lesser-known church with centuries of history beneath it?"

"Sounds intriguing," I said.

He navigated us through traffic past the Colosseum and parked near the Basilica di San Clemente, which was pretty but looked like any old church. In Rome, that is. In Seattle, it would be considered outstanding. I was getting spoiled by Rome's many splendid ancient structures.

"Are you ready to descend into history?" Mario led the way and paid our entrance fee. "The basilica is composed of three layers. The present was erected during the medieval period. During the second century, the location on which the church stands was a Roman mansion occupied by one of the first Roman senators to convert to Christianity. A century later, a temple was built on the same spot. It is believed it remained in use through the third century, when Christian persecution ended." He glanced over to me. "Am I boring you?"

"No, not at all," I said. "I was just thinking an art historian could spend her life studying Roman architecture here."

"Maybe you'd enjoy spending time here doing just that."

"I would, if you were here," Maureen said. "I mean if you were our tour guide."

Oh, brother. I gawked up at numerous intricate mosaics.

"Those are twelfth century," Mario said, following my gaze. "Come on, the best is yet to come. The entryway to the fourth century church is just through the sacristy."

Despite the humid darkness, I admired frescoes on the walls and fragments of mosaics on the floor. "This is unbelievable," I said. "Beautiful." We submerged down moist passageways.

"I feel claustrophobic," Maureen said, hanging on to Mario's elbow. "What's that water?"

"We are looking at the ruins of the Roman manor. The water flows through the Cloaca Maxima, ancient Rome's primary sewer system. This is now considered pure water, but I wouldn't drink it."

"Gross." The corners of Maureen's mouth stretched back reminding me of a lizard. Not a kind thought, but true. I wished she would slither away, out of my life

"I find it fascinating," I said. "I could spend hours down here."

"Not me." Maureen turned toward the exit.

I recalled climbing St. Peter's Basilica. I'd felt closed in from all sides, short of breath and cloaked in fear. Yet down here, I found tranquility and the sound of the water restful.

"You two go ahead without me," I said. "I love this place." I recalled why I studied art history in college. In Seattle, anything over seventy-five years old was considered an antique. Here, the past unfolded itself like an intricate tapestry spreading out past the birth of Jesus.

"Okay, Mario," Maureen said. "Let's go."

"No, I won't leave Lucia." He brought our group to a halt. "We came together, and we'll leave together. Unless you want me to call your mother, find her location, and get you a car or Uber."

Maureen folded her arms. "Trying to ditch me?" She brought Tabatha to mind.

"No," Mario said, "but I won't leave Lucia."

"I suppose I could return here another day," I said.

"And I could escort you," Mario said. "I have the whole week off."

I turned to Maureen. "How do you feel."

"Fine, I guess." Yet she looked fatigued, and her gate was unstable.

"Maybe we should go somewhere for lunch and rest," Mario said. "Maureen, would you rather spend time with your mother?"

"No, she'll just fuss over me and drive me nuts."

"For good reason," I said. "You know, we were in a plane—"

"You were there," she said. "It wasn't exactly a crash."

"Maybe not, but you were unconscious." It was too dark for me to see her eyes clearly. Her pupils were huge, but maybe mine were, too, a natural occurrence in a dim chamber.

"I know a nice place near here for lunch," Mario said.

"Absolutely," Maureen said. "Anything to leave here. I need to get out in the light."

Her words dug deep into my brain. In the light is where I needed to be. Honesty. No more secrets.

Ten minutes later, stepping outside into the sunshine, I was bathed in warmth. As I strode across the cobblestone street, I considered how different Rome was from Seattle. The roadway had filled with locals jabbering in Italian, tourists, and zipping little cars—some honking. Would I like to live in this mad-dash environment amid ancient remnants of history? Yes, I'd love to give it a try.

When we were situated at a table by a window in a small restaurant and had ordered food, Mario checked his messages. His mother had called him while we were in the basilica, below street level where reception was minimal. "So sorry," he said, "I'll be right back."

Through the window, I watched his handsome silhouette. I glanced across the table to see Maureen staring at him too. "What a hunk," she said. "Does it bother you that he's putting the moves on me?"

He was? "I hadn't noticed," I said. "Nor do I care." I opened a white cloth napkin, placed it in my lap. "Since you and I are by ourselves," I said, "now might be the perfect time to speak candidly."

"Here it goes." She narrowed her eyes. "Mom warned me about you and your mother. Not to believe either one of you."

I sat stunned. Getting to know Maureen was going to be tougher than I thought. Maybe impossible. "I figured you came on this trip so we could get closer," I said.

"I came so I could see Rome at Christmas, and I haven't been disappointed." She grinned, her teeth pearly white. "Mario is an unexpected treat." She took in my stare. "If he was my Christmas present, thank you very much," she said.

The waitress brought us an antipasto platter. Maureen positioned cheese and a slice of salami atop a cracker. "My guess is you want him for yourself." She chomped into her creation, savored the taste. "But what we want and what we get are often two different things. Am I right?"

Elbows on the table, I rested my chin on my hands to keep venomous words from spewing out my mouth that could never be retracted.

Mario sauntered into the restaurant and settled next to me. "I hope it's all right with you, Lucia. My mother wants to drive down here to meet you and spend New Year's Eve with us. I should have asked you first."

"What about me?" Maureen asked.

"If you and your mother—and yours, too, Lucia—wish to join us *va bene*."

"Oh yeah?" Maureen said. "Who will you kiss at midnight?"

My question exactly, but I was glad I hadn't voiced it.

CHAPTER 43

"YOU SHOULD HAVE invited Mario in," Aunt Anna said when Maureen and I entered the *pensione*'s main sitting room. "I want to have a better look at this fellow who has both you girls chasing after him."

"No, Mother," Maureen said, "he'll think I'm groveling like I'm desperate."

"And you're not?" Mama stepped into the conversation. "What's going on? Mario is Lucy's friend, and Maureen's trying to muscle in?"

"Can I help it if he finds me more attractive?" Maureen asked, her volume raised.

A couple entering the *pensione* walked by and paused to listen in. Not that I blamed them. Let's face it, everyone enjoys hearing a family squabble.

"Hold on," Mama said. "Lucy met him first."

"So?" Maureen sat next to her mother, crossed her legs at the ankles.

A text message pinged on my phone. I decided to ignore it for the time being. We dispersed to our own rooms. I kicked off my shoes and plunked down on my bed, its springs creaking.

"How did you do with Aunt Anna?" I asked.

"Better than expected. She loves shopping, and there's plenty to be had." She removed her shoes and massaged her feet. "Aren't you going to answer your text message? It could be from Mario."

I took a peek and saw Gretchen Williams. Ugh, could I deal with her? A moment later, the phone rang insistently; I recognized Gretchen's number.

"Aren't you going to answer?" Mama asked.

"It's Tabatha's mother," I said.

"You might as well take her call. Or I will and tell her you're in the shower."

"Nah, I'd better."

"Lucy, have you heard from Tabatha?" Gretchen asked, skipping formalities.

"No, I haven't spoken to her since she left with you Christmas Day. Are you sure she isn't hiding somewhere in your house?"

"But you're back in Rome, right? I saw your face on TV."

"What does that have to do with anything? I'm travelling with my mother. We're finishing our perfec Christmas," I realized I'd revealed too much. I needec to terminate this call. "My mother's waiting for me righ here. I need to run. Goodbye."

"Sorry, Mama, I shouldn't have told her you were here."

"So? If she comes to the house, she'll find Tom manning the fort." She winked.

Moments later, I received a call from Mario. I felt my heart flutter in a silly schoolgirl way. "Maureen called and said she wants to have *la cena questa sera*—I mean supper—together tonight."

"She called you?" They must have exchanged contact info. I wondered whose idea that was.

"She asked for my number," he said. "I couldn't say *no*. Not when my mother is wanting to meet you and your family."

"I guess, okay." His heart was in the right place.

MY DINNER WITH Mama, Anna, Maureen, Mario, and his mother at a posh, bustling restaurant that night was fantastic. His mother, a brunette in a black silk sheath and stiletto heels, looked as though she'd just stepped out of a hair salon. Everything about her said sophisticated—expensive but understated. She was on the cool side at first as she examined me from across the table, making me wonder what Mario had told her about me. But with Mama's help, she warmed up to us.

We enjoyed delicious food, laughter, and a flirtatious waiter who paid all his attention to Mario's mother. Maureen acted her usual vivacious self.

Mario's mother called me a *bella ragazza*, which Mario translated for me: beautiful girl. I don't know which I liked the most, the beautiful or the girl part. In any case, I felt young and attractive when I was with Mario.

I wore my new Christmas dress. Mario told me I looked fantastic wearing it in Seattle and had suggested bringing it, along with an evening jacket or sweater. I chose an ebony sweater with jet-black decorative beading.

At the end of our meal, Mario insisted on paying and made a final toast. "May this be the best Christmas ever for these charming ladies." All clinked glasses. Maureen's was the first to touch Mario's, then she emptied it and asked for a refill.

"Maybe we should all gather again for New Year's Eve," he said.

"Absolutely," Maureen clinked his glass again. "Can't wait," she said.

Mario leaned against me and spoke in my ear. "How about if you and I meet for breakfast tomorrow? Just the two of us. Early, before the others get up, if you don't mind."

CHAPTER 44

THE NEXT MORNING, as I showered and dressed, I thought about Mario and his generous Christmas gift. I wouldn't be here without him, stressful though the landing had been. I'd learned I was braver than I thought.

Mama seemed to be asleep, her covers pulled up around her chin. She was probably dreaming about Tom. How wonderful that she'd found her true love. But how about me? Was I in love with Mario or just venturing through a silly case of infatuation that would fizzle out as soon as we returned to Seattle? And did he love me?

I sneaked out of the room, not that I thought Mama would try to stop me. But to be on the safe side, I tugged the door shut without allowing the knob to click. I trotted down the stairs and saw a flash of red as Mario pulled his car up front. The brilliant color made my heart skip a beat. No, it was my anticipation of seeing the man who had captured my heart. Before I could reach him, he'd hopped out, rounded his car, and opened the passenger door. I slid in, and he closed my door without slamming it. I'd left Mama a hand-written note telling her not to worry. I'd call or text her before lunchtime. I figured she'd be okay. After dinner last night, she'd given me a nod of approval. "Mario's delightful," she'd said in the privacy of our room. "You have my blessing."

I imagined the snarl on Maureen's face when she found out I'd left with him, and I smiled. Okay, I was acting like a brat, but it was my turn.

Mario zipped away and down the hill. Few vehicles were on the streets. "Morning traffic hasn't started up yet." He took us to the Victor Emmanuel, its white marble glowing in the golden rising sunlight, to see the splendid Christmas tree again. I thought of Tabatha and of Maria as my gaze zeroed in on Maria's former apartment.

"Let's stop in that little café where I found Tabatha," I said. "They had the best pastries and yummy fresh croissants. And cappuccinos. I need coffee."

"You poor thing." Mario cranked on his steering wheel. "No caffeine yet?"

Mario tucked his car in a small spot. The café's front door was opening when we arrived. "*Un momento*," Leonardo said. "Good to see you again."

"*Un cappuccino* and an espresso for me," Mario said. "And hurry."

"*Sì, sì*, but I'm not quite ready. Take a seat wherever you like."

"Are you warm enough to sit outside?" Mario asked me. He draped his jacket over my shoulders, pleasing me no end. He wore a turtleneck wool sweater, his muscled arms filling it nicely.

"Yes, I'd rather stay outside if you don't mind." I felt warmth from the morning sun and figured the temperature would only improve. And we'd lose this primo table with its spectacular view of the Victor Emmanuel if we sat inside. I let my gaze travel up to Mussolini's balcony and decided to ignore it. My glance wandered around the square and behind us to where Maria used to live.

When Leonardo brought us our drinks, I asked him about renting the place for a week. "Whom should I speak to?"

"*Mi dispiace, è occupato.*"

"It seems someone is already renting it," Mario said.

"I believe you know her," Leonardo said.

"You mean Maria and her baby came back?" I asked.

"Yes."

I glanced up at the window overlooking the café and saw movement as a head dipped out of sight. Tabatha? I must be seeing things.

"Who is that upstairs?" I asked Leonardo as he brought a platter of pastries and croissants.

He hesitated.

"Never mind."

Mario scanned the building behind us. "I don't see anyone."

Maybe I was imagining things. How could a fifteen-year-old girl just pop up on the other side of the world? Next thing I knew I'd see Mussolini.

But I was right. Minutes later, impish Tabatha appeared and plopped down at the remaining seat at our table as if she'd been expected. I was speechless.

"*Signorina* Tabatha," Leonardo said. "How did you sleep, *cara*?"

"Like *una bambina*."

He chuckled. "*Bene*. I'll bring you hot chocolate."

"*Grazie*," she said. Wow, her accent was perfect.

"Good to see you," Mario said smoothly, "but your parents are sick with worry."

"Nah, they don't care." She pilfered a fruit-filled croissant from our platter and chomped into it.

"But . . . how did you get here?" I finally found my voice.

"Duh. The same way you did. By jet." She sipped her hot chocolate and licked her upper lip. "I talked some guy at the airport into telling the airline I was his niece for one hundred dollars. I have my own passport and my parents' credit card. Any idiot could do it."

I reached toward my purse for my phone. "I need to call your parents."

"No, please, please, please don't call them," Tabatha begged me. "For once, let them wonder where I am. They never tell me what they're doing. I have yet to get a Christmas present from them." She snagged another tasty morsel. "If it wasn't for your family, I would have missed Christmas all together."

"I'm sure they meant to be there for you." I attempted to sound convincing.

"That's because you're so nice," she said. "You think they'd act like you."

As the tables around us filled, she ordered another hot chocolate. Leonardo gave her a small bow as if she were royalty. "How about freshly squeezed orange juice instead, *signorina*?"

"Okay, thanks." She sent him her sweetest smile.

"How are you paying for everything?" Mario asked her.

"I have a stash of money. And I have my folks' credit card in case I need it."

"They could close that card any time," I said.

"But they won't, because they don't want me to come back. I'm too much trouble." She nibbled from the platter. "And before you ask, I turned off the locator on my phone."

"You live here all by yourself?" Mario asked.

"No, Maria came back. She'll pay me to babysit so she can get a job. Isn't that the coolest? It means I'll live right across from my favorite balcony."

"Are you planning to drop out of school?" Mario asked. "When does your vacation end?"

"Who cares?" She steepled her fingers. "I don't need to graduate from high school. I can pass that dumb old GED test."

"Knowing you, I bet you could pass the test in the blink of an eye," I said. "But you'd miss out on going to the prom." As soon as I said it, I knew it was a mistake.

"Like anyone would ask me." The corners of her mouth dragged down.

"I thought girls went to proms without dates these days." I recalled the miserable evening my date stood me up for the senior prom. Well, I was making up for it now by being in the heart of Rome with Mario.

I felt his leg against mine and experienced a flood of passion expanding in my chest. I longed to be alone with him.

Tabatha obviously had a problem, but nothing I'd done to help her had worked. I was done with the Williamses' family games. She needed a psychiatrist.

A familiar puppy gallivanted over to our table and sat beside Tabatha. She fed it a snack from the platter.

"Isn't Puppy getting big?" Tabatha asked. "Pretty soon, when she jumps on you, she'll just about knock you over." Tabatha stood and patted her leg. "I'd better get her back upstairs, so Leonardo doesn't throw a fit."

"You can't just walk away, Tabatha. I insist you contact your parents immediately, or I will." I held up my phone.

"But Maria is counting on me." She sank back down on the chair.

"Here, give me your phone," Mario said, his voice still gentle. "I'll reset the locator so they know where you are. Promise me not to turn it off again?"

"Yeah, I promise," she shot me a glare, "but only because it's you who's asking."

I refused to give in. "Go pack your things," I said. "You're coming with us."

When Tabatha scampered up to Maria's apartment, I rang Gretchen and told her the good news. She thanked me but didn't seem as relieved as I thought she should be.

"Why would Tabatha do such a crazy thing?" Mario asked me after I hung up.

"To give her parents a chance to prove they love her is my best guess."

"I can understand that thinking." He sipped his drink. "After my parents got divorced, I rarely saw my father, who moved to Milan. I would have done anything to gain his attention, but nothing worked except getting into trouble."

I could relate.

"I was surprised when my mother told me he was coming here on New Year's Eve," he said. "To meet you."

"Meet me? I'm honored."

"Yes, they've agreed to a temporary truce for my sake. This has never happened before." His gaze penetrated mine. "But she told him I was head over heels in love with you, and he'd better hurry up, or he'd miss out on planning the wedding. She'd invite only her friends and family. That got his attention. He called me right away."

"And what did you say?" I asked.

"That it's all true. I've found the love of my life."

"Seriously?"

"My darling, can't you tell I love you?"

I leaned back to scrutinize his marvelous face. "What about Maureen? It seems as though you're attracted to her."

"No. She's a lot of fun, but she's not you. I have a cousin who likes that flirty type. We can introduce them. But you are the woman who has captured my heart." He took my hand, brought it to his lips. "I adore you, Lucia, and hope to marry you. If you'll have me."

The suddenness of his proposal caught me off guard. I couldn't speak. He cupped my chin and coaxed my mouth to his until our lips met, then melded into a luxurious kiss that I never wanted to end.

When our lips parted, he said, "And how about you? Do you love me—just the smallest bit?"

"Yes, I do. But we hardly know each other."

"I know all I need to know."

So did I.

"We could come back here for the wedding next Christmas?" I whispered.

"All right." He sunk down on one knee, drawing the attention of everyone around us.

"Will you marry me next Christmas?"

"Yes." My uncertainties evaporated.

He dipped his hand into his pocket for a small box, then opened it to expose an emerald ring. "This color will echo your eyes," he said. "It belonged to my maternal grandmother. My mother's idea. But we can buy you a new one if you prefer."

"No, this is perfect," I said.

A round of applause erupted as he slipped the ring on my finger, then kissed me again.

EPILOGUE

Five months later

"YOU MAY KISS the bride," the preacher says from the sumptuous terrace at Hotel Hassler—adorned with white and yellow flowers to match my bridal bouquet.

Mario and I couldn't wait until next Christmas to tie the knot, as was our original plan. We couldn't even wait for this wedding. Mama's pastor from a modest church in Seattle made our marriage official a couple of weeks ago. A small, family-only affair. For fun, I wore Mama's old midi-length lace cream-colored bridal gown since mine was still being sewn in Italy under Mario's mother's watchful eyes.

Mario and I decided to hold our second wedding and reception in Rome so all his family could attend. And because I've come to treasure the city.

Mario's hands glide over my white satin gown—a present from his mother—around my waist, and his full lips find mine. I will never grow weary of kissing him. As we embrace, I try to hold on to this moment forever. Because, let's face it, life and relationships are hard.

Tabatha, my flower girl, tosses handfuls of yellow rose pedals and yells, "Yay!"

Mama and Tom, newlyweds themselves, lift their glasses. I can't recall seeing Mama happier—her face radiant, making her look ten years younger. She and Tom beat us to the altar by a month and are on their honeymoon.

Our guests, including Tabatha's parents, clap and cheer. Enthusiastic toasts abound, with fluted glasses filled with champagne and sparkling cider. Some words of congratulations are in Italian, and I can't understand them verbatim. But I get the gist: long life together and happiness.

I sip my cider, as does my cousin Maureen. Good for her. She's off opioids and booze. We agreed to attend NA meetings together. Maureen and I have become as close as sisters. She's sitting next to Mario's handsome cousin and told me she hopes to move in with him when he relocates to Seattle, much to Aunt Anna and Uncle Karl's disapproval.

Mama and Tom couldn't afford Hotel Hassler, but Mario's parents insisted on paying to have the celebration on the hotel's largest terrace. And they put Mama and Tom up in a suite as a wedding present to them. Seems I married into a wealthy family.

Both Mario and I work at Amazon now, but in different departments and locations. He works in Bellevue,
and I in Seattle, where we reside in a condominium on
Capitol Hill with a splendid view that still can't compare
with Rome's beauty.

My gaze drifts above the rooftops of the spectacular city where Mario promised to bring me for Christmas next year.

Several mysteries still remain in my life, such as what
happened to my father that horrendous day he died.
I have let go of the notion he committed suicide. He
may have, or he may have gotten himself caught in a
wind shear and lost control of his aircraft. I am powerless to change the outcome.

Another riddle: who legally owns the angel painting by Rembrandt? Maureen had been doggedly determined to claim it as hers alone, so I was blown away
when she and Aunt Anna gave it to Mario and me as a
wedding present.

Several mysteries have been solved: Maureen is not
my half sister. Last month's DNA test confirmed we
are indeed cousins. We felt both sad and ecstatic. We
hugged each other after we received the results, as did
our mothers.

Another conundrum resolved: Tabatha was recently
diagnosed with bipolar disorder and is on medication,
which seems to help her erratic behavior and depression. I was delighted her parents allowed her to take
part in our wedding this glorious afternoon. I hope
she will always be a part of our life.

Our honeymoon—as if coming to Rome isn't
enough—will be to drive up through Tuscany all the

way to northern France. This leg of the journey we've kept a secret, even from Mama. It seems I've caught Maureen's bug: to find our great-grandfather's stolen art collection. At least find out where he lived and the location of his gallery.

Much priceless artwork is still missing since WWII. I pray his collection will resurface. Stranger things have happened.

RECIPE

Panna Cotta

IN ITALIAN PANNA cotta means "cooked cream." It requires very few ingredients, and is basically a mixture of cream, sugar, and vanilla. Gelatin is added to set the mixture and create a custard-like consistency. The final product is rich and silky smooth. In spite of the heavy cream, it is perfect as a light not-too-sweet dessert after a heavy meal. If you wish to make an even lighter panna cotta, you can replace some of the heavy cream with a lighter cream or milk.

INGREDIENTS

1 envelope powered unflavored gelatin (1/4 ounce)

2 tablespoons milk

2 cups heavy cream

6 tablespoons sugar

1 ½ teaspoons pure vanilla extract

INSTRUCTIONS

1. Pour the milk into a small saucepan, then sprin-
   kle the gelatin on top. Let stand one minute, then
   place the pot on low heat until the gelatin has dis-
   solved (1-2 minutes). DO NOT BOIL. Immediately remove from heat.

2. In a separate pot, add the cream and sugar, heat on
   medium/low heat just until the cream starts to boil.
   Immediately remove the pot from the heat.

3. Add the gelatin mixture and the vanilla to the cream
   and sugar, and combine well with a whisk. Pour into
   4 ramekins or glasses and let the mixture cool, then
   refrigerate for at least 5 hours, preferably overnight,
   or until the panna cotta is firm.

4. Serve panna cotta in the ramekins, or to unmold, dip the ramekin in boiling water for about 3-4 seconds, gently slide the tip of a knife around the edge and invert onto a plate.

5. Dress it up by drizzling with berry sauce, lemon curd, or honey, or garnish with strawberries and mint.

6. Panna cotta can be covered with plastic wrap and refrigerated for up to 3 days.

AUTHOR'S NOTE

FROM ROME WITH LOVE is a work of fiction. My contemporary characters sprouted from my imagination. My historical characters are based on real people, although I took a few liberties.

My family lived in Rome while my professor father taught classics (Latin and Ancient Greek) to university students from across the United States. I loved Italy so much I studied Italian as my college language and have visited Italy often as an adult. And I have enjoyed a lifelong interest in art, my major at the University of Washington. Today, many pieces of valuable art stolen from Jews by Nazis during WWII remain missing. I find this to be both fascinating and tragic. The story took root in the back of my mind and deprived me of sleep more than once until Beth Jusino helped me untangle it. Thanks, Beth! A round of applause to Mary Jackson for your encouragement. And many thanks to you, my readers. Each and every one of you!

ABOUT THE AUTHOR

BESTSELLING AUTHOR KATE Lloyd is a passionate observer of human relationships. A native of Bal-
timore, she now lives in Seattle, WA. She's the author
of half a dozen novels, including the bestselling Legacy
of Lancaster series.

Over the years, Kate worked a variety of jobs, including car salesman and restaurateur. For relaxation and
fun, Kate enjoys walking with her camera in hand,
beachcombing, and singing.

Find out more about Kate Lloyd:
Website: www.katelloyd.com
Blog: http://katelloyd.com/blog/
Facebook: www.facebook.com/katelloydbooks
Instagram: katelloydauthor
Twitter: @KateLloydAuthor
Pinterest: @KateLloydAuthor

Kate loves hearing from readers!

CPSIA information can be obtained
at www.ICGtesting.com
Printed in the USA
LVHW041654061120
670968LV00005B/808

9 781735 241128